# Spotted Pony Casino Mysteries

Poker Face
House Edge
Double Down
The Squeeze
The Pinch

# Down and Dirty

Spotted Pony Casino Mystery
Book 6

Paty Jager

Windtree Press
Corvallis, OR

DOWN AND DIRTY
Copyright © 2024 Patricia Jager



Windtree Press
Hillsboro, Oregon
http://windtreepress.com

Cover Art by Covers by Karen

PUBLISHING HISTORY
Published in the United States of America
ISBN 978-1-962065-59-7

**Special Thanks**
To the Crimescene online group, my critique partner, and beta readers. Without you, this book wouldn't ring true.


**About the Book**
This series is set in and around a fictional casino on The Confederated Tribes of the Umatilla Reservation in NE Oregon. The reservation is real. I have researched, and while I've made up people and where they live, I will try to stay true to the life people live on the reservation.

# Chapter One

Dela Alvaro, head of security for the Spotted Pony casino on the Umatilla Reservation in NE Oregon, sat at her desk, thinking about how much she'd enjoyed the First Salmon Ceremony she and Heath attended the day before. The ceremony celebrating the return of the first spring Chinook salmon was something she would remember every time she peered into a river or ate the fish that had nourished the Umatilla and other tribes of the Pacific Northwest for centuries.

Heath had invited her to attend the annual celebration. In the past when he'd invited her to what she felt were tribal celebrations, she had always come up with an excuse not to attend, feeling like an interloper. However, now that she believed she was half Umatilla not Hispanic, she had wanted to go and learn more about their traditions and their connection to this land.

After coming across a photo of a man with an incredible likeness to her and having someone she didn't like tell her the mugshot was of her father, Dela had become obsessed with discovering the truth. She'd yet to confront her mom about the man Dela believed to be her father.

Changing her thoughts from her parents, she smiled remembering how welcoming the tribal members had been to her participating in the celebration. She knew that was because of Heath, whose family had a long history in the Umatilla tribe. And Grandfather Thunder, the man who lived next door to her and her mother during Dela's childhood, and who she now believed to be a relative, even though he told her to never mention the man she believed to be her father.

She and Heath had been digging up information through the court systems, newspaper accounts, and her father's diary they'd found in a Thunder family cabin in the Blue Mountains. Theodore (Dory) Thunder's face bore a strong resemblance to Dela's. What she hadn't told Heath was she felt something stir in her when she looked at Dory's photo. Something that made her want to find out the truth about him. Her gut didn't believe he was a serial rapist. Or that her mom had been one of his victims.

The phone rang, shaking Dela out of her thoughts.

"Dela, it's for you," Margie, the security staff member on the desk, said, holding the phone out to her.

Rolling her chair across the space between her desk and Margie's, Dela grasped the phone. "Dela."

"It's Gus Sander."

Dela let out a disgusted sigh. She was having too good of a day to talk to a man who had manufactured and sold drugs on the rez.

"Don't hang up." His voice went up an octave as if

he was scared.

"Why shouldn't I?" she asked, wondering why he'd called her.

"You're the only person I can trust. You gave me back money knowing it was gained illegally and you ruined me, but didn't put me in jail. I respect that."

"Why are you buttering me up?" She tapped a pen on the edge of Margie's desk. While she didn't care for the man, she found it interesting he called her for help. Her curiosity would keep her from hanging up.

"I need to talk to someone who will listen and not just lock me up. I think there is something—" he inhaled a sharp breath. "Meet me on the River Parkway in two hours." The line went dead.

Dela stared at the phone and wondered what that was all about. Handing the phone back to Margie, Dela glanced at the time clock. Two hours from now would be midnight. Good thing Heath wasn't home waiting for her. He was helping out this week taking regular patrols for the tribal police rather than his regular detective hours. Tonight and tomorrow night he had the graveyard shift.

"I'll be headed out at eleven-thirty, but if anything comes up, give me a call," she told Margie.

"Got it, boss." The woman smiled and went back to reading a book.

"I'm going to do a walk around before I leave."

Margie waved a hand as Dela left the security office. She made her way around the gaming tables and slot machines, talking to the security personnel and checking in with surveillance. By the time she finished her rounds, it was time to meet Gus. While she'd wandered around the casino checking that her employees were doing their job, her mind had tumbled around reasons Gus would come to her for help and what he might be caught up in. From her past experiences with the man, she figured it had to do with drugs.

The April night didn't feel as if spring had arrived. Dela walked as briskly as she could with a prosthetic leg to her car. At the door of her new mid-size SUV, she curled her fingers under the door latch and the locks didn't click. She tugged on the latch and the door opened. The doors had been locked when she went to work at 2 PM. She glanced around the parking lot. The employees' cars were all in nearly the same spots they always parked and there wasn't one that looked out of place.

How had her car become unlocked? Dela slid behind the wheel and did a quick scan of the interior. Everything seemed to be where it belonged. She was glad she hadn't taken Heath's advice to keep a handgun in her glove compartment. If she had, and it was stolen, she'd never forgive herself if it ended up being used to kill someone.

Her phone rang as she drove out of the parking lot behind the Spotted Pony. It was Heath. She hit the call button on the monitor in the dash. "Hello. I didn't expect to hear from you tonight."

"Are you home yet?" Heath asked.

"No. I am leaving the casino. I received a weird call from Gus Sander." She waited, knowing Heath would have something to say about her meeting with the man.

"Sander? What did he want?" Heath's voice rang with suspicion.

"He said he trusted me and needed help."

"That doesn't sound good. Don't go alone. Take someone with you."

"Who am I going to get to go with me at this time of night? I'll be fine. He sounded scared. I don't think he'll harm me." At least she hoped he wouldn't try to harm her.

"I don't like it. Call Travis. He's always up half the night." Heath insisted.

"I'll call you when I get home and tell you all about it." Dela ended the call. She hated to do that to Heath but she wasn't worried. In her gut, she could tell Gus was scared and wanted her help, not to harm her.

*But what about the people he was scared of?* Her mind spat out this tidbit for her to worry about the rest of the way to Pendleton.

She exited I-84 onto Emigrant Avenue. Zigzagging through the streets, she headed to the River Parkway. It consisted of a concrete and brick walkway along the Umatilla River that wound its way through Pendleton. The main starting point to the walkway was five blocks from the Pendleton Stampede grounds.

There were plenty of parking spots along the street at this time of night and year. Plants were starting to come out of winter hibernation, as were the people. She doubted anyone other than she and Gus would be out walking as cold as it was tonight. After parking, she shifted in her seat to reach behind and grab a heavy coat she kept in the back seat during the winter. She spent most of her time indoors, however, having a warm coat to wear when she came home kept her from freezing while she tossed hay to Jethro, her donkey.

Dela tucked her phone and car fob in her coat

pocket and stepped out. Pulling the coat on, she glanced up and down the street. It was quiet except for the wind rustling the new growth on the trees that welcomed visitors. She walked up the incline to the statue of a pair of herons dancing on a large rock. A slanted sign at the edge overlooking the river gave an account of the wildlife that inhabited the waterway.

Scanning the walkway in both directions, Dela wondered if she should stay here or follow the path. Where the hell was Gus? She pulled the hood up on her coat and shoved her hands into the pockets. Standing in one place wouldn't keep her warm. She decided to walk and set off to the right, walking briskly for about fifty yards.

Just as she started to pivot, she noticed someone on a bench. They were hunched forward as if in pain.

"Gus?" Dela asked, walking toward the person. As she drew closer, she recognized a brand of fuzzy woman's boots on the person's feet.

The woman's head came up. The little bit of moonlight wasn't hindered by the trees. The woman's eyes lit up and a smile spread on her face. "You've come. I knew you would. Adam and I so want to help you spread love." She reached out to Dela with long slender fingers wrapped in tightly knitted gloves.

"I'm sorry you have mistaken me for someone else," Dela said, turning away.

A hand grabbed her arm.

When she spun back around the woman was on her feet. Her eyes no longer held warmth, but wariness and a fierceness Dela had never seen in another's eyes.

"I know where the bodies are buried," the woman said in a loud whisper. "Ask me. Ask me where the bodies are buried."

Dela studied the woman's face. There was a craziness in her eyes. Her eyelids fluttered and the eyeballs rolled upward. "Ma'am, are you all right?" Dela reached out to take the woman's arms. With a quickness that belied her fragility, the woman dove down the embankment toward the water.

Dela started to follow but balked at the steepness of the river bank. A muffled cry rang out in the cold night air. Following the sound, she jogged back to the herons and past them.

Up ahead a concrete bridge spanned the river. She spotted movement in the shadow of the bridge. Dela picked up her pace, keeping an eye on the space under the bridge. Someone ran out the other side into the moonlight, she called out, "Gus! Stop, it's Dela!"

The person picked up speed.

She accelerated into the best run she could do without her running prosthesis. Ducking into the darkness under the bridge, her foot caught on something and she fell forward. Her arms stretched in front of her to keep from smacking her face on the asphalt. They pressed into something soft, warm, and sticky before her body made contact.

Instantly, she scrambled to her feet, wiping a hand on her coat and digging in her pocket for her phone. She pressed her thumb on the screen and it opened. A quick hunt of the apps and she turned on the flashlight mode.

In the beam of her phone lay Gus Sander, bleeding from his neck, his eyes open and unseeing. Moving her phone back and forth, the light searching the body, something glinted at the edge of the beam.  She directed the light to the glint and discovered a knife on the ground beside the man's head. Just as she thought it was lucky the killer left the weapon behind, her gaze noted the carved initials on the antler handle. Shit! It was the knife Heath gave her on her 18th birthday. Now she knew why her car was unlocked.

# Chapter Two

The Pendleton City Police came within fifteen minutes of Dela calling them. First to arrive were two officers Dela hadn't met before. One pulled out his notebook to take her statement while the other set up large outdoor lights.

She'd answered the first officer's question of who she was when Detective Fletcher arrived.

"Ms. Alvaro, shouldn't you be at work at the casino?" the detective asked.

"I was at work. Earlier tonight, Gus Sander, the victim, called me and asked me to meet him here at midnight." She kept her gaze on the detective as the officer wrote down what she said.

"Why would he call you?" Fletcher crossed his arms. The man was known for intimidating suspects. But she wasn't a suspect and knew more about the detective than he knew about her. Heath had been to several instructional conferences with him.

"I don't know. He said he knew he could trust me."

She shrugged.

"Trust you? Why would he need someone he trusted?"

Dela raised her hands, "I don't know. That's why I was meeting him. To find out what he'd gotten messed up in."

"That sounds like you two have done business before." The man uncrossed his arms and stared at the body now lit up like the star of a play. "His throat was slit. Bag that knife."

Dela had called Heath while waiting for the police. He wasn't happy she was involved in another murder, not just by being here, but because her knife was the possible murder weapon. He also told her she didn't have an alibi since she hadn't taken anyone with her to vouch for the fact she didn't kill the man. She'd told him about the strange woman, but he hadn't thought that was an alibi. As Detective Fletcher turned his attention back to her, her gut twisted and she knew she had to tell him about the knife.

"That knife looks like one I keep in my car. When I left the casino to come here, my car was unlocked. I know I locked it. I've had enough run-ins with unscrupulous people to know to lock my car. Even at home."

Fletcher studied her. "Continue with what you did when you left the casino."

She told him about arriving, walking first in the opposite direction, and meeting the crazy lady.

"What crazy lady?" Fletcher asked.

"There was a woman, hunched on a bench that way." She pointed to the east. "It was cold so I walked about fifty yards to the east wondering where Gus was.

I spotted the woman. At first, she talked about the love she and Adam would spread and I could help, then her eyes became fierce and they fluttered and she said she could tell me where the bodies were buried." Dela shivered thinking about the change in the woman. "When I asked if she was all right, she took off down the bank toward the river. Then I heard a cry in this direction and jogged this way. I saw someone run out of the shadow under the bridge." Dela held out her hands. "I ran into the shadow of the bridge and tripped, landing on the body."

Fletcher's eyebrow rose. "You're telling us that you fell onto the body and that's why you have blood on your hands and coat?"

"Yes, because that's the truth." She crossed her arms and glared at him.

Fletcher snapped his fingers. "Donald, take Ms. Alvaro to the station. I want to check out the crime scene before I finish interviewing her."

"I gave my statement. Can't I go home and you can catch up to me tomorrow?" She didn't want to sit around the city police station all night as the crime scene was investigated. Not to mention Heath would be worried.

"You are a person of interest. I'd prefer you to be at the station."

"But I didn't—"

"If you did scare someone away who used your knife to kill the victim, you could be in danger." The detective looked her in the eyes. "The station is the best place for you until Heath can come get you."

She didn't see the venomous glare that she'd always received from Detective Jones of the Tribal

Police. This detective acted as if he believed her. Or was he just saying that because he knew Heath?

"Fine. Can I call him and let him know where to find me?"

Fletcher nodded as he squatted down beside the body.

She followed Officer Donald to a city car. He held the door as she sat in the back. Dela hated riding in the back seat of a police car. She didn't feel safe. She felt like a hostage.

Pulling her phone out of her pocket, she dialed Heath. Tears burned the backs of her eyes. She was tired, and deep down, she knew she should have waited to talk to Gus the next day with Heath present.

"What's happening?" Heath answered.

"Detective Fletcher has an officer taking me to the station for more questions and to keep me safe." She sighed, thinking about the hours of sleep she would miss.

"Safe? Why would he say that?" The exasperation in Heath's voice reminded her that he stuck by her more times than she wanted to think about when she'd been involved with the law.

She told him about seeing someone running away and calling out to them. She drew in a deep breath and blurted out the real reason she believed she was being taken to the police station. "I told him it was my knife lying on the ground next to the body. I didn't tell you before, when I ran into the dark under the bridge I tripped over the body, getting blood on my hands and coat."

"Damn, Dela! They think you did it, don't they?"

"I couldn't tell. Fletcher is hard to read. He seemed

sincere, but he also seemed intent on digging up all the evidence." She looked up when the vehicle stopped. "We're at the station. Fletcher said I couldn't leave until you came to get me. I have a feeling I'll be here all night. Finish your shift before you come. We can both take a nap when I get home." She ended the call as the officer opened her door.

The car was parked on the side entrance where the on-duty staff entered and suspects were brought in. Only the obligatory nighttime lights were on. Officer Donald walked her down the hall to a door he opened, revealing a dark room. He ushered her into the room and the light came on blinding her with its brightness.

"You can wait in here for Fletcher. Want something to drink?"

"Since it looks like I'll be here a while, coffee, black and can I use the restroom?" Dela shed her coat.

"I have to take a photo of your coat and hands before you can use the restroom." He pulled out his phone.

She held her hands out, then turned them palm up, and spread her arms so he could take a full-body photo.

"Spread the coat out on the table, please."

Dela did as instructed, making sure the blood showed that it wasn't spattered as it would be if she had slit Gus's throat.

After the officer took the photos, he pulled on gloves and started to fold her coat.

"Wait. I need my phone and car keys out of the pocket." Dela grabbed at the coat and shoved her hand into the pocket. She came up with her phone and keys.

"Do you want to check the other pockets?" Officer Donald asked.

"That should be all that's in there." But to be safe, she stuck her hand in the other pockets. She pulled out a used tissue, a receipt for gas from the Mission station, a candy bar wrapper, and a folded flowery paper she didn't recognize. "Okay. Bag it."

The officer studied her a second then put the coat in a large evidence bag. He wrote on the bag and told her to wait, he'd show her to the restroom after he'd taken the coat to evidence.

Dela stood by the table, waiting for him to leave. As soon as the door clicked shut, she unfolded the flowery paper. Her fingers shook as she read the scrawled writing.

*I can tell you where the bodies are buried. Follow Adam.*

When had the woman placed the note in her pocket? And why? What had she been doing on the river bank at that time of night? Was she homeless? Dela had so many questions pinging around in her head, she barely heard the officer outside the door soon enough to tuck the note in her pants pocket.

Officer Donald returned. This time he had a long tube. He took the top off and pulled a long-handled cotton swab out. "I need to get a sample of the blood on your hands."

Dela sighed deeply and stretched her hands out to the officer. It would match the victim. One more strike against her.

♠ ♣ ♥ ♦

Dela heard the footsteps coming down the hall. She'd dozed off for a bit after she'd used the restroom and the officer brought her a cup of coffee. One sniff of the coffee, she knew it would taste burnt. She'd pushed it to the center of the table after the officer left her, put her head on her crossed arms, and napped. But it had been a fitful nap with the crazy river lady invading her mind.

She felt slightly fresher from the nap and sat up straight as the door opened. To her surprise, Special Agent Quinn Pierce followed Detective Fletcher into the room.

"What are you doing here?" she asked, not sure if she was happy to see him or perturbed.

"Heath called and filled me in." Quinn sat in the chair across the table from her beside the detective.

She peered at Fletcher. "You're letting this Fed butt into your investigation?"

Fletcher's gaze drifted from Quinn to her and back to Quinn. Confusion wrinkled his wide brow. "You said she was a tribal member and you needed to be here."

"You know how tribal people feel about the FBI." Quinn shrugged and when Fletcher settled his gaze on her, the FBI agent gave her a look that said, play along.

Dela sighed deeply and leaned back in her chair. "What else did you learn at the crime scene?"

Fletcher frowned. "I'm the one asking the questions, not you. You are a person of interest."

"Only because Gus asked me for help." She muttered under her breath, "Some help I was."

"You have no idea why Gus wanted to meet with you?" Quinn asked. He knew she and Gus had met before when she was accused of killing Gus's meth cook.

"Not a clue. He called, tried flattering me with how he respected how I'd treated him in the past, and then said he wanted to meet to… That's when he had a sharp intake of breath and ended the call. So no, I don't know what he wanted to talk to me about." She leaned forward, staring at Quinn. "Has he stayed out of the drug business since his wife kicked him out?"

"Wait a minute!" Fletcher interjected. "What is this about a drug business? Is that how you knew him?"

"I was accused of killing his meth cook a couple years ago. The victim had been given a bag of money by Gus to buy product and make another batch. Before the victim's death, his wife had taken the bag of money and their son and fled. I found the wife and she asked me to return the money to Gus so she wasn't worrying someone would kill her. He appreciated that I returned his money and kept the police out of it. And I was the reason his wife divorced him. I told her he was fooling around with her best friend's daughter." Dela shrugged. "We women have to stick together."

"That's your history with the victim?" Fletcher asked. "All of it?"

"That's it. That's why his call surprised me. My guess is whatever trouble he was in he didn't want the police involved." Dela picked up the coffee cup, caught a whiff, and set it back down. "Can I get some water?"

Fletcher walked to the door, whistled, and then asked someone to bring in three bottles of water. He wasn't out of the room for Dela to ask Quinn anything.

The detective sat back down. "Let's start at the beginning of when you arrived at the walking path."

Dela repeated everything she did and saw from the time she stepped out of the car and put her coat on to when the first officers arrived on the scene.

During her recitation, the water arrived and she took several long drinks as she told the sequence of events. At the end, she asked, "Did you find Gus's vehicle anywhere along the parkway?"

"I have an officer looking. So far it appears he either walked there or parked some distance from the river." Fletcher studied the notes he'd scribbled. "That's all for now. But we'll keep your coat and expect you to come in tomorrow and sign the typed statement."

Dela glanced at Quinn and back to the detective. "Does this mean I can go, without Heath coming to get me?"

Fletcher nodded. "Special Agent Pierce said he'd take you back to your car."

Dela stood, smiled at the detective, and held out her hand.

He appeared unsure if he should take it.

"Thank you for doing a thorough job. I'm sure once all the evidence is looked over, I'll be cleared of this." They shook hands and she walked to the door, opened it, and walked down the hall, Quinn's footsteps following behind her.

# Chapter Three

The sun peeked over the Blue Mountains as Dela drove up to her house and parked. On the short drive from the police station to her car, she'd asked Quinn if he knew anything about a homeless woman living along the riverwalk. He said he didn't but he'd keep an ear out if he heard anything. Even though the woman had spooked her, Dela wanted to know more about her.

Heath's work vehicle sat beside the shed where they stored Jethro's hay and grain. She'd called him and told him she'd be driving herself home, he didn't need to come get her.

As she pulled her body out of the driver's seat the front door opened. Mugshot, her three-legged large mutt, hop-trotted up to her. She patted his head as she held Heath's gaze. The smell of breakfast grew stronger as she walked up to the porch. "How did you know I was starving?"

Heath kissed her and led her into the house.

"You're always starving when you are up all night."

He waited for her to hang her purse on the coat rack by the door and slump into her recliner, before asking, "Did having Quinn there make a difference?"

She smiled up at him. "Yes, I think it did. But he told Fletcher he was there because I was a tribal member." While she liked the idea of being a member, she didn't know for sure yet if she was. She only had her gut feeling that her father was Umatilla tribal member Dory Thunder.

"I told him to say that." Heath disappeared into the kitchen. As he returned, he said, "Otherwise, he would have had to say you were a person of interest in an FBI investigation and that would have made you look more suspicious."

"That's true. But I felt like Fletcher, having analyzed the scene, could see I was telling the truth. I think he was hoping I could help him discover who might have killed Gus." She frowned thinking. "I'd like to know what he was messed up in. Why he thought I could help him."

"Do you want to eat in the recliner or at the table?" Heath asked.

Dela held up a hand and he pulled her to her feet. "I want to get out of this prosthesis and take a shower." She held up her hands. "I can't see it but I still feel his blood on me."

"I can hold everything over. Let me help you out of the prosthesis and you'll be able to shower quicker."

She smiled. "I like that idea." A year ago she would have squirmed and told him she could do it herself. But since she'd finally given in to her feelings for Heath and allowed him to see all of her and her flaws, their relationship had grown stronger.

After a quick shower, Dela felt better. She was clean and sitting at the table in shorts and a T-shirt when a knock on the door startled all of them. Mugshot started barking and Heath shot to his feet.

Dela glanced at the kitchen clock. It was 8:12. Who would be coming here this early in the morning?

"Where is she?" her mom's urgent voice traveled into the kitchen.

"I'm in here, Mom," Dela said.

Deborah Truman rushed into the kitchen, putting her arms around Dela. "I heard you were brought to the Pendleton Police Station last night. What are you caught up in now?"

"Deborah, have a seat." Heath pulled out the chair next to Dela and her mom sat.

"I came across a body on the River Parkway last night. They took me in for questioning." Dela picked up her cup of chamomile tea.

"You came across a body? What time of night were you there? Why were you there?" Mom turned her gaze on Heath. "Why are you letting her run around at all hours of the night?"

Heath shrugged as he placed a cup of coffee in front of her mom.

"Heath isn't my boss," Dela said, wondering about how her mom could have thought her daughter would have someone tell her what to do and what not to do. In the Army she'd followed orders, it was a matter of life or death for them all. However, as a civilian, she answered to no one but herself.

"Well, someone needs to keep you safe if you can't

do it yourself," her mother said, before taking a sip of coffee.

"I can take care of myself, and I have been for many years."

Heath placed a hand on her shoulder. Dela breathed out slowly and then back in. He knew how crazy her mom could make her. Since Deborah had married Lance Truman, she seemed to have changed. Before, when it was the two of them, her mom believed in her and understood why she did what she did. Since becoming Mrs. Truman, Dela rarely saw her mom and when she did, she didn't like the woman her mom was becoming. She acted as if her life revolved around her husband. That she only had time for him and his needs.

Dela didn't like thinking these thoughts but she wanted her old mom back. The one who would listen to what she said and then help her logically make decisions. Not this one that seemed to worry about proprieties and keeping her man happy.

"I worked the night shift last night, and Dela was helping the police all night. We'd like to eat and then go to bed," Heath said, taking his seat across from Dela and picking up his fork.

"Oh, that's right. Dela did tell me you were doing the night shift while someone was on vacation. I'm sorry. But when Cheryl called me and told me what she'd seen, I had to come over and make sure you were okay." Mom finished off the coffee and placed the cup down as she rose to her feet.

"Did Lance mind that you ran out of the house so early this morning?" Dela asked.

"No, he had an early breakfast meeting with a man he's thinking about hiring as a foreman. Lance doesn't want to ranch anymore. He wants us to travel while we still can." She smiled. Growing up her mom had talked about how fun it would be to see other countries. Now she was getting her wish. Dela didn't want to spoil anything for her mom. She'd spent 30 years raising a daughter by herself and teaching. Now that she'd retired and married, she deserved happiness and no stress.

Dela pushed on the table to stand.

"Don't stand, you have to be exhausted." Mom leaned down and hugged her. "I'm glad you're okay," she whispered and straightened. "I'll let myself out. You two get some rest."

Mom walked out of the room with Mugshot right behind her. The front door opened and closed. Mugshot returned and sat down by Dela.

Dela and Heath ate in silence for several minutes.

"Is it just me or has your mom changed since her marriage?" Heath asked, picking up a glass of orange juice.

"She's changed. I'd like my old mom back, but I have a feeling with Lance giving her everything she wants, she'll hang on to him." Dela realized when she caught Heath staring at her that her tone had been snarky. "I don't begrudge her happiness. I just don't like the person she's turned into since marrying Lance."

Heath nodded. "I understand." They finished eating and did the dishes.

"I'll toss Jethro some hay and put Mugshot out with him. Then let's get some sleep." Heath dried his hands on the towel Dela had used to dry the dishes.

"I'd like that. Don't wake me if I'm asleep when you come in."

♠ ♣ ♥ ♦

Braying and barking woke Dela with a start. Her heart pounded against her ribs making it hard to breathe. The bed shook and her blurry gaze cleared as Heath pulled on sweats and headed out the door.

Dela swung her leg over the edge of the bed and grabbed her crutches from the hook on the nightstand drawer. She rose, sliding her left foot into a slipper, and headed down the hall.

The animals were quiet now. She swung over to the French doors that led out into the backyard. Jethro and Mugshot stood in the yard, staring at the gate on the side fence. It led out to the shed and the vehicles.

She stepped out the door and both animals came to her. Jethro nodded his head, showing off his teeth and Mugshot sat down beside her. She patted both their heads wondering what had set them off.

The gate opened and Heath entered. Sweat dripped down the side of his face and he was breathing hard.

Dela's stomach tightened. "Did we have an intruder?"

He nodded and waved for her to go inside.

Mugshot followed her in and Jethro started eating the lawn.

"Someone was trying to get in the house from the yard?" She sunk onto a kitchen chair. It was like Deja Vue all over again. Detective Dick, a corrupt tribal detective, had come after her several years ago. She'd been in the bath when the dog and donkey had alerted her. She'd had enough time to put some clothes on, grab her handgun, and take a position behind her bed to have a clear shot at him when he came through her bedroom door.

"This door was open when I came down the hall. I followed the intruder out the gate and lost him when he jumped in a vehicle with another person driving."

Dela peered at Heath. "Someone was waiting for him? Did you get the license number?"

"It didn't have one." He studied her. "Whoever you chased off last night must think you can identify them."

She shook her head, spinning the night before through her mind. "I didn't see anything. The person was in the shadow of the bridge and by the time he went under the next lamp, I was pushing myself up off of Gus."

"But he doesn't know that. He must think you saw him when he ran under the light." Heath rubbed a hand over his chin. "I don't like this."

"Neither do I, but I'm not hiding or going into protective custody. I want to go through Gus's things and see what he'd been doing lately." Dela glanced at the clock. They'd only been asleep a couple of hours. "You can go back to sleep. I'm going to make some phone calls and go to work."

Heath stared at her. "I'm only going to sleep while you make calls. You wake me up when you are getting ready to go to work. I'll take you."

"You can't take me to work. I'll need to come home before your shift is over," Dela protested. Not that this incident hadn't scared her a little, but she didn't want to be a burden on him or anyone else.

"I'll ask Jacob to pick you up. All you'll have to do is call him." Heath put his arms around her. "I don't want to lose you. Promise you won't go anywhere without someone with you. The intruder trying to get to you during the day with me here wasn't very smart."

"That means they don't know much about me, do they?" She leaned back to look up into his face. "Which means we can use that to our advantage."

"How?"

"I can go to places I don't normally go and see if they are following me."

"Not alone," Heath said firmly.

"I won't be alone. You have two hours more to sleep and then I'll be ready to go to work."

Heath kissed her and headed down the hall to the bedroom.

Dela used her crutches to gather a notepad and pen, then on her way to the couch, she grabbed her laptop. Setting all of the items on the couch, she returned to the kitchen to make a cup of coffee. If two hours were all the sleep she would get, it would take a lot of caffeine to keep her mind energized enough to ask coherent questions.

Settled on the couch with the notepad, she wrote down, Vivian Sander, Sander Construction, and Trace Talent. By now the police would have notified the next of kin. While his ex-wife probably wasn't notified, his daughter would be and she would call her mom. Dela needed to ask Vivian if she knew anything about her ex-husband's dealings.

# Chapter Four

Heath walked down the hall as Dela finished talking on the phone to Detective Fletcher. "Did you get the information you wanted?"

Dela smiled. "I have managed to get a meeting with Vivian Sander at the casino this evening, I left a message for Trace Talent to call, and Detective Fletcher told me he'd let me go into Sander Construction and look at the job files with him this afternoon. He'll pick me up at the casino at four." She stretched and handed her notepad to Heath. "I don't have much yet, but you can read it while I get dressed."

"You better hurry if you want to get to work early enough to get anything done before Fletcher shows up."

Dela swung her way down the hall and into the bathroom.

"Hey, do you think it's a good idea to be seen with the police if the killer is watching you? It might make them even more anxious to get rid of you," Heath said from outside the bathroom door.

"It will also give Fletcher a chance to see if anyone is following us."

♠ ♣ ♥ ♦

Dela had just finished talking to her second in command, Kenny Proudhorse, to let him know she would be gone for a while and he was in charge when Detective Fletcher arrived. She spotted the detective talking to Alfred their retirement-aged valet. He was her eyes and ears in the casino. He had a mind like a computer and could tell her who came and went and what vehicle they were driving.

"I'll call when I finish up with the detective. If all is calm, I'll leave you to run things tonight," she told Kenny.

He nodded his head. "You are the boss and you need time off too." His soft voice and earnest words put a smile on her face. She walked out from behind one of the Appaloosa horse statues at the base of the waterfall cascading down from the ceiling.

Detective Fletcher spotted her and strode forward. "I didn't think you'd be happy to see me."

She shrugged and walked by him toward the entrance. "I'll be happy when we get Gus's murderer caught."

The man caught up to her at the door.

"Leaving so soon?" Alfred asked, his gaze flitting to the man beside her.

"I'm helping the city police with a murder investigation. Kenny has things under control." She smiled at the old man and he winked.

"What was that all about?" Fletcher asked as they walked over to his unmarked police vehicle.

"Alfred? He sees and hears everything that happens in the casino and on the reservation. I'm sure that by the time I return, he'll have some information for me about Gus's death."

Fletcher started for her side of the vehicle, she quickly stepped forward and grasped the door handle. The only man she allowed to open the door for her was Heath. She knew he did it because he wanted to make her feel special. She didn't want someone opening the door for her out of habit.

When they were both seated in the vehicle, Fletcher asked, "How will he know to look into Sander's death? You didn't give him a name." He started the car.

"He'll find out where I'm going and what happened to me last night and then he'll start digging for information. That's how Alfred is." She shrugged as they pulled out of the casino parking lot. She glanced in the side view mirror to see if anyone followed. She didn't see any vehicles moving behind them. Settling back in her seat, she began asking the questions she'd had tumbling around in her head since Heath chased the intruder.

"Has anyone seen the vehicle I described driving around Pendleton without a license?"

"No. And before you ask, there are a lot of that type of vehicle registered in the state and Umatilla County. I do have the county and state law enforcement looking for the vehicle. It just reinforces that you are in danger."

"Am I no longer a suspect?" Dela asked, studying Detective Fletcher.

"You were ruled out as soon as you told me about

the knife and falling on the victim. A murderer wouldn't point out the weapon was theirs and the blood on your hands and coat were all smeared as if you had fallen on him, and not because you snuck up behind him and slit his throat." The detective glanced at her and grinned. "And your previous run-ins with the law have all been well documented. You don't play well with others, but you are usually helpful in finding the killers."

Dela huffed out a breath. It was good to know she wasn't a suspect but aggravating that they just felt she was useful, not good at her job. "Where had Gus ended up after his divorce?"

"He still has the construction business. It appears his wife, Vivian, took everything but the business from him. What I learned is he's been living in the office. He had a shower installed in the men's bathroom."

Dela thought that was smart of the deceased. He wouldn't have to pay for a place to stay while he built his business back up. She knew Vivian had kept the house and all the money, even the money Gus had made through drugs. She'd put the drug money back into the community through various philanthropic means.

At the construction office, Dela was surprised to see Evelyn, Gus's daughter, talking to the receptionist.

When the woman turned toward them, her eyes narrowed. "What are you doing here? I heard you are the one who stabbed my father." Evelyn put her hands on her hips and glared at Dela.

"I didn't kill him. He called me for help but I was too late." Dela crossed her arms. "Looks like you're jumping into your father's shoes pretty quick."

"He'd been teaching me everything so I could take over the business. It's pretty easy to step in when I've been with him at every one of the job estimates and contracts for the past year."

Detective Fletcher cleared his throat. "We're here to take a look at the jobs your father was working on. Maybe you can help us figure out who did this."

Evelyn's gaze landed on Fletcher and she did a brief nod. "Tara, I'll be in my office if anyone needs anything."

"Yes, Ma'am." The receptionist was a good twenty years older than her new boss.

Dela followed Evelyn into the office that had previously been lorded over by her father. Now it had the subtle touches of a woman. Not so many renderings of buildings and more floral accents.

"What do you want to know?" Evelyn asked, sitting in the chair behind the desk.

Dela sat in one of the chairs facing the desk. Detective Fletcher perched on the edge of the chair to her right.

"What are some of the projects your father was working on and which company of those projects would he be scared of?" Dela asked.

Evelyn glanced at the detective. He nodded.

"I don't understand. Father wasn't scared of any of the people we were constructing buildings for. Why would he be?" Evelyn's gaze flicked back and forth between them.

"He called me asking for help. He was scared of someone. Was he back dealing drugs?" Dela asked.

"No! I made sure of that. I didn't want any of that kind of gossip to discredit the construction company. Not when he was handing it over to me. I want to be known for quality workmanship and competitive pricing." The pride in her voice made Dela hope the young woman could pull it off.

"What are some of the recent builds the company has done?" Fletcher asked, pulling a notebook out of his pocket.

"I can't believe any of those would have anything to do with what happened," Evelyn said, staring at the detective.

"We will be discreet in asking them questions," Dela said.

Evelyn swung her gaze back at her. "What do you mean we? Are you now a policeman?"

Fletcher cleared his throat. "Dela is working with us as a specialist."

The woman crossed her arms. "How could a person of interest be helping you? I heard that her knife was the murder weapon. Why are you even bringing her in here?"

"I had no grudge against your father. He called me for help. When I went to meet up with him, I found him dead. I saw someone run off, but I didn't get a good look at him. How my knife got there is a surprise to me. I know my car was unlocked when I left the casino to meet your father. Whether he'd taken the knife from my car for protection or someone else did it to incriminate me because he'd called for my help, we won't know until we catch the killer." Dela leaned forward. "Evelyn, I didn't kill your father. But I want to find out who did just as much as you. I want to know who framed me and why they wanted Gus dead. What did he know that they didn't want him telling me?"

"Ms. Sander, if we could see all the construction jobs your company has undertaken in the last year, it could help us to figure out why your father was killed," Detective Fletcher said in a kind voice.

Dela glanced over to see if it was the same man she'd walked into the building with.

Evelyn locked gazes with Fletcher and then she nodded and stood. She walked over to a file cabinet, dug through the top two drawers, and pulled out files. Placing the files on the desk closest to Detective Fletcher, Evelyn asked, "Do you really think one of these people killed my father?"

"We won't know until we question them." Fletcher stood and gathered the files into his arms.

"Thank you, Evelyn. We'll find the killer." Dela stood and walked toward the door to open it for the detective with his full hands.

"If it's one of those people, it will make me think real hard whether or not I keep this company."

Dela understood the young woman's hesitancy to continue in her father's footsteps if he had been mixed up in something that would get a person killed.

# Chapter Five

Dela and Detective Fletcher took the files to the city police station and began writing down the names of the Sander Construction Company's clients.

Dela wrote down a company name and Keenan Cristo, the owner's name. "Have you ever heard of Oregon Trail Brewery?" Somewhere in the back of her mind, she'd heard the owner's name, but she wasn't sure where.

Fletcher looked up from the file he was reading. "I heard someone applied for permits and licenses for a brewery. Why?"

"A Keenan Cristo contracted Sander Construction to build the brewery at the corner of the Umatilla River and I-eighty-four." Dela's mind calculated where that would be. "It's across the river from the correctional facility and behind Walmart." She stared at the paperwork. "That seems like an odd place to put a brewery."

"Not if you plan on using the water from the river to run it." Fletcher held up a file. "I'd be more worried about this apartment building that cut corners. Notes are jotted down saying the construction company wouldn't be at fault if the structure is found unsound. The owner spent the least amount of money he could by using economy lumber. I think the first person we need to contact is Delbert Malik, the owner of the apartments. He would have a reason to keep Gus from talking about the inferior quality lumber used in the apartments."

"Where are the apartments located?" Dela asked. There had been new ones built in Mission over the last year.

"Near Rice-Blakely Park."

Dela felt bad that she was relieved it wasn't on the rez, but also feared for the people who didn't know they were living in housing made from poor-quality products.

"I think we need to check out both of these people," Dela persisted.

Fletcher held out his hand.

Dela slapped the folder about the brewery in it and snatched the folder about the apartment building from him. As they read the files, her phone buzzed. A glance showed Heath's name.

"Hi," she answered.

"How did the trip to the construction office go?" Heath asked.

"We're reading through the files of the jobs the company did over the last year. I found an interesting one and so did Fletcher." She didn't go into detail with the man sitting in the room with her.

"What time do you need to meet Vivian?"

"Seven."

"Want to have dinner with me before or afterward?" Heath asked.

"Where?"

"At the casino. That's where you're going after you finish reading files isn't it?" His voice held suspicion.

"I thought about going home for a quick nap when we finish here." She was getting sleepy as she stared at the paper in her hand.

"If Fletcher drops you off at home, I can take you to the casino for our dinner and your meeting."

Now she knew the true reason he'd called. To make sure she wasn't running around by herself. While one part of her loved that he cared, the independent obstinate nature of her, felt he was being controlling.

"I'm sure Detective Fletcher has better things to do than be my chauffeur."

"What are you talking about?" Fletcher asked, setting down the file.

"Hand the phone to Fletcher," Heath said.

Dela heaved a disgusted sigh and gave her phone to the detective. She went back to reading and listened to the one-sided conversation.

"Sure, no problem. I'll drop her off at home in thirty minutes. We've read all the files that were given to us." He listened. "Copy."

"Here's your phone," he said, holding it toward Dela.

She grabbed it and shoved it in her purse. "Did Heath talk you into babysitting me?" she couldn't keep the contempt out of her voice.

"No, he asked me to take you home so you can rest and he'll take you to the casino when you're ready."

Fletcher stood. "Do you want copies of any of these?"

Dela flipped open the Cristo file and took photos of the information that interested her. Then she did the same with the Malik file. "I'm good."

"I'll put these away and take you home." Fletcher disappeared out the door.

Dela wanted to hurry from the room and call her friend Molly to come get her, but she knew that would only upset Heath when Fletcher said she did a runner.

The detective returned and smiled. "Let's go. You'll have to direct me. I have no idea where you live."

Dela didn't acknowledge him. She just walked out of the building and over to his car.

He started the vehicle and asked, "Which way?"

"Head east on eighty-four."

He maneuvered out of town and onto the interstate headed east. "Do you live on the reservation?"

"Yes. I live in Tutuilla, a small community on the south side of the interstate." When they came to the exit for the casino, she told him to exit and go right. She lived only four miles from the casino which made it easy when she was called back in on nights when the customers got out of control.

At her house, she opened the door to the sound of barking and braying.

"Do you have a zoo here?" Fletcher asked, chuckling.

"No, that's my alarm system. Thanks for the ride." She closed the door and walked up to the front door. She'd expected to find Heath at home but his truck was missing and the door was locked.

Fumbling for her keys, she noticed Fletcher hadn't

backed out of the driveway. He was watching to make sure she made it into the house safe. She should be flattered but it only annoyed her. Why couldn't she be like other women and enjoy a man making sure she was safe?

She sighed, unlocked the door, shoved it open, and waved to Fletcher. As soon as she closed the door, she locked it and headed to the French doors that led to the backyard.

The donkey and the dog had their faces pressed against the glass looking in.

Dela laughed and opened the door, easing both the animals back so she could sit on the step and pet them. "You were good boys this morning chasing away that intruder. I just wish you could have stopped him so we could know who we are dealing with."

Mugshot licked her hand and Jethro put his large head on her shoulder. She laughed. "I wouldn't know what to do without you two." Dela pushed to her feet and stepped into the house to grab an apple off the counter.

"This is your treat." She held it in the palm of her hand as Jethro grabbed it with his large greenish teeth. When he walked away with his treat, she reached back in and held out a dog bone for Mugshot. "I didn't forget you." She ruffled his ears as he ate the crunchy bone.

Once the two were satisfied, Dela and Mugshot entered the house with her locking the French doors and walking over to the recliner. She'd slept in this for several months as her house was being remodeled. It made a great place to take a nap.

Barking and braying shot Dela's eyelids up and her

mind awake. She listened to a car door being closed and Heath calling out to Jethro.

Dela put her hand on Mugshot's head. "Shh, it's just Heath. We're okay." She didn't bother to get up and unlock the door. Heath had his keys. Instead, she remained in the chair, allowing the initial adrenaline surge to slow and her mind to slip back into a drowsy state.

Keys jingled, the doorknob jiggled, and a cool rush of air swept across her body as Heath opened the door and walked through.

The door closed.

"Did Jethro wake you?" Heath asked, from beside the chair.

She opened her eyes and smiled up at him. "Yeah, but that's okay. I've been asleep long enough." She pulled on the lever that lowered her feet and sat up straight. "Where have you been?"

He tossed his keys on the television stand before lowering onto the couch. "When I took on the night patrol shift, I didn't realize they still expected me to do my day job." He stifled a yawn. "I was called in to question Morty Bell. He was caught stealing from cars at the casino last night."

Dela leaned forward. "Did you ask him if he stole something from my car?"

"He swore he only stole from the people losing money at the casino, not the employee's parking lot." Heath shrugged. "I believed him. He had it in for people wasting money and figured they could afford to miss the valuables in their cars."

Dela leaned back. "Did you happen to ask him if he saw anyone lurking around in the employee's parking lot?"

"No, but I did ask Marty to send me video from last night of the front and back lots." He raised an eyebrow. "I was surprised you hadn't already asked him to do that."

Her cheeks heated. She hadn't thought to call on her surveillance team to check on who had broken into her car. "I guess being hauled into the police station and little sleep has me not thinking clearly."

He reached over and took her hand. "I understand. What did you say to Alfred? He was asking everyone questions when I arrived to ask Marty for the video."

A smile tipped her mouth. It made her feel like a tribal member when others jumped in and helped her out. "I just mentioned that I was mixed up in a murder."

Heath smiled. "You knew he'd start asking around and put his mind to figuring out what was going on."

"Kind of. What I'd really like to know from him is if he saw a vehicle that didn't belong in the employee's parking." Alfred would have noticed any out-of-place vehicle back there.

"Good idea. Get dressed and I'll get in my uniform. We can head to the casino and you can ask him." Heath stood, reached down, and grasped her hands, pulling her to her feet. But instead of releasing her, he pulled her into his arms and held her tight. "I know you will never be out of harm as long as you live, but I would love to go a year or two without you being in the middle of a murder."

She held him tight. He was her tree. Strong, whispering encouragements, and faithful to try to shade her from herself. "I'm sorry trouble seems to follow me. But I'm glad you're here to keep me from doing something stupid."

He leaned back, a smile on his lips and in his eyes. "As you've learned, I'm not going anywhere, *timnáki*."

When he used the endearment 'my heart,' Dela knew Heath was telling her the truth. "*qayciyáẃyaw.*" After growing up at Nixyáawii, she'd learned the polite words. And thank you had been the first word Grandfather Thunder taught her. It always made the elders smile when she thanked them.

Heath hugged and released her. "Let's get ready for work."

She nodded and walked down the hall ahead of him. He had been her rock growing up, and now, he was here always believing in her even when all the evidence pointed at her being the killer. How she was so lucky to have him in her life, she would never know.

# Chapter Six

At the Spotted Pony, Dela and Heath stopped to visit with Alfred.

"I've been talking to people and no one knew much about the death of Gus. But no one believes that you killed him," Alfred added, nodding, making his gray braids rub up and down the breast pockets of his Western shirt.

Dela smiled. "That's nice to know. Last night, or any time on your shift, did you happen to see a car in the employee parking lot that didn't belong there?"

Alfred studied her for several seconds and then snapped his fingers. "I did see a small dark SUV drive along the edge of the main parking lot and go toward the back. It caught my attention because it didn't have a license plate."

Dela caught Heath's gaze. He nodded.

"What time was it that you saw the vehicle?" Dela asked.

"Around eleven last night." Alfred narrowed his eyes. "Do they have something to do with the murder?"

"I think they got into my car and stole the knife that killed Gus." Dela held Heath's gaze. The car had arrived after her phone call with Gus. Someone knew he'd called her and was going to tell her something.

"Thank you, Alfred. And if you see that vehicle again, let me know." Dela put a hand on his shoulder.

"I will. And I'll keep a watch out for anything unusual in the employee parking lot."

"Thank you." She grasped Heath's arm. "Let's get dinner before I talk to Vivian."

Her phone buzzed. It was Marty in surveillance.

"Hey, Marty," she answered.

"Dela, I saw you and Heath enter the casino. I have the video he requested. Want to come back to surveillance and take a look?"

"Only if you have popcorn," she said, joking.

"I do."

"Heath and I were just going to get some dinner."

"No problem, which restaurant?" Marty asked.

She asked Heath, "Which restaurant are we eating at?"

"Stallion or the Pony?"

"I like the Pony better." She said into the phone, "We'll be at the Pony."

"I'll see you in ten."

Dela put her phone away. "Marty is bringing the videos to us it sounds like."

"That works. Why did you pick the Pony? I was ready to pay for a nice meal."

She shrugged. "I like the less proper atmosphere of the Pony over the Stallion."

"I should have known you were a bar and grill and not a fancy dinner date." He squeezed the hand he held as they walked through the jingles and voices of the slot machines and players. The energy from the machines and people always gave Dela a burst of adrenaline. The flashing lights and bright colors added to the liveliness. Moving through the slot machines to the gaming tables, there was a subtle change in the energy. Not so flashy and bright, but more intense.

They stepped through the opening to the Pony Bar & Grill. Dela did a scan of the patrons. While the Pony was noisier than the Stallion, she felt more at home here. The servers were friendlier and the food was more her style.

"Where do you want to sit?" Heath asked.

"Somewhere that we can look at the video without others seeing," she replied, pointing to a corner booth.

They hurried across and both slid to the middle in the corner. A waitress came over. She smiled at them and said, "We generally keep the booths for more than two people."

"A third person is meeting us and," Dela reached into her pocket and pulled out her security card. "We're having dinner and a meeting with someone from surveillance. This is the best spot to have privacy."

The woman's face reddened. "I'm sorry. I didn't realize you were security."

Dela glanced down at her polo shirt which sported the Spotted Pony Casino logo and wondered how long the woman had been working here. All the security staff wore the same dark blue shirt with the casino emblem and the word Security written underneath along with khaki pants. She just didn't have the mic and belt with various means of subduing a rowdy patron.

"I'll have an iced tea," Heath said, cutting into the awkwardness.

"I'll have lemonade, please," Dela said. "And we'll take a basket of waffle fries to start."

The waitress nodded and hurried away.

"I'd say she's a new hire," Heath said.

"Yeah. She's not very observant if she didn't notice my security uniform."

The waitress returned with their drinks, a basket of waffle fries, and various dipping sauces.

Before she left the table, Marty arrived. "Hey, Sara, how's your second day on the job?"

The woman gave him a wan smile. "It's going okay. There's more to learn about this than I knew."

"How so?" Marty slid in next to Dela. "Hi," he said and nodded to Heath.

"They can tell you. Did you want to order, now?" Sara asked Dela.

She and Heath gave her their orders and she hurried away.

"What did you say that has her worried?" Marty asked.

"How do you know her?" Dela asked. After all, he was married to her best friend and she didn't think he was the cheating type but all the years she'd worked as an M.P. in the Army and now here in security, she'd learned you never really knew anyone.

"She's a cousin on my mom's side." He bumped her shoulder. "Did you think I would step out on Molly? Never! She's the best thing that ever happened to me."

"That's good to hear. I'm sorry I upset Sara. We sat

here and she told us since there were only two of us, we couldn't sit here. I showed her my I.D. and told her you were coming." Dela shrugged. "I didn't do anything wrong."

Marty leaned around her and said to Heath, "Did she have her 'I don't take shit off anyone' look?"

Heath laughed and nodded.

Dela humphed and said, "Show me what you found."

Marty chuckled and opened the laptop, he had in his hands, on the table in front of her. "Someone did pull up to your car, get out, push a button on something in his hand, and open the passenger side door." He ran the video.

Even though Dela parked under a light, the person had on all black and a hoodie pulled over his head. She could tell by the build and how the person moved it was a male. But that was about it. When he closed the door, she didn't see anything in his hand, but he had to have taken the knife.

"Okay, we can't see much about him. What about the car?" she asked.

"Not much there either. A dark smaller SUV without a license. No stickers or anything else to distinguish it." Marty ran another video of the car pulling into the lot and another of it driving off.

"This is proof someone got into your vehicle," Heath said. "Marty, send a copy to Detective Fletcher at City Police. I'm pretty sure he knows Dela didn't kill Gus but this is proof someone had access to her car and the knife."

"I can do that." Marty closed the computer and slid a little farther from Dela, placing the device on the bench seat next to him. "Mind if I catch up on news and then split?"

Dela smiled and said, "Not at all. What kind of news do you have?"

"Molly and I have finally saved up enough to build a house out in your area. With us moving out of the living quarters at the vet clinic, Travis has been getting pretty serious with a girl he met at the last powwow."

"That was last July. Is she from around here?" Dela asked. She was happy for Travis but wondered if he was a little too young to jump into marriage. He had only recently turned twenty-one. She and Heath had attended his birthday party. It had been pretty mellow for a coming-of-drinking-age birthday. "Was she at Travis's birthday?" She was trying to remember if she saw him hanging out with one girl more than any other.

"No, she had to work that weekend. She seems to have her priorities figured out. She's taking courses at Blue Mountain and is helping Molly at the clinic." Marty smiled when Sara arrived with their dinner and a soda for him. "Thanks, Sara. I'm sure you weren't formally introduced. This is Dela Alvaro, head of security for the Spotted Pony, and her squeeze, Heath Seaver, Detective with the Tribal Police."

"Oh! You're both in security," she said in a tone of admiration.

"Yes," Heath said.

"Dela and Heath, this is Sara Rush."

"Pleased to meet you, Sara. You'll see quite a bit of me because I like to use the bar and grill for meetings," Dela added.

"I'll remember that for next time." The young woman's cheeks reddened. "Thank you for the introductions," she said to Marty and hurried away.

"She's a good kid. Had a tough upbringing, but she's come out one of the good ones." Marty picked up his soda. "So, what's new with you two, other than another death being pinned on Dela."

She sighed. It did seem like every disreputable person killed was pinned on her. "Not much. Life was moving along smoothly until last night." She felt Heath's gaze on her and pivoted her head to peer into his eyes. What was he thinking behind that penetrating stare?

"Who were the two people you and Fletcher came up with that you were interested in?" Heath asked.

She looked at him in confusion. What did that have to do with their life lately? Stuttering she said, "K-Keenan Cristo and Delbert Malik. Why?"

Heath's gaze shifted to Marty. "Look these guys up and then see if they frequent the casino. It would be good to learn more about them. Someone had to tell the killer which vehicle was Dela's and know that she would have a weapon to use to implicate her."

"That means someone who knows her well talked to them, even Dela herself." Marty and Heath both peered at her.

Raising her hands, she said, "I don't tell anyone anything personal about me."

Heath nodded. "That's true. Trying to get anything out of her is like trying to pull Mugshot through a miniature doggie door."

Marty laughed. "I'll find photos of the men and see what I can find in videos. I'll start with the most recent and work my way backward."

"Sounds like a plan," Heath said, picking up his

fork and digging into his meal.

Dela thought about what Heath had suggested. Had someone from the casino been talking about her? And if so, why would they give a patron her information? For money or what?

# Chapter Seven

Dela stepped out of the security office and spotted Vivian Sander entering the casino. The woman was ten minutes early. Dela strode down the walkway toward the tall fashionably dressed woman who carried herself with confidence.

Vivian caught sight of her and smiled, walking in her direction. Men of all ages watched her.

When they met, they both nodded.

"Let's go in the coffee shop, it's quieter," Dela said.

Vivian's smile drooped. "I was hoping you'd say the bar."

Dela laughed. "You can go there when we've finished talking." While they were worlds apart, Vivian from money and dressed like a model in a magazine and Dela grew up on the reservation and preferred workout clothes to anything else, they had bonded over their disgust of Vivian's husband.

Once they were seated in a booth on the far side of the coffee shop, Vivian set her purse on the bench beside her and peered at Dela. "This is about Gus, isn't it?"

Dela nodded and ordered coffee when the waitress arrived. Vivian ordered the same and once the woman had left, she said, "I don't believe you killed him. That was too good for the bastard."

"We agree on that. He needed to wallow for a while longer. But he called me, asking for my help. Out of curiosity, I showed up to meet with him. That's when I found his body with my knife lying beside him." Dela's anger rose every time she thought about how someone had broken into her car, took the knife given to her years ago, and used it to kill the man.

"I didn't have someone kill him, though I'd thought about putting my hands around his throat a few times when I discovered all the illegal crap he'd been doing behind my back." The woman's usually calm face was taut and her eyes sparked with anger.

"I ran into Evelyn at the construction company. I'm sure you know she's taking over." Dela waited for the woman to nod. "Do you think she knows the clients as well as she told Detective Fletcher and myself she does?"

"You mean do I think there might be one who my ex-husband double-crossed and that's why he ended up dead and that person could go after Evelyn?" The woman's eyes narrowed. "Just let them try. I've already hired bodyguards for her. She thinks I'm being overprotective. She doesn't believe one of their clients killed him. But I see you think the same as I do."

"If he was truly out of the drug business then the

only other thing I can see is his construction company that would tie him with someone who wanted to kill him. Detective Fletcher took files about the clients from the past year. Can you get Evelyn to let someone look at the books to see if Gus might have been using cheaper lumber than was paid for or charged someone more than the work or supplies were worth? We do know he has records on Delbert Malik who built apartments by Rice-Blakely Park. Those records show Malik requested all the cheapest materials be used. Then he had Gus sign a paper saying he wouldn't tell anyone. I didn't get a chance to ask Evelyn if she knew her father had agreed to keep quiet. Makes me wonder if he was having second thoughts and Malik decided to shut him up. But there is the paper he signed that anyone can read and has read." Dela shrugged.

"That sounds like Gus. He probably pocketed five grand to sign that paper." Vivian picked up her coffee cup and sipped. "I think Evelyn would have told me about that if she'd known. She has been telling me all about the ways she was keeping her father straight.

"What about a Keenan Cristo and his Oregon Trail Brewery?" Dela asked.

"He is a smooth talker and a very handsome man. He's popped into a few of the Chamber meetings and some of the charities I help with. When I asked him what made him pick Pendleton to build his brewery, he said he wanted to give the economy a boost." She shrugged. "I've heard he starts brewery businesses in all kinds of smaller communities."

"Do you know where he's based out of?" Dela asked.

"One person said Seattle, another said San Diego.

I'm not sure. I can ask him if you'd like. I'll see him at a charity meeting tomorrow."

"No, it's best to just act like I never asked you questions." Dela picked up her cup of coffee and wondered how to ask her next question. "Not that I think you have been keeping tabs on your ex, but do you know if he was still messing about with younger women?"

"You think a mad father or mother could have had him killed?" Vivian asked.

"It is one of the things that got him into trouble before." It was the straw that had ended his marriage. When Vivian found out he'd been sleeping with her best friend's teenage daughter, she'd started divorce proceedings and took him for everything but the construction company.

"I haven't been keeping tabs on him, but Evelyn has. She said as far as she could tell he'd thrown himself into work since the divorce because it was his only means of making money and he didn't have extra to throw around. In fact, he'd been losing weight according to Evelyn." Vivian's eyes glazed over for a few seconds as if she were remembering something. Then she shook. "I can't help you much but I can keep an ear out if I hear anything."

"That would be helpful, just don't go asking questions. If the wrong person hears you inquiring about your ex-husband's death, they might think you know something you don't." Dela put a hand on Vivian's arm. "Promise you won't ask questions, just listen and let me know if you hear anything that pertains to what we talked about here."

"I promise I won't ask questions. And I'll talk with

Evelyn. I'll tell her to help you and the police and not to go asking any of her clients any questions." Vivian finished off her coffee and slid to the end of the bench. "Thank you for contacting me. That's what I like about you. You were willing to talk to my ex-husband even after all he'd done, and now you are trying to solve his murder. I'll help you all I can." She gracefully rose to her feet and strode out of the coffee shop.

When Dela focused on her coffee cup to finish the drink, she noticed Vivian had left a twenty-dollar bill to pay for the coffee and as a tip to the waitress. That was what Dela liked about the woman. She always thought of everyone and not just herself.

The lack of sleep from the night before had her eyelids drooping. Putting her hand to her mic, she asked for Kenny's location.

"Office, boss," he replied in his soft drawl.

"Stay there until I get there," she replied.

"Copy."

Dela slid out of the booth and headed to the security office. On the way, she scanned the casino floor, noting where the security personnel were stationed. She stopped by the water feature near the entrance and texted Heath. *I'm ready to go home. Is Jacob available to take me?*

*He's in the parking lot where you normally park.*

*That's convenient.* She meant it sarcastically. Why hadn't she figured Heath would have Jacob waiting for her when he finished his shift with the Tribal Police?

*It was his idea, not mine. But I thought it was good.*

Heath knew her too well. He'd understood she was upset.

*Talk to you in the morning.* She replied and headed

to the security office.

Kenny swiveled his chair when she walked into the room. "What's up?"

"I'm heading home. No sleep last night and only a couple of hours today has me beat. Things look quiet. Call if you need anything." She stopped at her desk, pulled off her mic and radio, placing them on her desk, and grabbed her purse out of a desk drawer.

"Want me to walk you out to your car?" Kenny shrugged. "I heard what happened last night."

"Thanks, but Jacob's waiting to drive me home." She hated the fact that it made her feel safer than driving home alone. Something she had done for several years at this time of night and it rarely bothered her. However, knowing someone had breached the lock on her car last night and stolen something from it, had her wondering what else they could do to harm her.

"Jacob's a good man," Kenny said.

"He is." She walked out the back door of the security office and spotted Jacob in a car where she usually parked. She'd first met him when he was in grade school. His big sister was Dela's best friend. Robin had been like a sister to Dela. They'd shared everything.

Until the day they'd gone to Pendleton and Dela had to return for basketball practice. Robin wasn't ready to return and said she'd find a ride home. Dela had driven off believing her friend would call a family member to pick her up.

The next day she found out Robin never made it home. A day later they found her abused body alongside the freeway. Dela had regretted her decision every day since. She had thought Jacob would hate her. Instead, they had bonded over the loss and she counted him as one of her closest friends.

His car pulled up alongside her. "Hop in, I'm your ride home," he said, reaching across and opening the passenger door.

"I'm glad it was you that Heath sent to pick me up." She smiled and settled into the passenger seat. It was kind of nice being driven home when she was so tired. She had a hard time keeping her eyes open as Jacob asked about her mom and how she liked married life. He parked in the driveway behind her car.

Dela opened the door to exit the vehicle and said, "You don't have to check the house. If someone was here the boys would be making more noise." Mugshot's happy bark, followed by a happy bray from Jethro, filled the air.

"They can make more noise than this?" Jacob asked, jokingly.

"Try to break in some time and you'll find out."

"I promised Heath I'd make sure no one was in the house when I brought you home. And I agreed with him that it was a good idea." He put up a hand to stop her objection. "And I could use a cold one after today."

She got the hint. He wanted to hang out and talk a bit. She was tired but never too tired to visit with a friend. After her mistake over twenty years ago, she never refused a friend anything. That, and losing another best friend just a year ago had solidified her vow.

"Come on, I'll unlock the door and while you're prowling around the house I'll get you a beer." Dela strode to the door, put the key in the lock, and twisted. The door opened and Jacob went in ahead of her.

When he headed down the hall, she walked into the kitchen and opened the French doors to let Mugshot in and pet Jethro. By the time she'd finished talking to the animals and closed the door, Jacob entered the kitchen.

"Let's sit in the living room," Dela said, pulling two beers out of the fridge. She led the way to the other room and handed Jacob a bottle before she sat down in the recliner. Using the lever on the side, she made the footrest raise and felt immediate relief taking the pressure off her stub.

"Have you figured out how the killer had your knife?" Jacob asked.

"We saw a video today of them using something that looked like a key fob to unlock my car door. I don't understand why they didn't relock the door, so I wouldn't have known they had been in my car." She sipped her beer.

"Do you have two key fobs?" Jacob asked.

"Yeah. One in my purse and the other is in this drawer." She tapped the top of the end table between the couch and her recliner.

Jacob placed his beer on the table and opened the drawer. His hand swished around inside making scraping and clanking noises. "There isn't a key fob in here."

Dela's heart started thudding in her chest. "It has to be." She plunked her bottle on the tabletop as she lowered the footrest. Leaning forward, she pulled the drawer out of the table, placed it on her lap, and began going through it. She looked through it twice. There wasn't a fob to be found. She handed the drawer to Jacob.

"My car and house aren't safe," she whispered.

Fear had been her friend on many occasions in Iraq as an M.P. in the Army and she'd known fear the night Detective Jones broke into her house to kill her, but this was different. This was feeling as if she would never be safe again. She started shaking.

"Hey. It's okay. You can get a loaner for a while and keep both keys with you. I'll stay until Heath comes home and you can get someone to install better locks and a security system. You can be safe in your home." Jacob knelt in front of her and pulled her into his arms.

She hated feeling vulnerable, hated being scared. With a gentle push, she eased out of his hold. "I'll be fine. You're right. I can rent a car and get top security on the house tomorrow." She pushed to her feet. "I think I'll go to bed. Not enough sleep has made me react emotionally."

Jacob leaned back and smiled. "Dela, if not getting enough sleep makes you human then you need to miss more sleep."

She shoved him, making him fall back on his butt.

Jacob laughed, and Dela walked down the hall to her bedroom.

She heard the television go on and headed for the shower.

# Chapter Eight

The door creaked open and Dela shot up in bed, her hand pulling the Glock out from under the pillow.

"*Timnáki*, it's Heath. Put the gun down."

His soft voice broke through the fear that pumped her heart and whooshed in her head. Dela dropped her arm holding the weapon and slumped back against the headboard.

Strong arms wrapped around her. "You're safe and always will be." He placed the gun on the bedside table and rocked with her in his arms until her heart stopped racing.

He kissed her face and said, "Jacob told me about the key fob and getting a security system. We'll take care of all of that today. I have the day off and we'll make sure the house and you are safe."

Dela nodded against his shoulder. "I hate feeling scared," she said through clenched teeth.

"I know. That is what makes you so strong. Your

fear of being vulnerable. This is something we can take care of. You will be in control by the middle of the day. I promise. Get dressed and I'll have breakfast ready for you."

"Don't you need to sleep?" Dela focused on his tired face.

"Not until you have a rental car and the house is secure. Then I'll sleep." He kissed her forehead and left the room.

Mugshot placed his basketball-sized head on the bed and nuzzled her. "Thanks for being here last night," she said, patting his head. He'd awakened her during the night when she was having a horrible dream about someone entering the house and killing everyone she cared about. The dog had climbed up on the bed and snuggled with her until she'd fallen back to sleep.

He licked her hand and walk/hopped to the door.

Dela swung her leg over the bed and grabbed her crutches. She swung to the door and opened it for the dog to go out. She listened for voices. When she didn't hear any, she swung down the hall and into the kitchen.

Heath had his back to her as he made coffee. She moved up behind him and put an arm around his shoulders, leaning against his strong back. "Thank you for understanding."

He spun around and wrapped his arms around her. "You know how I feel about you and I would do anything to make you feel safe and happy." His gaze drifted down her body. "How did you know Jacob had left?"

She felt foolish now, standing in the kitchen in her clinging tank top and skimpy shorts. "I didn't hear any voices."

He grinned, kissed her long and sensual, and then picked her up. "Grab your crutches. You need to get dressed so I can concentrate on breakfast and making you feel safe."

She wrapped one hand around her crutches and the other arm around his neck as he carried her down the hall and deposited her on the bed.

"Get dressed. We have a lot to do today." He left the room whistling.

Dela shook her head. She would never understand that man. But she was willing to spend her life trying.

She put her prosthesis on and dressed in less than thirty minutes. She walked into the kitchen and found Quinn buttering toast. "Who invited you?" she asked, taking her usual seat at the table.

Quinn lifted his toast and pointed to Heath. "He wanted to know what would be the best security system that can be installed today." Quinn took a bite of his toast and a sip of coffee and said, "I asked why and he told me about your intruder and missing key."

Dela studied Heath. Why had he brought the Special Agent into their problem?

"I didn't know who else could hook us up with a security system around here as fast as someone from the FBI."

True, Pendleton wasn't a place with high-tech security systems. But still. "Fine. What can you get for us?" she asked Quinn, picking up the coffee cup Heath had set in front of her.

"I happen to have two very good systems out in my car. One even has motion sensor video."

"I like the sound of that, but does that mean it would video anyone, even us if we walked in front of it?" Dela wasn't sure she wanted video footage of what she and Heath did on a daily basis where someone could possibly get hold of it.

Her phone buzzed. She glanced at the name. "I need to take this." Picking up her phone, she walked into the living room. "Hello, this is Dela."

"It's Trace. You left a message for me to call you." His voice was hesitant.

"I did. Were you still being Gus Sander's bodyguard when he died?"

"No! If I had been he wouldn't be dead. Once his divorce was final, he put me back on construction work. But I was upgraded to bodyguard again yesterday. That's why I couldn't call until this morning. I was watching Ms. Sander all night."

Dela was glad to learn Vivian had picked Trace as one of the bodyguards for Evelyn. "More pay I imagine."

"Yeah, Mrs. Sander has always been more generous than Gus."

Dela nodded and said, "Did you happen to work on the apartments by Rice-Blakely Park?"

"No, but Stan said that the boss and Mr. Malik argued a lot over that job."

That was good to know. "Stan who?"

"Stan Gould. Why?"

"Just want to ask him a few questions. What about the new brewery, did you help with that job?"

"Yeah, Mr. Cristo was easy to work for. I think Gus only came around to check on that a couple of times. Everything went smoothly."

"Okay, thank you for returning my call. Keep an eye on Evelyn. We think Gus's death had to do with the business." She wanted him to understand there could be a threat to the woman's life, unlike when he was bodyguard for Gus over a small disagreement.

"I understand. Mrs. Sander made it clear what would happen to any of us that didn't keep her daughter safe."

Dela smiled. She could see Vivian giving the bodyguards instructions. "Good. I may contact you later for more information about the jobs over the past year."

"That's fine." The line went silent.

Dela glanced up from where she'd been staring at the floor and found Heath and Quinn watching her from the kitchen doorway. "Did you think I was setting up a clandestine meeting with the killer?" She dropped her phone into her pant pocket and walked into the kitchen.

"Who was that?" Heath asked.

"Trace Talent. I'd asked him to call right after Gus was found, but he just now had time to call. Vivian has hired him to guard Evelyn."

"You think the daughter could be next?" Quinn asked.

It was obvious Heath hadn't caught him up to date on what had been happening with the murder investigation. "We believe Gus's death had to do with his construction business which Evelyn has taken over since the death of her father."

Her phone buzzed again. Dela pulled it out of her pocket and read the name. Mom. She sighed and answered, "Hi, Mom."

"Dela, would you and Heath be available to attend a dinner at our house tonight? I know it's late notice but one of the guests can't make it and Lance wants to have a full table. You know, to make a good impression."

"We're kind of busy with the police thinking I might have killed someone…"

Heath rolled his eyes and Dela held in the chuckle tickling her lips.

"This is very important to Lance. He's trying to get a new business in town interested in his barley and wants to make a good impression on the owner."

The hair on the back of Dela's neck tingled. Cristo, that's where she'd heard the name before. "Who will be at the dinner?" she asked as innocently as she could.

Heath's eyebrows rose and Quinn crossed his arms.

"Oh, Mayor Temple and his wife, Zaria from the Chamber and her husband, Keenan and Annie Cristo, and if you and Heath can come that will make an even ten."

"What time do we need to be there?" Dela asked, holding up a hand as Heath started to protest.

"Six for before-dinner drinks. You know this is the first big dinner party I've hosted since Lance and I married. It's kind of fun putting it all together and not having to do any of the work."

Dela heard the excitement and nerves in her mom's voice. "I think you will be a great hostess. If you aren't cooking, who is?"

"Lance told me to get it catered since he wanted me by his side all night and not dealing with food and serving. I asked Kattie Wells."

"That's an excellent choice. We would love to come. See you tonight." Dela ended the call and turned to Heath. "You need to get some sleep. We have a dinner party to attend tonight."

"I heard. Why do we have to go?" he asked, dishing scrambled eggs with ham and tomatoes onto her plate.

"Because Keenan Cristo and his wife will be there."

Heath stopped serving Quinn and stared at her as the FBI Agent stopped his cup of coffee halfway to his mouth.

When Heath pulled himself together, he asked, "How do your mom and Lance know Cristo?"

"From what I gather, Lance is trying to get Cristo interested in using his grain for the brewery. Which kind of makes sense. Locally grown grain in locally made beer is good advertising." She sat down at her place and started eating.

"We're going to have to eat quick and get the rental car and the security system installed so I can get some sleep." Heath finished dishing eggs to Quinn and sat down to eat.

"I can take care of the system install while you take Dela to get a rental," Quinn said.

Dela stared at Quinn. Lately, he had been overly nice to her and she didn't like it. She preferred thinking of him as the nasty Fed. "Why would you take time off to help me?"

Quinn's eyes dulled with disappointment when he looked at her. "I wish you would quit thinking the worst of me. Marion and I have talked about you more than I care to talk about anyone, but she wants us to be friends because her brother respects you."

"Who's her brother?" Dela asked, unsure she wanted him talking about her to a woman she didn't know.

"State Trooper Gabriel Hawke." Quinn smiled.

"Hawke's sister is who you're dating and being all

moony-eyed over?" Dela held back a snort. "Does he know she's dating a Fed?"

"He does. I attended the Tamkaliks Powwow in Eagle with them last July. The Native American culture is fascinating. I've always had an interest in it but learning things from Marion and her mom, I'm becoming even more enthralled."

Dela was still trying to wrap her head around the State Trooper, who helped her find the human traffickers working out of the Spotted Pony and ultimately captured her the job of head of security, being okay with an FBI agent dating his sister.

Heath slapped Quinn on the back. "Good for you learning about Marion's culture. It is an asset to a marriage when both people embrace the other's culture." He glanced over at Dela.

She had been embracing Heath's all these years and she was hoping they were hers as well. They would know when they were able to get back to pursuing more information about Dory Thunder.

Everyone had finished eating. Dela rose and started clearing the table. "Heath, go shower and change and we can go to the car rental." She loaded the dishwasher while Heath changed.

Quinn was on the phone the whole time she did the dishes. When she finished, she caught him walking around in the living room.

"What's wrong?" she asked.

"Nothing. I was just figuring out the best spots to set up the cameras."

"I don't want any in the house." She stopped in front of him and crossed her arms.

"No, we won't put them in the house. I'm trying to

decide if we hardwire or use battery cameras. We'll definitely put a couple on the shed in front." Quinn rattled on about the cameras until Heath joined them.

"I've heard more than I need to know about security cameras," Dela said, walking toward the coat rack to get her purse.

"You need to know this before you go to your dinner," Quinn said, stopping her movements.

"What do we need to know?" Dela asked, facing Quinn as Heath stepped beside her.

"I called Milo and he sent me information on Cristo. The name rang a bell when you said it. We don't have anything on him, but DEA has been trying to catch him for a while. They believe his breweries are making more than small-batch beers. But they haven't been able to catch anything going in or out that shouldn't be." Quinn studied both of them. "What I'm saying is don't ask too many questions. We don't need him figuring out someone is on to him before DEA can get some people in there undercover."

"We'll stick to how he brews beer and how my stepfather is part of that," Dela said.

Heath opened the door for her. "We'll tread lightly."

They walked out to Heath's pickup and once Dela was seated in the passenger side, she shifted to study Heath who was backing out of the driveway. "Do you think Gus was going to go into the drug business with Cristo and pushed too hard?"

Heath shrugged. "We aren't going to know what happened until we gather all the evidence."

# Chapter Nine

They arrived home by noon. Quinn and Milo stood on the front porch looking at Quinn's phone.

Dela parked her rented Rav4 and walked up to them. "Are you watching videos to see how to install the cameras?"

Milo faced her and grinned. "They're installed. Quinn's trying to figure out how to send the encrypted code for the videos to you and Heath."

Dela glanced at the corners of the house. She could barely see the cameras.

Heath joined them. "I like the cameras on the shed. They're pointed in good directions to capture anyone sneaking up to the back of the house."

"Let's go in. We brought pizza and pop if you're hungry." Dela pushed between the men to open the door and enter.

Mugshot started howling.

"Do you smell pizza?" she asked him and

scratched his head after she'd placed the two pizza boxes on the counter.

Heath followed her in with the pop. He placed it on the counter and pulled plates out of the cupboard, setting them on the table.

Quinn and Milo entered the kitchen.

"Can't you make that dog stop howling?" Quinn asked, holding his hands over his ears.

Dela opened the lid of the three-meat pizza and picked the smallest piece. She walked over to the French doors and opened the door. Before she could offer the pizza to Mugshot, he hopped up and captured it in his mouth. He carried it over to his dog house and went inside.

She returned to the house. "He just wanted a piece of pizza." Dela washed her hands and joined the men at the table. They ate and talked about the cameras. Milo showed Heath and Dela how to download the app to use the code Quinn sent them to see the videos from the cameras.

"You can watch it in real-time too, if you're signed in," Milo added.

"Sounds like a good system," Heath said. "What do we owe you?"

"I'll let you know when I get it all added up," Quinn said, wiping his mouth with a napkin and standing. "I need to get to work."

"Me, too. Be careful at the dinner tonight," Milo said, scooting back from the table.

"We know not to ask the wrong questions," Dela said, wishing the two men would leave so she and Heath could work on their strategy for the dinner now that they knew more about the man they would be meeting.

♠ ♣ ♥ ♦

Del stood on the front porch of her mom and stepfather's large ranch-style home six miles from Pendleton in the middle of wheat country. She wore a denim jacket over a flowered blouse and a mid-calf denim skirt with her one pair of cowboy boots. Heath said she looked good, but she feared she was underdressed.

Heath was handsome with his long hair in a braid down the back of his emerald green button-up shirt that was untucked from his khaki slacks. He wore beaded moccasins his mother gifted him on his last birthday.

Mom answered the door. Her face was flushed and her eyes danced with good humor. "Dela, Heath, I'm so glad you're here." She ushered them into the living room.

Lance walked over, embraced Dela, and shook Heath's hand. "Glad you two could come. It makes Deborah happy to have you around."

"We're happy to help out Mom," Dela said, not trying to look too interested in their other company.

"Come, I'll introduce you to the others." Mom walked over to Mayor Temple and his wife first.

"George and Linda, this is my daughter, Dela, and her boyfriend, Heath." Mom had her hand on Dela's arm.

"Pleased to meet you," Dela said, shaking hands as Heath did the same.

"Your mom talks about you all the time," Linda said, smiling.

Dela smiled at her mom and then at the woman. "It was just the two of us for a lot of years. I talk about her all the time as well."

Her mom blushed and led them over to Zaria Landis and her husband. Dela knew Zaria from working with the Pendleton Chamber of Commerce. "Zaria and Darren, this is my daughter, Dela, and her boyfriend, Heath."

Zaria nodded to them. "Dela and I have met while putting together functions at the casino."

"Hi, Zaria. Nice to meet you, Darren," Dela added, making sure the husband received attention since Zaria seemed to be ignoring him. She wondered if the two fought before they arrived. There was definitely a chill between the couple.

"Nice to meet you," Darren said, flicking a glance at his wife and reaching out to shake their hands.

"I'll take them over to meet the Cristos." Mom ushered them away.

"Did they come here so icy?" Dela whispered to her mom.

"I'll tell you later," Mom whispered back and stopped in front of the couple Dela had presumed were Mr. and Mrs. Cristo. "Keenan and Annie, this is my daughter, Dela, and her boyfriend, Heath."

The man was handsome in an exotic way. He beamed a warm smile on them both and shook hands. "Pleased to meet you."

The woman, who had been talking to Lance at the small bar, turned toward them and Dela caught her breath. It was the crazy woman she'd met on the pathway before finding Gus's body. The woman smiled wide, warmth shining from her brown eyes just as it had done when they first met.

She took Dela's hand in both of hers and said, "It's

nice to meet you. Your mother has been so welcoming, I don't know how to repay her."

"P-pleased to meet you." Dela studied the woman. Annie didn't seem to remember meeting her that night. Dela knew this wasn't the place to bring it up.

The woman turned her attention to Heath. "Oh, you two make a beautiful couple. And I can feel your auras. You spread love and light wherever you go."

Now this sounded like the woman from the other night. But she was fashionably dressed and held herself with grace. Not the fierce gaze, hunched posture, and fright that had emanated from her on the river path.

"Thank you, Mrs. Cristo," Heath said, smiling at Dela. The woman had won him over.

"Please, call me Annie." She smiled and released his hands.

"What would you like to drink?" Lance asked them.

"I'll have iced tea," Heath said.

Dela nodded. "Me, too."

"You're being light drinkers tonight," Lance said, dropping ice cubes in two glasses and grabbing a pitcher of tea.

"We both have to work tomorrow," Dela said, by way of moving him off the subject. They both wanted clear heads to hear everything Cristo talked about.

"So do George, Linda, Zaria, and Darren, but they're having one drink." Lance handed them the glasses and walked out from behind the bar, carrying his cocktail.

"Our work demands all of our attention," Heath said, taking Dela by the elbow and wandering them over to the group of Mayor Temple and Cristo.

"Ahh, it's been a long time since I've seen you, Dela. I must say I've heard good things about you at the casino," Mayor Temple raised his drink to her.

"Thank you. I'm just doing my job." She sipped her tea.

"What do you do at the casino?" Cristo asked.

"I'm head of security." Dela noticed Annie flick a glance in her direction. Now she wondered how much of the act the night of the murder was just that, an act.

"Really? Someone as young as you?" Cristo asked.

She didn't think he looked a day over forty so that made him not that much older than her. "I spent ten years in the Army as an M.P. before coming home. I know how to handle myself and how to pick out criminals."

He frowned. "I guess that would be a good trait for a person of your occupation." He turned his attention to Heath. "And what do you do?"

Heath smiled and said, "I'm a detective with the Umatilla Tribal Police."

Cristo looked back and forth between them. "That must mean you don't get a lot of time together."

Heath put his arm around Dela. "We get as much as we want."

She laid her head on his shoulder. "You make time for the people you love. Just like coming here tonight when Mom asked." As she talked, Dela watched Annie. The sadness aimed at the back of her husband said they didn't have a good marriage.

Cristo cleared his throat and asked Mayor Temple a question about how the plans for an upcoming event were going.

Dela whispered in Heath's ear, "I want to talk to Annie." She slipped out of his arm and over to the woman, standing with her back to the room and staring out a window.

"What do you do while your husband is setting up the brewery?" Dela asked, walking up behind the woman.

Annie startled and swung around, her eyes wide with fear.

"I'm sorry. I must have caught you daydreaming. I didn't mean to sneak up on you." Dela reached out to steady the woman. She drew away from her touch.

"I'm fine. Just thinking about something." Annie pulled herself together and shot a worried glance toward her husband.

"I asked what you do when your husband is busy setting up the brewery." Dela sipped her iced tea.

"I stay in the house we're renting. It's pretty and there's a nice view of the valley." She spun the glass in her hands slowly but didn't drink.

Dela noticed the woman's long thin fingers and her gaunt face. She worried the woman wasn't getting enough to eat. But surely her husband would make sure she did. Unless she was ill. "Do you always travel with your husband when he's setting up new businesses?"

She nodded. "He keeps me close."

That was odd wording. Dela studied the woman who every thirty seconds cast a glance at her husband.

"Are you two having a nice conversation?" Mom asked, joining them.

"Yes. I asked Annie what she did while her husband was busy." Dela hoped her mom would add more to the conversation.

"We are going out to lunch tomorrow." Mom smiled brightly at Annie, who returned her smile but without the wattage of Mom's smile.

"That sounds fun. Where are you going?" Dela asked.

"I thought I'd take her to Hamley's but she said Keenan has already taken her there. Any suggestions?" Mom asked.

"Bring her to the casino. The Stallion has some nice specials going on this week." Dela wanted to get a chance to watch the woman without her knowing.

"That's a wonderful idea. Is that okay with you, Annie?" Mom watched the woman eagerly.

"Y-yes. Though I'll have to ask Keenan if he minds." The woman appeared to be slowly losing her confidence.

"Let's ask him now. If he doesn't approve, we can think of something else." Mom raised her hand and called, "Keenan, we have a question for you, could you join us?"

"You should just let me ask him," Annie said, becoming agitated.

Dela stepped next to the woman, wondering why she feared having Mom ask her husband about a lunch date.

"Yes, what do you ladies want to ask me?" His gaze landed on Annie. Dela saw the flash of anger before he moved his gaze to her mom and appeared inquisitive.

"As you know, Annie and I plan to go to lunch tomorrow. Since you two have already dined at Hamleys, I thought I'd take her to The Stallion at the casino and then we could go to the Tamástslikt Cultural

Institute next door to the casino. It has a fabulous display this month."

"That sounds like a wonderful treat. Do you want to go there, Annie?"

Dela picked up on the undertone of his questions. He was making her turn Deborah down instead of him. What was his hold on her? Why didn't he want her to have a nice lunch and outing?

"It sounds like fun, Deborah, but I'm not sure after being out tonight if I'll feel up to that much." Annie's gaze was on her husband as she talked.

Deborah faced Keenan. "Why are you keeping your wife from enjoying lunch and seeing the museum?"

Keenan's face reddened and his eyes sparked. "She turned you down, not me."

Mom put her hands on her hips. "She didn't turn me down. She was staring at you while she said it. I've been around enough abused women to know when something isn't right."

Now the other guests had gathered around.

Dela stepped closer to her mom. "Don't ruin your dinner party."

Mom shrugged Dela's hand off her arm. "I won't have a dinner party for someone who abuses his wife." She pointed to the door. "You Mr. Cristo may leave. But your wife is staying here and enjoying dinner."

Keenan glared at Mom and spun around, his gaze landing on Lance. "Your wife has accused me of abusing Annie. Are you going to stand there and let her get away with it?"

Lance shrugged. "Deborah has lived on the reservation for decades and has been a teacher. She has witnessed abused women and children. This is her house too. She can throw out whoever she wants."

Her stepfather's words were the first time Dela truly believed he loved her mother. He was siding with her over the man who could make him richer.

"I'm not going without Annie," Keenan ground out.

Heath and Lance stepped between the man and his wife.

"We'll see that she gets home if that's where she wants to go," Heath said.

"You don't understand," Keenan insisted. "She's not abused." He ran a hand through his perfect hair, messing it up. He said, "Annie, tell them why you can't go to such a long outing."

Dela studied the woman. Tears glistened in her big brown eyes. Her lips trembled.

Annie pushed between Heath and Lance, flying into Keenan's arms. She sobbed on his shoulder.

"It's okay. These are friends. Can I tell them?" Keenan asked in a soft voice.

Annie nodded but kept her face buried.

Keenan sternly peered into each person's eyes and said, "Annie has a mental illness that can be quieted by medicine for short periods of time. But the longer she goes without the next dose the worse her condition becomes." He shifted his attention to Dela's mom. "She can come to something like this because I can tell when we need to go home. But when she goes anywhere alone, she doesn't think about time and slowly lapses into the illness."

"Would just taking her to lunch be okay?" Mom asked.

"As long as you don't have her gone for more than three hours. That's all she can handle." Keenan gave his wife a squeeze and her head lifted from his shoulder. "Would you like to go to lunch with Deborah tomorrow?"

"Not tomorrow. Maybe the next day?" Annie said in a quiet voice.

"Did you hear that?" Keenan asked.

"Yes. I'll pick her up on Saturday at noon." Mom glanced at Dela. "Would that make it so we aren't in the middle of the lunch crowd?"

"Yes, you should arrive after most of them have already eaten." Dela wondered at her mom's strong attachment to the woman Dela thought was crazier than her husband knew.

"She'll be ready. I think we've had enough for tonight. We'll leave and let the rest of you enjoy your dinner."

"You don't have to go," Mom said, moving toward them.

"It's best." Keenan shook hands with Lance. "No hard feelings. I was just protecting my wife as you were standing up for yours."

"I understand." Lance walked them out to their car.

"I'm so embarrassed!" Mom said, peering around the room at everyone. "She acted so scared of her husband I thought for sure he was abusing her, not keeping her safe."

Linda and Zaria moved toward Mom, wrapping their arms around her and saying she couldn't have known and had done what she thought was best.

Dela met Heath's gaze. He was digesting what they'd seen as well. They would have a lot to talk about on the way home.

Lance returned and everyone entered the dining room for dinner.

Dela listened to the conversations and let Heath ask questions that led them to learn the mayor had helped Keenan get the permits to build the brewery and Zaria had suggested the Sander Construction Company.

"What made you suggest Sander over, say Blue Eagle or Teller?" Dela asked.

"I knew Gus needed work and the other two were turning people away," Zaria said without looking up from where she swirled a piece of French bread in the juices on her plate.

Dela caught the eye roll from her husband. Studying the woman, Dela realized she was the type that Gus liked. Her dress hung off her shoulders showing cleavage, her skirt was short, and she had a curvy body. And she was still in her twenties. Had she and Gus been hooking up?

# Chapter Ten

Friday morning, Dela woke with a list of people she wanted to see. When she and Heath returned from the dinner the night before, they'd spent over an hour discussing what they heard and saw. While they both sympathized with the Cristos, Dela still didn't quite believe the husband's story. She'd seen how crazy the woman had been the night of Gus's death. Hadn't the husband missed his wife while she was out running around Pendleton that night?

Whatever she felt about the couple, Quinn and the DEA suspected the breweries Keenan owned were transporting illegal drugs. Drugs had been Gus's downfall before and could have led to his death.

"When do you plan to go to work?" Heath asked as he placed his breakfast dishes in the dishwasher.

"After I talk to Zaria and Stan Gould. Why?" She played innocent but she knew he was trying to figure out how to go with her.

"Jacob and I can't get out of work today. There's a mandatory meeting. I don't want you running around talking to people without someone with you." He stood by her chair and put a hand on her shoulder. "I want you to call Travis or Molly or someone to go with you and then follow you to the casino."

Dela let out a breath to keep from exploding. She hated it when Heath became overprotective. If she'd wanted someone to hover, she would have remained living at home with her mom. "Whoever thinks I know something isn't going to do anything in broad daylight. They're cowards and will only attack when they think I'm vulnerable. Which I won't be from now on."

"Humor me and take someone with you this morning." He cupped her chin, raising her face to look into his eyes. "You take too many risks when you're alone."

She sighed. "Fine, I'll see who I can find."

He shook his head. "No, you will find someone now so I know who you are with before I leave this house." He kissed her on the top of the head and walked down the hallway to finish putting on his uniform.

Dela cursed under her breath and tapped her fingers on the table. Who should she call? Marty? He usually didn't go in to work until afternoon, like her. She picked up her phone and scrolled through her contacts, touching Marty's name.

As she listened to it ring, she used one crutch to get to the French door and let Mugshot in.

"You've reached Marty. Leave your name and phone number and I'll return your call when I get the message."

The phone beeped and she said, "Marty, I need a

wingman this morning. Call me as soon as you get this." She ended the call and cleared her dishes from the table, before grabbing her other crutch and swinging down the hall to the bedroom to get dressed.

Heath stepped out of the bedroom as she arrived at the door. "Did you get someone?"

"Yeah, Marty. I'll call you when I'm headed to work."

Heath angled his body so he filled the doorway. "Don't say anything to give away what Quinn told us."

"This isn't the first time I've questioned people." She narrowed her eyes. "Why all of a sudden do you sound like you don't trust my instincts or my interview technique?"

He grinned. "I trust everything you do, but sometimes, when you're on a mission, like, oh vindicating your name, you tend to push harder than you should." He leaned toward her. "I want you to get the answers we need, not alienate the people you talk to."

She shoved on his chest with one hand. Instead of pushing him out of the way, it tipped her backward.

His arms swooped around her, pulling her close. "I am always on your side, even when I have to rein you in." He covered her mouth with his and kissed her until she forgot what they'd been talking about.

Her phone buzzed in her shorts pocket.

"Get that. I have to go to work." Heath made sure she was steady on her crutches before he strode down the hall.

Dela raised the phone, saw Marty's name, and swiped. "Dela."

"Got your message. I can hang with you until noon.

Then Molly and I have an appointment with our builder at one."

"That works. I can swing by and pick you up." Dela ended the call, entered her bedroom, and dressed.

An hour later she pulled up to the vet clinic, parking near the door to the living quarters. She was happy Molly would finally have a house separate from her business. And she'd finally found a good man to share that life with.

She knocked on the door to the living quarters and waited. The door opened and a tousle-headed Travis grinned at her. "Mom and Marty are in the kitchen."

"Shouldn't you be working somewhere? Like in the clinic?" Dela asked, following him into the house.

"Toby, Melvin, and I are building Mom and Marty's house."

Dela stopped and hugged him. "I'm happy for you but I thought Marty said he had an appointment with the builder at one. You live together, you can have a meeting any time you want."

"That's the guy doing the concrete foundation. Once he's done, then we take over. My girlfriend is working in the clinic with Mom. Come on, I'd like you to meet her." Travis headed toward the door to the clinic.

"Um, I think you might want to brush your hair and get dressed first," she said, motioning to his messed-up hair, shirtless torso, pajama pants hanging on his hip bones, and bare feet.

"She's seen me in less." Travis winked.

"Does your mom know that?"

"Know what?" Molly asked, walking out of the kitchen.

Travis's cheeks reddened. "Nothing. I'm getting dressed." He did an about-face and disappeared into a room.

Dela laughed and followed Molly into the kitchen.

"What are you and Marty doing this morning?" Molly asked, pouring a cup of coffee.

"I need to talk to some people and after someone tried to frame me for Gus's death and then tried to get into my house, Heath doesn't want me going anywhere alone." Dela sighed and slid onto the stool next to the breakfast bar.

"When a man loves you, they worry about you. And that man loves you. When are you going to open up and tell him you feel the same?" Molly sat on the stool next to her.

"I already have." Dela smiled at her friend's shocked face.

"You have? When?"

"When we were in Lincoln City. After losing another friend, I decided it was time to tell him how I felt before something happened to one of us."

"And? What did he say?" Molly set her coffee down and watched her.

"He was happy I finally voiced my feelings. But he said he knew, he was just waiting for me to say it."

Molly laughed. When she stopped, she said, "I always said you two were perfect for one another and you are."

"Just like us." Marty walked into the kitchen and put an arm around Molly's shoulders.

Molly patted his arm. "Yes, just like us. You two be careful today."

Dela slid off the stool. "We will. I'm just asking

some questions that came up at Mom's dinner party last night."

Molly's eyebrows arched. "You went to a dinner party hosted by Deborah and Lance? How did that go?"

"It was interesting. I'll tell you about it later. We need to go so Marty will be back here in time for your appointment." Dela led the way out to her rented car.

"Nice rental. Did you get the security set up?"

"Yeah. Every side of the house is covered by a camera. I can even see what Mugshot and Jethro are doing whenever I want."

She headed to Pendleton and the Sander Construction office to find out where Stan Gould was working today.

The receptionist wouldn't give them the information until she'd talked to Evelyn. While Dela and Marty waited for Evelyn to arrive at work, Dela filled him in on why she wanted to talk to Stan.

Evelyn walked into the building with her arm linked through Trace's. Dela studied their features. They seemed happy. Had the bodyguard and his client become intimate?

"Ms. Sander, these two are requesting information about one of our workers," the receptionist blurted out.

"Dela, come into the office and I'll talk to you." Evelyn waited for Trace to open the door for her and they all entered.

Once they were all in the room, Trace closed the door and stood by it.

Dela smiled at him and stopped in front of the desk. "Seems you and your bodyguard are close."

Evelyn glanced at Trace. "We are pretending he's my boyfriend to keep people from wondering why I need a bodyguard. It was all Mother's idea. I don't see why I need a bodyguard but to make her happy, I'll put up with it." She sat down at the desk and asked, "What do you need and why?"

"I'd like to know where Stan Gould is working today. I need to ask him questions about the apartment building your company built for Delbert Malik." Dela studied the woman. She seemed surprised.

"Why would you need to know about that building?"

"In the files Detective Fletcher borrowed, we found a note signed by your dad to keep something quiet about the building. Delbert Malik was the one who requested the signed document."

The woman stared at the pen in her hand as she mulled things over. Finally, she said, "Do you think Mr. Malik had something to do with Dad's death?"

"I don't know. It's just one lead we are following. Could you find out where Stan is working today, please?"

Evelyn picked up the phone and asked the receptionist the question. She nodded and replaced the phone. "He's doing finishing touches to the brewery today."

Dela hid the smile tickling her lips. Not only could she talk to Stan but she'd get to snoop around the brewery as well.

♠ ♣ ♥ ♦

Dela drove to the brewery. The building looked complete on the outside. She figured Stan must be doing some finishing work on the inside. There were three Sander Construction vehicles in the parking lot and two sedans. She hoped Keenan Cristo wasn't here.

She didn't want him to know she was looking into the murder of Gus.

She and Marty exited her car and walked to the front door which consisted of two 4 by 9 feet sliding doors, making the inside open to the seating outdoors. Half a dozen large leafy trees were planted on the patio perimeter. They would provide shade in the summer and let through warm sunshine in the winter. If she wasn't here investigating a murder, she would be impressed with the setup.

Stepping inside the building it was dark except for the light shining through the 9-foot glass doors and windows across the front.

"Hey, no one without hard hats allowed in here," a male voice called out.

# Chapter Eleven

Dela peered into the darkness as a man as broad as he was tall and all muscle, stepped out of the shadows. He wore a hard hat, thick gloves, flannel shirt, cargo pants, and athletic shoes. Dela's gaze stayed on the shoes. Why would a construction worker wear athletic shoes and a hard hat? Wouldn't he have on boots?

"I think you should leave." The man now stood five feet in front of them. His face was as round and flat as a bulldog, jowls included.

"We're here to talk to Stan Gould," Dela said.

"Are you police?" the man crossed his arms. They resembled two steel beams in front of his broad chest.

"No. He's having trouble with his cable. We can't do anything until we find out exactly what the problem is. No one was at home and he told us where to find him," Marty said, handing a business card to the man.

Beefy arms flipped it over a couple of times. "Stay put. I'll get Stan. Don't wander around, things aren't all attached yet." He stomped off to the back of the building.

"How do you know Stan even has trouble with his cable?" Dela asked.

"Everyone has cable trouble. Besides, who wouldn't use any excuse to take a break when you're doing hard labor." Marty winked at her.

Dela shook her head and spotted a tall man with broad shoulders dressed in jeans, t-shirt, and boots walk out of the shadows.

"Stan Gould?" Dela asked.

"Yeah, you don't look like the cable company," he said, but not loud enough for anyone else to hear.

"We're not." Dela tipped her head toward the doors. "Let's go outside."

The man followed them out. "I didn't think it would be someone from the cable company when Balto handed me the card." He grinned. "We don't have cable."

"Then why did you come out to talk to us?" Marty asked.

"Curious why someone needed a ruse to talk to me." He glanced back and forth between them.

"We're helping the police with inquiries into Gus Sander's death," Dela said.

"I can't believe it happened. I mean who would want Gus dead? He got along with everyone." Stan seemed genuinely confused.

"We heard he and Delbert Malik had some heated discussions. Do you know what about?" Dela asked.

Stan nodded. "Malik cut corners everywhere he could on those apartments. I've been telling people not to rent them, they'll end up with the roof falling in on them. I'm sure Malik greased some inspectors' palms because there was no way that building should have passed inspections. Gus argued with him over several things that should have been built with better materials."

"Did you hear the full conversations and did Malik know you heard?" Dela asked, thinking if the two argued in public, then Malik would have a lot of bodies by the time he took out everyone who knew he was a crook.

"Yeah, everyone who worked on that building got an earful at one time or another."

Dela glanced at the brewery. "How's the work going here? Do they have a projected opening date?"

Stan grinned. "This is one hell of a fun job. I've never built a brewery before. I'm learning all kinds of things. Balto has been at every brewery Mr. Cristo has built. He's knowledgeable and explains why we build things the way we do."

"When do you think they will be ready to open?" she asked again.

"He's hoping to have a few batches brewed and ready to open Stampede weekend."

Five months from now. Dela thought about that. Would they wait to start moving illegal products until then or would they start before? "That should make a lot of Stampede goers happy," she said.

"How many brews are they making?" Marty asked.

"I'm not sure. Balto says they have three standard ones they make at all the breweries and then they play off what they can get ahold of in the area."

"You're taking a long time to talk about cable!" Balto shouted from the doorway.

"Gotta go. I hope you find out who killed Gus." Stan jogged into the building.

Dela and Marty walked to her car.

"I don't think we can consider Malik a suspect. He would have had to kill too many people to keep his miserly ways quiet," Dela said, opening the driver's door.

"I was thinking the same thing," Marty said, sliding into the passenger seat.

"Let's go see if we can wind Zaria up and get her to tell us if she was sleeping with Gus." Dela buckled her seat belt and started the car. She caught a movement from the corner of her eye and spotted a guy in a hoody jogging toward a dark SUV.

"Hold on." She put the car in drive and spun the tires, leaving the parking area and heading toward the City and State Police building. It was fortunate the two were housed in the same building on Airport Road. She figured once the people following them figured out where she was headed, they'd leave her alone. The only problem would be getting out of there without them noticing her, now that they knew what she was driving.

Marty unbuckled his seatbelt and slid between the seats.

"What are you doing?"

"Trying to get closer to them so I can take a photo of the car."

"It won't do any good if there isn't a license plate." Dela took the corner onto Airport Road nearly on two tires. She heard a click.

"I got the front and the side view as it passed this street. You can slow down now," he said, turning around as they entered the parking lot of the Oregon

State Police and the City Police offices.

Dela stopped the car and sat for a minute pulling herself together. "Let's see if Detective Fletcher is in." She stepped out of the vehicle and felt her knees wobble. It had been a while since she'd tried to outmaneuver another vehicle. The adrenaline was diluting and she now realized how stupid it had been to drive like a lunatic. But when she'd seen the car, her thought was to go somewhere they wouldn't want to be seen. And what stalker wanted to be at a police station?

Marty held the door open waiting for her.

She shook herself and walked through. Dela walked up to the officer behind the glassed-in counter and asked to see Detective Fletcher.

"Who do I tell him wants to talk to him?" the woman behind the desk asked.

"Dela. He knows who I am."

The woman nodded and picked up the phone. The protective glass between them didn't allow Dela to hear what was said.

The woman nodded and said, "He'll be right out."

Dela paced back and forth for five minutes before Fletcher appeared from a door to their right.

"What are you doing here?" he asked, walking into the lobby.

"We were talking to one of Gus's construction workers at the new brewery. As we were leaving, I spotted the car that was used when someone tried to get into my house and the one that we saw on video footage the night they stole my knife from my car. When they followed me, I drove here."

"Fast!" Marty added, holding out his hand. "Marty Casper, surveillance at the Spotted Pony."

"What were you talking to a construction worker about?" Fletcher asked, shaking Marty's hand but keeping his gaze on Dela.

"He had overheard arguments between Gus and Malik. The client we spotted as a possible suspect from the Sander Construction files."

"Ahh, yeah. We wrote him up for fraud due to defective materials being used in the building of the apartments. He has an alibi for the night of the murder."

"It would have been nice if you had communicated that to me," Dela had thought working with Fletcher would be a relief from dealing with Quinn, but now she was thinking differently.

"Hey, that goes both ways. You should have told me you planned to talk to the worker and I could have told you Malik isn't the killer." Fletcher had his hands in his pockets and he shrugged his shoulders.

"I'm going to talk to Zaria Landis. I discovered that she was the one who suggested Mr. Cristo use Sander Construction. From what she said, and the coldness between her and her husband, I think she and Gus were hitting the sheets." Dela studied the detective.

His eyes widened. "You think Zaria and Gus were…" He laughed. "I don't see that."

"You don't know the way Gus had over women. She is exactly his type. The complete opposite of the woman he married." Dela glanced at Marty. "Do you think we can go back and see Zaria without being followed?"

Marty shrugged. "We don't have much choice. But you know, I don't think they followed us there. That vehicle was parked in that spot when we arrived. I remember seeing it."

Dela smiled. "Then we know who they are working for."

"Wait a minute. What are you talking about?" Fletcher pulled his hands out of his pockets and looked like he was going to grab the back of their shirt collars.

Dela glanced around to make sure there wasn't anyone else listening. "An FBI friend told me that the DEA has been watching the breweries Keenan Cristo has built across the country. I think Gus saw something he wasn't supposed to at the brewery and that's why he was killed."

"You think Cristo is behind it?" Fletcher had a skeptical expression on his long face.

"We'll know when we put all the pieces together." Dela pivoted to the door. "Let's get going so you make your appointment," she said, pushing through the door and stepping out into the sunshine.

Shading her eyes, she scanned the parking lot and the street. She didn't see the black SUV anywhere. But they could be on any side street waiting for them to come out. There was only one way to go to avoid the black SUV.

"Where are you going," Marty asked as she headed toward the airport.

"We'll take Airport Road all the way out to Barnhart Road and come back into Pendleton on the Freeway." She drove by the airport and put the accelerator down as she sped the five miles down the two-lane road toward Barnhart Road. She used the onramp to get on I-84 and head back to Pendleton.

She took the exit that put her the closest to the Chamber of Commerce building and dropped her speed down to normal town driving.

"How do you know Zaria will even talk to us?" Marty asked.

"I'm going to drop in as if I'm there from the casino, then talk about what happened at my mom's last night, then talk about Gus and ask her about their relationship." Dela found a parking spot that might hide her car if the SUV happened to drive by.

"Do you think it's a good idea for me to be with you? It sounds like you're mostly talking about things I don't know?"

"It will look more legit that we are there on casino business if you're with me. After all, surveillance is part of security." Dela exited the car and walked into the red brick building.

"Can I help you?" A middle-aged woman behind the counter asked.

"We'd like to talk to Zaria, if she's in. We're from the casino." Dela handed the woman one of the casino business cards.

"I'll see if she's busy." The woman took the card and walked into the rooms behind the lobby.

"What if she doesn't have time to see you?" Marty asked as Zaria and the receptionist returned.

"Dela, this is a surprise. I didn't think we had anything from the casino to discuss," Zaria said, waving them to proceed down the hall in front of her.

Dela walked ahead to the woman's office. She entered the small office and sat in the chair in front of the desk. Marty pulled a chair from the side of the room over beside hers.

Zaria sat behind the desk and clasped her hands together on the wood top. "What is this about?"

"Did you get the information from communications

about the MMIW event to be held at the casino in May?" Dela asked.

"I don't remember getting anything." The woman started digging through a pile of papers on her desk.

"Glenda said she was sending it to you last week. Maybe it hasn't reached you yet." Dela cast her voice to sound sympathetic.

"It must not have. I know I would have remembered seeing it."

"That was interesting what went on at my mom's last night, wasn't it?" Dela dropped her voice to a conspiratorial volume.

Zaria flicked a glance at Marty.

"I told him all about it," Dela said.

"Yeah, man, that had to have been something crazy to watch," Marty said.

That was why she liked taking him along when questioning people, he could fall into a conversation not even knowing what was being discussed.

"I had wondered why Keenan never brought his wife to any of the charity events. He didn't even bring her to the groundbreaking for the brewery. I guess he thought a quiet dinner at a home wouldn't be too much for poor Annie." Zaria leaned back in her chair, relaxing.

"I felt bad for my mom, thinking Keenan had abused his wife. But there were all the signs." Dela had discussed the things she'd witnessed with Heath the night before as they drove home. The woman did have all the characteristics of an abused person. But not knowing what her mental illness was, it could replicate those actions.

"I can tell you. I will never be a woman who is

abused. I like men but I'd never fall for anyone that I would allow to hit me more than once." Anger sparked in Zaria's eyes as she spoke.

"Not all women are as strong as we are," Dela said. She glanced at Marty. Molly's first husband was abusive. It had taken Dela years to talk Molly into leaving him. Marty knew that about his wife. "But the strongest women are the ones who break away."

Marty smiled at her. "They are."

Zaria studied them. "You two know someone."

"My wife. I'm her second husband and I will never treat her like that piece of crap she married the first time." Marty's tone said it all.

Dela nodded in agreement.

Marty caught her gaze and said, "You're lucky to have Heath, he knows you would never hurt anyone."

Zaria leaned forward. "What do you mean by that?"

"Didn't you hear? Dela found Gus Sander's body and her knife was the one used to slit his throat. But she didn't do it and the police think it was a frame-up." Marty nodded his head.

Zaria's gaze landed on Dela. "You found Gus? How?"

Dela told her about getting a call from Gus, at which point the woman's eyes narrowed, and going on with how she heard something and saw a person run out from under the bridge, then how she landed on the body and called the police.

"Why would he call you for help?" the woman said in a pouty tone.

"I helped him out of a tough spot before. Before your time as his lover." Dela watched the woman's eyes widen and her cheeks flush.

"What makes you think I was his lover?"

"You're his type, and you set him up to get the brewery job. You would only do that as a favor for something. Did he ask you or did you do it because you were sleeping with him?" Dela wasn't going to let up on this.

"We had a fling for a short period of time. But I decided I liked my fit athletic husband better than an over-the-hill lover. I got him that job to keep him from saying anything to Darren." She narrowed her eyes. "And I'll expect you two to not tell him."

"Are you sure he doesn't already know?" Marty asked. "A guy can tell when his girl is getting it somewhere else."

Zaria's eyes widened and her mouth dropped open half an inch before she said, "No. You're lying."

"I'm not. Usually when the girl is getting it elsewhere, she's wearing sexier underclothes, she's too tired to do it with her husband or guy, and she has a lot of meetings or appointments she didn't have before." Marty leaned forward with his elbows on his knees. "If you were doing any of that, he knows."

"Shit!" Zaria tapped a pen on the desk. "That's why he kept hounding me about some of the meetings I said I had. I noticed he followed me to a couple of the legit meetings. Now I wonder if he followed me to the meet-ups with Gus."

Dela stood. "Is that why you two were so frosty last night?"

Zaria shook her head. "Darren thought I should have dressed more appropriately last night. He said I looked like I was fishing for a rich lover." She smiled.

"I wouldn't mind getting into Keenan's bed, but I have a feeling the way he treated his wife last night that he only has eyes for her. Even if she is crazy."

# Chapter Twelve

Dela dropped Marty off at the clinic and drove to the casino alone. She used the road from Riverside to Mission and turned right to head to the casino. She felt safe on the reservation roads. While the people in the unlicensed SUV could drive here, they would stand out.

She entered through the employee entrance at the Security Office. Her friend Margie was on duty at the podium by the door. "Heard you are back in the cops' sights, again."

Dela put her purse in her desk drawer and attached the mic and radio to her clothing. "Not really. They figured out I was set up. I just wish I knew who knew about the knife in my car and why they would want to frame me."

"You know if you asked, we'd all keep a listen to conversations and see if we could get you some information." Margie slid off the tall chair behind the podium.

"I know. But I don't want to put anyone in danger." Dela knew the word to look for that car would go around the rez faster than an email if she asked.

"No one would be in danger and we would be keeping you out of danger. We already know about the car. Alfred told us to keep an eye out and let him know when it's seen on the rez." Margie smiled and put her hands on her hips. "Is there anyone else you need us to watch for?"

Dela shook her head. "No, just the people in that car."

Margie nodded and went back to the podium.

Dela did a mic check asking one of her staff to respond. They did and she headed out to the hallway to the gaming floor where she could visually check up with everyone. As she made her rounds, Dela kept an eye out for anyone she considered of interest in Gus's death.

Her phone buzzed. Heath. "Hi. I'm at the casino," she answered.

"Who followed you there?" he asked.

"No one. The people in the black SUV did follow us from the brewery. But they fell off when I drove to the police station." Dela told him about the visit with Stan and Zaria as well as the detour to lose the SUV.

"I dropped Marty off at the clinic and used Mission Road to get to the casino." She scanned the casino and thought she caught sight of someone familiar going into the bar. "Hey, I need to check something out in the bar. I'll catch up with you later."

"Don't hang up. I was calling to see if you wanted to have a late lunch with me. In say, an hour?"

"Sure. You coming here?" She walked faster

toward the bar, trying to keep the conversation going and bypass the early weekend gamblers.

"Yeah. See you at two." The silence on the other end was a relief.

Dela stepped into the Pony Bar and Grill and scrutinized the tables. The bar and the casino were filling up. This was only Friday, she wondered what tomorrow would be like. The cooler spring weather must have brought the people inside to gamble rather than try to tackle outside chores and hobbies.

Walking farther into the room, Dela spotted the back of the person she was interested in. The person appeared to be ordering a drink. As the woman turned with two drinks in her hands, Dela ducked behind the nearest tall table with people to not be seen.

Farley's voice in her earbud said, "Dela, why are you hiding from someone? Do I need to send in security?"

She shook her head so Marty's second-in-command would know she didn't want help. Then she pulled out her cell phone and called Farley. When he answered she asked, "Why are you watching me?"

"Marty told me to keep an eye on you when you're here. Something about you found another body and someone is trying to frame you. He figures if we had footage and someone watching you, you would always have an alibi."

She rolled her eyes and stepped even farther behind the table as Keenan Cristo joined his wife at a table. Something wasn't adding up. They looked like a normal couple. She spoke into the phone, "See the couple at the tall table by the end of the bar. Keep an eye on them. When they leave the casino, I want to see the footage."

"Are they the people framing you?" Farley asked.

"They are persons of interest in Gus's death." Dela ended the call and left the bar even though she would have preferred to stay and try to hear their conversation. Before she walked out, she noticed who was waiting on the Cristos. It was Cherry, and Norma was the bartender today. She'd talk to both of them when she and Heath had lunch.

♠ ♣ ♥ ♦

"Why are we having lunch in the noisy bar and not the coffee shop?" Heath asked as Dela led him into the bar and grill.

"Because I saw Keenan and Annie in here earlier. I want to talk to Cherry and Norma about them." Dela took the same table where the Cristos had sat.

Norma came out from behind the bar. The tables were less than half full now that the lunch rush was over. "Good to see some friendly faces," she said, bringing them iced tea. Today her gray and purple hair was pulled up into a ponytail that reached the middle of her back. She was a tall, thin woman. Her right arm had a green vine with purple and red roses climbing along the length and disappearing under her short-sleeved purple t-shirt with a skull and crossbones on the front.

"That was quick service," Heath said, raising his glass and drinking.

"I saw you enter. Figured with you in uniform and Dela on duty it would be your usual non-alcoholic beverage. Do you need menus?" Norma asked.

"Yes, we are here for lunch." Dela glanced around the room. "Is Cherry still here?"

"She's taking a break. I'll take your order but she should be out before you finish. Do you need to talk to

108

her?" Norma darted a glance at the bar. "I'll be right back with those menus."

"What makes you think Cherry knows anything?" Heath asked.

"Because she was waitressing this table where Keenan and Annie sat. Norma would have caught glances at them and possibly heard some of what they were talking about." Dela picked up her iced tea and her phone buzzed. Farley.

"Are you still spying on me?" she asked.

The exuberant young man laughed and said, "No, not when you're with your squeeze."

"He's not my—" Dela stopped when Heath's eyebrows rose. "Why are you calling?"

"I have that video of the couple you requested. It is interesting."

Dela sat up straighter and peered into Heath's eyes. "How?"

"The woman seemed out of it by the time they left the casino. You'll have to see for yourself."

"I'll be there in an hour." Dela leaned back as Norma placed a menu in front of her. Ending her call, she asked Norma, "Do you remember a couple who were here about an hour ago? They sat at this table."

Norma rested her forearms on the table and leaned close to Dela. "We're not supposed to talk about the people who come in here, but I'm guessing with you being head of security, it's okay and you asked me, I didn't just divulge anything."

Dela nodded.

"They were interesting. Well-dressed and talked refined. She ordered their drinks. A Shirley Temple for her and an Old Fashion for him. Cherry took their order.

I was curious so I stayed down at this end of the bar. They didn't act like the usual customers that come in here. You could tell they weren't here gambling. He did most of the talking. She just sat there sipping her drink and listening."

"Could you hear what they were talking about?" Dela asked.

Norma shook her head. "No, he kept his voice only loud enough I guess she could hear." She glanced at the bar and said, "What're you eating? I have to get back to the bar."

Dela ordered a burger and fries and Heath ordered a club sandwich. When Norma left, Dela said, "I know something weird is going on with those two."

"It could be Keenan was acclimating Annie to the casino to see if she could handle it tomorrow with your mom." Heath picked up his drink.

"That would make sense, I guess. But why pick the bar when they are going to the quieter restaurant?" Dela leaned back in her chair and scanned what she could see of the room. "There had to be a reason they came in here." She hoped to find out more when she watched them on the video.

Cherry arrived at their table with the food. "Who had what?"

"I had the burger," Dela said, reaching for the plate. "Do you have a couple minutes to talk to us?"

Cherry set the club sandwich in front of Heath and nodded.

"I'm curious about the couple who sat at this table an hour ago. Did you overhear anything they said or see anything that seemed odd?"

"That guy was good!" she exclaimed.

"What do you mean?" Dela asked, confused.

"The man at the table asked if that was you watching them. I glanced over as you were walking out the door and I said, 'Yeah.'"

Dela shot a glance at Heath. He shrugged. Nothing she could do about it now. "Did he ask you anything else?"

"He wanted to know what hours you worked and I told him, no one really knew. You just come and go as you please, sometimes staying long hours and sometimes only popping in for an hour or two."

Dela liked that Cherry gave Keenan nothing concrete. "Good. I like keeping everyone on their toes. Especially people like him. What about the woman? Did she say anything?"

"At first she was polite and asked me questions about the bar and how I liked working here. But the longer they stayed, she started saying weird things and he would cut her off, and start talking. He finally tossed money on the table and practically carried her out. She was wobbly-legged and her eyes were rolling back in her head. I asked if I should call a doctor. He said, no, he'd handle it." Cherry glanced at the bar and then back at Dela. "Did I do the right thing?"

"Yes, you offered help and he didn't take it. Thank you. If you think of anything else, contact me, please." Dela cut her burger in half.

"I will. Enjoy the meal."

Dela waited for the waitress to move on to another table before she said, "I bet they call and cancel on Mom tomorrow if she couldn't handle being here an hour today." Dela leaned forward over the table. "And frankly, I would be happy to know my mom wouldn't be hanging around with that woman. She was creepy the night I met her on the parkway and she sounds like she was being creepy in here today. I don't want Mom riding around with that woman in her car."

Heath stared at her. "If the woman has a mental illness she can't help it."

"I know, but if you had seen her talking about buried bodies, you would know what I'm talking about. She looked like the person who buried the bodies when she was saying it."

"It makes you wonder what kind of trauma caused her to become unstable," Heath said, picking up the third quarter of his sandwich.

Dela thought about that as she finished her burger and then the fries.

Norma walked over and handed them the bill. "How did everything taste?"

"Good. I need to walk around the casino a dozen times to wear off all the food," Dela said.

Norma laughed and picked up the empty plates. "You know, there was something familiar about that woman but I can't place it. If I come up with it, I'll let you know."

"Thanks," Dela responded, sliding off the tall chair and wiggling her leg with the prosthesis. Her leg hung long enough that the knee felt stiff.

"I have to get back to work. What time will you be heading home?" Heath asked, walking beside her to the gaming floor.

"Not until after midnight." She stopped and studied him. "I can drive home without an escort."

"I'm off tomorrow. I'll be sitting in my pickup in the lot waiting for you." He squeezed her hand and strode to the entrance.

She wanted to be angry with him, but she wasn't. As Molly said earlier in the day, he loved her and wanted to keep her safe. Dela crossed through the gaming tables and headed for the surveillance office. She tapped her security card against a small box in the design on the wall and a door opened. She stepped through moments before the door closed.

The large room with dozens of monitors and eight men and women watching them was quiet.

"Hey, Dela. Good to see you," Lionel, one of the oldest casino employees, said.

"Hi, Lionel. How are things?" she asked, as she walked the length of the room to enter the back room and office.

"Not bad. Heard about your car being broken into. We're keeping a lookout for that black SUV for you."

"Thank you." She opened the door and entered.

Farley and Marty sat at the table in front of three monitors, their heads bent together, studying something.

"You had something for me to look at?" Dela asked, causing the two men to start.

"Hey! You are sneaky," Farley said, pushing his chair away from where they'd been looking at something and over to a keyboard. "I'll pull up that footage you wanted to see."

Dela walked over to where Marty sat. "What are you doing?"

"Farley found some software that can enhance images. We've been trying to see into the SUV that followed us this morning from the photos I took." He glanced up at her. "So far, no luck."

"We'll catch them." She turned her attention to the

video playing on the monitor in front of Farley. He stood and motioned for her to take the chair. She did, all while watching every move the Cristos made. She noticed the slow deterioration of the woman's calm. Seeing the moments of clarity in the woman's face and then the lengthening moments of confusion, fear, and anger, Dela found herself worrying for the woman and wondering why a man with the money Keenan had, didn't get her a good nurse and settle her in a small apartment in his home.

Surely, the woman would be more stable in the same environment every day instead of being dragged all over the country while her husband set up more breweries.

The last minutes before they left the Pony and exited the casino, Dela could see the woman had no control of her body and didn't seem to know where she was. "That's so sad," she said in a whisper.

"What?" Farley asked.

"Nothing." Dela wished she could learn who the woman's doctor was and discover her true condition. "Thank you for getting that for me."

"No problem. Anyone else you want me to keep tabs on?" Farley asked.

"No. As far as I can tell, none of the suspects frequents the casino." Dela shoved the chair back and stood. She placed a hand on Marty's shoulder. "Thanks for going with me this morning and for trying to figure out who the guys in the SUV are."

"No problem. You know Molly would have my hide if I didn't take care of her friend." He smiled and winked.

She knew he was using Molly as an excuse to keep

from saying, he had her back. As she had any of her employees' backs at the Spotted Pony.

"Do you have an escort home when you get off work?" he asked.

"Yeah. Heath said he'd be waiting for me when I finish."

"He's a good man. Don't let him get away," Marty said. His tone and face said he wasn't joking around.

"I don't plan on it. I hope I don't have to come back in here tonight. That will mean it will be quiet." She put her hand on the door.

"You'll be back," Farley said. "Because Marty will have an image of those guys for you."

"Thanks for the vote of confidence." Marty held up a fist and the two bumped fists.

Dela exited the room and walked through the surveillance room. She raised her hand to open the door and a voice in her earbuds said, "Need help at the roulette table."

# Chapter Thirteen

Dela spun around. "Who has eyes on the roulette table?"

"I do," Kay said.

Dela hurried to stand behind the woman. "What's going on?"

"A guy is trying to make a bet but a woman isn't letting him." She pointed to the monitor to her upper left.

Dela focused on the people in the footage. The two were facing each other. She recognized the man, but not the woman. The man was Darren Landis. Interesting. "Keep an eye on them if they part ways." Dela headed to the door. As soon as she stepped on the casino floor, she headed for the gaming tables.

Two security guards were standing to the side. The man and woman weren't touching one another, they were shouting back and forth.

Dela walked up between them. "Darren, go with

Russ." She motioned for Russ to take hold of Darren. "Take him to the office."

Luckily the other officer who had arrived was female. "Nadine, bring this woman along. We'll figure out what's happening in the security office, not on the gaming floor." Once the two security officers led the man and woman away from the table, Dela smiled and said, "Now you can all return to having fun. I'm sorry for the interruption." As she walked away, the patrons at the roulette table clapped.

She followed the officers and the couple into the security office. "Nadine, stay here with—what's your name?"

The woman was younger than Zaria and dressed more conservatively. "Louisa. Louisa Tuttle."

"Nadine, stay with Louisa while I talk to Darren." Dela tipped her head toward the small room they used for holding people until the Tribal Police arrived.

Russ led Darren in and stood by the door, while both Dela and Darren sat down.

"What's going on? You were interrupting the other roulette players fun." Dela sat back in her chair as if she didn't have anywhere else to be.

Darren wrung his hands in front of him on the table, but he didn't make eye contact.

"Last night you and your wife were frosty at my mom's dinner party and now you're arguing in public with another woman. What would Zaria say?"

He raised his head. Angry eyes glared at her. "That whore wouldn't care. All she thinks about is how exciting it would be to screw someone other than her husband."

"Were taking your anger at your wife out on the

woman you brought to the casino with you?" Dela tried not to sound sarcastic but it didn't work.

"You think it's funny?"

She could see the pain in his eyes. "No, I don't think it's funny. I'm sorry your wife is sleeping around. But does that poor woman out there deserve to have you yelling at her in public?"

He shook his head. "No. She works with me. I made the mistake of saying I wasn't going home tonight to show Zaria what it felt like to be home wondering where your spouse was and Louisa said that wasn't a good way to fix things. How she figured out I came here, I don't know. She was trying to tell me to stop wasting my money and do what needs to be done. Tell Zaria we're through." He studied Dela. "How can a person love someone and keep getting their heart trampled and yet they can't fathom being separated from that person?"

Dela heard the hurt and saw the pain. He was as much a victim of a mental illness as Annie. And this was the reason Zaria slept with other men, she knew Darren would never leave her. "I'm sorry for your marriage being what it is but you can't come in here and take your frustrations out on the person who is trying to help you. And stop the playing on the roulette table."

Dela studied the man. He was at his wit's end. Was he so upset over his wife's sleeping with Gus that he would kill the man? He had the right build of the person she saw running from the bridge. "Where were you Wednesday night?"

"What? Wednesday night? I was sitting outside Hamley's watching to see who my wife left with."

"At what time?" Dela asked. It wasn't that far from Hamleys to where Gus was killed.

"I was there until nine-thirty. That's when Zaria left the restaurant. I followed her home and we argued. She didn't like me following her around."

Dela would have to ask Zaria about the time.

"Russ is going to escort you to the entrance. I suggest you get in your car and drive home. Then sit down with Zaria and have a heart-to-heart talk. If she doesn't love you, it might be in your best interest to walk away before she shreds your heart anymore." Dela stared at the man and wondered when she'd become a Love Doctor.

Darren nodded and stood. Russ opened the door and the two walked out.

Before Dela could rise and ask to have Louisa brought in, Nadine and the woman appeared in the doorway.

"You want to talk to her next?" Nadine asked.

"Yes. Thanks." Dela motioned for the woman to sit down.

Nadine took up the spot Russ just vacated.

"Louisa, I'd like to hear your side of what was happening at the roulette table." Dela leaned back in the chair and smiled.

"I work with Darren. He's been doing lousy work for the last month, month and a half. He's going to lose his job if he doesn't shape up. Then today he told me about his problems with his wife. I suggested he go home, pack his things, and see what she does. He seemed like that was what he'd planned to do, so I followed him. But he didn't go home. He came here instead."

She wrung her hands and said, "I watched him and saw he was displaying destructive behavior, so I stepped up and tried to talk to him. He started shouting and saying hurtful things, but he's a good man. That woman has made him mean and cruel. He feels devalued." She stopped with a wide-eyed expression as if she said more than she'd meant.

"It seems you care about Darren," Dela said.

"I know how he feels, I guess," she admitted.

"You'll have to be his friend if he does leave his wife. You might need to pick up the pieces." Dela stood. "If you come here again and get into a shouting match, disrupting our clientele, I'll have you arrested for disturbing the peace."

Louisa nodded. "I won't be coming back. I don't like the noise."

Dela nodded for Nadine to escort Louisa out of the casino.

When they left, she settled back in the chair and wondered at the strange relationships of people. Which brought her thoughts to her mom and the man Dela believed was her father. Had he raped her mother? Was he a serial rapist? She pulled the photo of Dory Thunder out of her pant pocket and studied it. His eyes appeared sad but not crazy. Not like Annie Cristo.

She shoved the photo back in her pocket and walked into the office.

"Did you get things settled?" Margie asked.

"Yeah, between them at least." Dela sat at her desk. She had a schedule to make and one more walk around the casino before she would leave.

Opening her computer, she clicked on the icon for the schedule then clicked on the internet and typed in mental illnesses. After reading about mental illnesses, mainly psychotic which kind of fit Annie, Dela realized she needed to do her rounds and she hadn't even worked on the schedule.

She stood, stretched, and headed out to the casino floor. All was quiet in the way of rowdiness, but the building was filled with the noise of machines, people, and music. Dela was ready to head home and the quiet.

As she passed by the deli someone called her name. She pivoted and discovered her friend Rosie behind the counter. "What are you doing working so late?" Dela asked.

"I'm filling in for Tiana. She's on vacation." Rosie leaned her elbows on the counter and studied her. "You look as tired as I feel." She yelled into the kitchen, "I'm done for the night, you can clean up."

Rosie walked around the counter, grabbing her purse out from underneath the cash register. "Do you have time to sit a minute?"

"Yeah." Dela followed her over to a table and sat. "What do you need to talk about?"

"Nothing. I'm just making sure you're okay. I heard about the police thinking you killed someone. Which I know you didn't do. And I haven't had a chance to talk to you since I learned some more about Dory Thunder."

Dela's heart stopped. "What did you learn?" She worried her friend had discovered the man's criminal record.

"He was Grandpa Thunder's oldest son. He and a cousin, Leonard Thunder, enrolled in the army and went to Vietnam. Leo died. Dory came home. They say that after Dory returned he blamed himself for his cousin's death." Rosie dug around in her purse and pulled out a small notebook. "This is what I found on Leo." She ripped several pages out of the book and handed them to Dela.

"Thank you for digging into this. How did you find out this information?"

"The tribal archives. I told you I volunteered to help get them digitized. I wrote down everything I found on Leo and Dory. I couldn't make copies without Nancy getting suspicious. You said you didn't want anyone to know."

"Rosie, you are a good friend. Thank you for doing this." Dela was happy she had friends like Rosie, Molly, and Heath.

"Not a problem, just let me know if you need anything else looked up. I have access to all the records." Rosie used the table to stand. "I'm ready to go home and get off these feet. One of these days I'm going to think about losing weight so they don't have to carry so much." She smiled and slowly walked toward the security office to check out.

Dela watched her friend who was as tall as she was wide and who had a heart as big as the Appaloosa horse statue at the water feature. She had told Rosie about Dory, hoping she could dig up more information about him since no one on the reservation wanted to talk about him, including his father. Grandfather Thunder had warned her not to bring Dory up to her mother. He said it would only bring her pain. If Dory had raped her mom, Dela could see why. But Mom had never said one bad word about how she was conceived or the man who'd made her pregnant. She only told Dela her father was Cisco Alvaro and he died before they could get married. But try as she might, Dela could never get more out of her mom. When she'd tried looking up Cisco Alvaro, she never found one that was the right age that died in the eight months before she was born.

Her phone buzzed. Heath.

*I'm outside.*

*Coming.*

Dela stepped into the security office to take off her radio and mic and grab her purse. She found Oliver at the podium reading a car magazine.

"Things are slow tonight," she said to him.

"Maybe from our standpoint but all the cars I saw in the parking lot when I came on shift, I'd say the casino is hopping out there." He put the magazine down and drank from a bottle of water.

"That's true. You can hardly move there are so many people." Dela put her purse strap over her head and said, "Kenny knows to call me if he has problems."

"Same as usual then," Oliver said. "Have a good night."

"Thanks, you too."

She exited the building and spotted Heath's truck not far from her car. While it irked that he felt the need to follow her, she did feel safer seeing him.

She was halfway between the building and the car when lights came around the corner of the building. Before she could register what was happening the sound of screeching wheels and two vehicles colliding filled the air.

# Chapter Fourteen

Dela stared at the two vehicles smashed together. Within seconds it registered the truck was Heath's. "Heath!" she screamed and ran to the vehicle, as voices behind her called out.

She ran around to the driver's side and tried wrenching the folded door open. It didn't budge. She peered through the glass seeing only the white powder from the airbags floating. Pressing her face against the glass, the powder finally settled and she could see Heath. Blood trickled from his nose, making a dark trail on his white upper lip. He appeared stunned but she didn't see anything worse. "You stupid fool. You could have killed yourself," she said, tugging on the door again.

"Marty called the police and the EMTs. They'll be here shortly," Kenny said, leading her back from the truck.

"What about the driver of the car?" Dela asked,

remembering the car had been coming at her before Heath hit it.

"The driver's gone. Marty saw the whole thing. I'm sure he'll have footage of the person." Kenny started to lead her back to the casino.

"I'm not leaving Heath. He saved my life." She shrugged out of Kenny's hold on her arm and hurried back to the truck.

The thought of not having Heath in her life nearly buckled her over. She staggered to the passenger door and tugged hard. The door opened. Ignoring the powder all over the inside, she slid in and grasped Heath's hand. "Did you hurt anything other than that thick skull?"

He turned his head and peered into her eyes. "I saved you. That's all that matters."

"Not if you aren't alive to grow old with me," she scolded.

Flashing lights appeared around the side of the casino. First a Tribal police car and then the reservation EMTs.

When the tribal exited the vehicle, Dela was happy to see it was the newest recruit, Officer Tabitha Shaw. Heath said the young woman was proving to be a good law enforcement officer.

The tribal officer pulled out her phone and took photos before she walked over to the open passenger door. "Oh God! It's Heath!" She stared at him until he opened his eyes and said, "Tabby, make sure you get all the details from Dela."

Dela felt him squeeze her hand. She knew he wanted her to tell everything she saw. "I was walking out of the casino leaving for the night." She glanced at Heath. "Heath came to escort me home because of the break-in of my car, the murder, and the man who tried to get into my house, not to mention the car that followed me earlier today."

Tabby was writing as fast as Dela was talking.

"Dela, you need to move so we can get Heath out," Spencer Flare, one of the EMTs and a classmate of theirs, said, touching Dela's arm.

She nodded, realizing she was blocking Heath's only exit. "I'm going to move so they can get you out of here," she told Heath and kissed his hand before releasing it.

"Tell Tabby everything," he said, just above a whisper.

"I will." Dela slid out and followed Tabby over to her car. The officer opened the driver's side door and told her to sit.

She didn't have to be told twice. Her knees were weak as she thought about how she would have been run over if Heath hadn't been here. And the fact he had risked his life to save hers.

"Tell me what you saw when you walked out of the casino," Tabby said.

"I saw Heath sitting in his truck waiting, then when I was halfway between him and the casino, a car came roaring around the corner of the building." She thought about that. "Someone must have been back here on a phone with the driver for him to know when I was the most vulnerable."

"I made a note of that. What happened next?"

"The lights of the car blinded me. I didn't see anything but I heard screeching tires and the crash. The impact removed the lights from my sight and I saw it was Heath's truck. I ran to check on him. I didn't think to look for the other driver."

"That's understandable," Tabby said. "But you didn't see anyone else? Like the person you think orchestrated the attempt on your life."

"Nothing." She stood as the EMTs put Heath on a stretcher. "I'm going to follow them to the hospital. Talk to Marty in surveillance. Kenny said he saw it all."

"I will. Are you sure you don't need someone to drive you? You're still shaken up."

A car raced into the employee parking lot and stopped by the police car. Dela smiled recognizing the vehicle. Molly stepped out of the passenger side and Travis was behind the wheel.

Her friend strode toward them. "Dela, are you okay?" She wrapped her arms around Dela and said, "Marty called me. He said Heath was hurt."

"The EMTs just took him to St. Anthony's. Could you drive me to the hospital?" Dela eased out of her friend's embrace.

"Of course, I'll drive your car and Marty can pick me up when he goes home." Molly faced Tabby. "Do you need anything else from her?"

"No. I'm going to go in and talk to Marty."

"We'll be at the hospital if you need anything else." Molly led Dela to her car. She brushed the white powder off Dela's clothes from sitting in Heath's truck.

They were halfway to Pendleton when Molly said, "Marty said the car was coming for you and Heath drove in front of it to save you."

Dela nodded and swallowed the lump in her throat. "The fool nearly killed himself."

"To save you," Molly said softly. "The woman he loves."

Tears burned her eyes and slid down her cheeks. She couldn't think of another person who would have sacrificed themselves for her. "I know."

At the hospital, they were told he was in the emergency room and one person could go in.

"You go. I'll be right out here," Molly said.

Dela followed the nurse to a small room. The head of the bed was raised so he could sit up. A nurse was cleaning up his nose.

"Are you his wife?" the nurse asked.

"Not yet, but soon to be," Dela said. She saw Heath's lips twitch. He was awake and heard her.

"The doctor examined him and doesn't think anything is broken. He'll have bruising. We're waiting to take him for X-rays and a CT scan to make sure he didn't injure the brain. He does seem to have a mild concussion."

"From the airbag," Heath muttered.

"Is it okay if I sit with him?" Dela asked.

"Yes. Keep him talking. We don't want him falling asleep until we've finished all our tests." The nurse rolled the stainless-steel tray away from the table. It was cluttered with bloody gauze and instruments.

Dela sat on the stool the nurse vacated. She grasped Heath's hand with both of hers. "Thank you for saving my life. I wish you hadn't been hurt in the process."

"You're worth a bloody nose and possible concussion." A lopsided smile tipped his lips.

"It has to have been the people who followed Marty and me this morning. But why are they still after me? I didn't see anything. I don't know anything." Frustration bubbled in her chest. Not only were they still after her, but everyone she was around was in danger.

"Did anyone besides us see what happened tonight?" Heath asked.

"Marty was watching it on a monitor. He sent Kenny out. I told Tabby to go talk to Marty." Dela hoped they caught a good photo of the person driving the car. If they did, they could get him on attempted murder and maybe he'd cough up who sent him to kill her.

"Good. Hopefully, they caught him." Heath squeezed her hand. "How bad is the damage to my truck?"

"I have a feeling you'll be buying a new one." She knew how much the vehicle meant to him. He'd bought it from someone in Pine Ridge who had said it had been his father's. A man Heath didn't get a chance to know.

"Damn! The truck isn't worth more than you but…"

"I know. It had been your father's. It had sentimental value." She leaned over and kissed him. "Maybe we can find one like it."

"No. If it needs to be replaced, I'll buy a new one."

"We're ready to take him for X-rays," a nurse said as she entered the room pushing a wheelchair.

"I'll be in the waiting area. Let me know when he comes back," Dela said, standing and releasing Heath's hand.

"You aren't alone, are you?" Heath asked, concern wrinkling his brow.

"No. Molly brought me to the hospital." Dela waited until the nurse wheeled Heath down the hall before she returned to the waiting area.

Molly sat in a chair, drinking from a paper cup. Another one sat on the table beside her. When she caught sight of Dela, she picked up the cup on the table.

"I bought us coffee. Figured it was going to be a long night."

"Thank you. He's not in too bad of shape. They're doing X-rays and a scan of his head to make sure there aren't any internal injuries." Dela sat, holding the cup in her shaking hands. She steadied them long enough to take a sip. Then she placed the cup back on the table, clutching her hands together between her legs. "I'm a mess. I don't remember being this shaken up when my platoon was hit."

"That's because you were in a war and knew something could happen at any moment. This is different. You're home where it should be safe." Molly put a hand on her arm. "You're mentally tough. That's what I've always admired about you. You helped me through some terrible years. It's my turn to return the favor. Marty, Travis, and I are here for you and Heath."

"I know. It's just. I feel like a hypocrite. All my talk about not sure I'm ready for marriage, not sure I love Heath." Dela knew in her heart that she did love him. Thinking he could have been killed trying to save her nearly tore her heart in two. "When I realized he'd driven in front of that car, I thought I'd lost him and he'd never know I would have done the same for him."

Molly smiled. "He knows. Why do you think he hangs in there when you push him away? He has known since you two were in high school you loved him. Shoot, we all knew it. You just couldn't or wouldn't see it. We also know you pushed him away because you were afraid you couldn't handle it if something happened to him. We all saw how wounded and emotionally raw you'd become after Robin. But you did what you needed to do and came back stronger and ready to commit to relationships."

Dela studied her friend. The words she spoke were from her heart and what she believed.

Shaking her head, Dela said, "I don't deserve the family and friends I have."

"You do. And you deserve the love of a good man. Stop putting him off and make an honest woman of yourself."

Dela laughed. "I haven't heard that expression in a long time."

"You know what I'm saying. Tell that man you are ready to get married."

"He knows I am. But I have one more thing I have to solve before I can chain Heath to me for the rest of his life." She had to know if she was conceived from rape and if that man was indeed her father. Since she couldn't ask her mom without spilling all she knew about Dory Thunder, she and Heath had to keep digging. The information Rosie gave her was still in her pocket. But she didn't want to read it now.

She wanted to share it with Heath. After all, her past would be part of their future.

# Chapter Fifteen

Dela was in the room with Heath when a nurse came in. "Your friend's ride is here. She wants to know if it's okay for her to leave."

"You'll stay here until they release me?" Heath asked.

"That was my plan. Molly drove me here in my car," Dela said.

Heath gave a slight nod. "Let them know it's okay to go. But ask Marty if he saw anything from the video."

Dela nodded and walked out of the room and down the hall to the waiting area. She spotted Marty and Molly sitting in chairs, their heads together deep in discussion.

"Hey," Dela said, walking up to them.

"Good to hear Heath isn't hurt bad," Marty said.

"Yeah, I think he had more damage from the airbag than the actual crash. Just a slight concussion. They should send him home in a couple more hours. I'll be here with him until we can leave."

"Good. After tonight, I don't think you should go anywhere without someone watching your back." Marty ran a hand through his shoulder-length hair. "I couldn't believe it when I was watching you walk out of the casino and then those lights came around the corner. I was yelling at you, but of course, you couldn't hear me or do anything blinded like you were by the headlights. Then Wham! Heath hit that car and sent it flying. The driver must not have had an airbag because the driver's door flew open and he ran out like his ass was on fire."

"Did you get a good enough look at him to identify him?" Dela asked.

"I'll know more tomorrow. I'm using that image-enhancing software on the best still image I could get of his face."

"Did you look for someone standing around in the parking area? Or possibly in a car that drove away after the crash?" Dela knew it was nearly impossible that someone would have been standing where the camera would get a view.

"I'll have Farley go through the footage tomorrow. We'll start a couple of hours before you leave the casino and an hour after the police and everyone else leave the scene." Marty stood and put a hand on her shoulder. "Don't worry. We'll all be watching our monitors better and keeping an eye on you."

"I'm not sure I like the idea of everyone spying on me." She hated attention and really hated people knowing her business.

"If it will keep you safe that's what we'll do whether you like it or not," Molly said, hugging Dela.

"I'll call you about noon."

"If I'm awake, I'll answer." Dela watched the two walk out of the emergency entrance. She turned to head back to sit with Heath when she heard her name. Spinning back around, she spotted Tabby walking toward her.

"I need to get Heath's statement if he's able to talk," she said.

"He can tell you what he saw." Dela led the tribal officer down the hall to Heath's room.

The doctor was checking his eyes when they walked in. He faced Dela. "We didn't see anything to be worried about on the X-rays or the scans. I'll release him, but he needs to have someone with him for the next twenty-four hours. Here's a list of things to watch for." The doctor picked up a paper from the tray by the bed. "If any of these symptoms intensify get him back in here. At this time, I don't foresee that happening but if he doesn't rest it could worsen the concussion."

"I understand. Thank you." Dela took the paper and scanned the symptoms. "When can I take him home?"

"I'll go finish filling out the paperwork and the nurse will bring in the discharge papers. Most likely within the next thirty minutes." The doctor left the room.

Tabby stepped out from behind Dela. "Hi, Heath. Good to see you're doing okay."

"Hey Tabby. I suppose you want to know what I saw."

"Yes, I need your statement." She opened up her notebook and poised a pen over a page.

Dela sat on the stool next to the bed. She hadn't heard his version of what happened. They'd talked about everything but that when he wasn't drowsy.

"I was parked about three cars over from Dela's vehicle waiting for her to finish so I could follow her home." He stopped and looked at Dela. "She's had a bad week and we knew someone was trying to hurt her after the break-in at the house."

Tabby nodded. "We have all of that documented. You believe this had something to do with the happenings earlier in the week?"

"Yes. She walked out of the building and as soon as she was too far from the building to get back in and too far from her car to get to safety, a car came barreling around the corner with its lights on bright. As soon as I saw it, I realized it was headed for Dela. I had already started my truck when I saw Dela walk out, so I slammed my foot on the accelerator and put it in drive. I wanted to get between the car and Dela before it was close enough to her to do damage."

He held out his hand and she grasped it. Dela knew his fear when he saw the car. It was the same she felt realizing it was his vehicle that had crashed into the car.

"Did you see who was driving the car?"

"No. I was focused on the front of the vehicle to stop it." Heath shifted his attention from Tabby to Dela. "I'm glad I stopped him."

She squeezed his hand. She was too.

"I talked to Marty in surveillance at the casino. He sent a copy of the video to the station. I'll take a look at it tomorrow. Hopefully, we'll be able to get something from that to help find this guy. Take it easy. I'll let the Chief know you won't be coming in for a couple days." Tabby closed her notebook and left the room.

Once they were alone, Dela told Heath what Marty

had said about the video. "There wasn't a plate on the car but they have the car and can use the VIN to find out who owns it." That was their best way of discovering who was behind the attempts on her life.

It was 4 am when Dela and Heath walked into the house. Mugshot and Jethro were making all kinds of noise in the backyard. She figured it was because they had been left so long without a person checking on them.

After getting Heath in bed, she stepped into the backyard and nearly toppled over from the donkey and dog heads pushing at her for attention.

"Sorry guys. It wasn't a good night. Heath has a concussion and he got it saving me." She searched the shadows of the fence even though she knew the two animals wouldn't have been so anxious to see her if there had been a stranger in the yard.

All of the incidents since Gus's death were making her paranoid and for a good reason. Someone wanted her dead.

Dela reached inside the house, grabbing an apple out of the basket on the counter. She gave Jethro the apple and let Mugshot in. She locked the door and gave her three-legged pet a treat. He carried it down the hall to the bedroom, where he lay in his bed and crunched.

She checked on Heath, who sat up with pillows propped behind him.

"My head hurts less if I'm elevated," he said. "Get changed and come lay by me."

She undressed, removed the prosthesis, and pulled on her tank and shorts before laying next to Heath.

"Tomorrow, when my head feels better, we will sit

down and figure out who is after you. I don't like not knowing. If we had something to follow, a lead of some kind, we could go after them, instead of always being surprised."

"I know. I don't want to change what I do, but I can't do my job if I think everyone around me could be out to get me. And all because I saw the back of someone running away from a murder. I know he was tall, thin, and had good form when running. I don't know if he's young or old, or what race he is. He wore a black hoodie, jeans, and running shoes."

"That could be a quarter of the male population in Pendleton." Heath had his arm wrapped around Dela. "Go to sleep. I'm here." He kissed the top of her head and she closed her eyes.

Her eyelids flew open. "I'm supposed to be keeping an eye on you." She wiggled her way to sit up beside him against the pillows. "What do you want to talk about?"

"Nothing. We need to sleep so we are at our best tomorrow."

"But are you okay to sleep?"

"Yeah. The doctor said they don't worry about that so much anymore. Close your eyes. Let's sleep. The sun is coming up."

"Okay." She closed her eyes, slid her head on Heath's chest, and fell asleep.

♠ ♣ ♥ ♦

Barking penetrated Dela's sleep. Her body sprang into a sitting position. She shoved the hair off her face and looked down at Heath. She placed a hand on his chest to feel if he was breathing. There was a steady rise and fall. She couldn't believe he was sleeping through Mugshot's barking, which was coming from the living room.

"I'm alive. Look on your phone and see who's out there. If it's no one important make Mugshot come back in here," Heath said, rolling over.

Dela picked up her phone and opened the app for the cameras. "Really?" She watched her mom bang on the door, walk away, then come back and pound on the door. "It's Mom."

"Just tell her what happened and we need sleep."

Dela started to get out of bed.

Heath grabbed her arm. "No. Text her and tell her."

*Mom, we were up all night. Heath was in a vehicle accident. We need to sleep. I'll call you later.*

Her phone buzzed.

*That's terrible! Is he okay?*

*He's fine. We need sleep. Please. I'll call later.*

*I love you.*

Dela sent her a heart emoji, called Mugshot to the bedroom, and snuggled against Heath. Her eyes closed, she drifted…

Buzz! Buzz! Her phone vibrated on the bedside table.

"Don't touch that unless you plan to put it on do not disturb." Heath's arm circled her body, holding her in place.

When he fell asleep, she gently eased out of his grasp and picked up the phone. It had been Zaria who called. Curiosity got the best of her.

Dela slipped out of bed, grabbed her crutches, and swung down the hallway. She lowered onto her recliner and held the phone to her ear to hear the message Zaria left.

"Thank you for sending my husband home last night. I understand he disrupted a game at the casino. He told me you gave him advice to leave me. How dare you think you can tell him what to do. I don't want you coming to the Chamber anymore. I want to work with someone else."

Wow! She'd hit a sore spot with Zaria. Did she really love her husband or just love having a doting husband? Dela hoped Darren left the woman. He deserved better.

Since she was up and had her phone, Dela checked her other voice messages. One was from a number she didn't know. She pressed play.

"Tonight was a warning. Stay out of our business or else."

She stared at the number, copied it, and sent it to the one person who had access to as much information as a law enforcement agency could get.

*Quinn, someone tried to run over me last night and Heath stopped them. Then I received a threatening message from this number.* She pasted the number in the message and sent it.

*Where did they try to run you over?* He replied.

*Casino parking lot.*

*Video footage?*

*Yeah. With Tribal Police.*

*We'll look into both.*

*Thanks.*

She received a thumbs up.

Her stomach growled. If she cooked anything, the smell would wake up Heath. He needed his rest more than she did.

She poured cereal into a bowl and added milk. A

cup of coffee sounded good, but that would have to wait. As she ate, she dialed her phone and called her mom.

"Dela, why didn't you answer the door if you're up?" her mom asked.

"I wasn't up when you were knocking. I planned to stay asleep, but the phone kept making noise. I slipped out of bed when Heath fell back asleep. He needs the rest." The scene of the crash played in her mind and she shuddered.

"What happened?"

To not worry her mom, she said, "There was a crazy driver in the parking lot. He swerved toward me and Heath drove his truck in front of the car to keep it from hitting me." It was a bit of a lie but better than scaring Mom.

"Oh no! Is he okay?"

"The airbag did most of the damage. He had a slight concussion and a bloody nose. The doctor said there could be bruising on his face and chest. We didn't get home from the ER until four this morning."

"I'm so sorry I disturbed you. I was trying to catch you before you headed out for the day. Keenan called and said Annie wouldn't be able to make it for our lunch today. I'm worried about her." The worry was evident in her mom's voice.

"I am too." Dela went on to tell her mom about seeing the couple at the casino yesterday. "I think he did it as a test run to see if she could handle it. And from what I saw, she couldn't."

"I don't understand how she can be so sane and nice one minute and crazy the next. Why doesn't he get someone to look after her?" Mom sounded as if she were ready to confront the husband.

"Mom, it isn't any of our business." What she really wanted to say was don't get mixed up with Keenan, but she didn't. The information she knew about the man's business wasn't something she could discuss with her mom.

"Don't take Annie on as a project you plan to fix. Once the brewery is up and running, they'll move on to the next project." Dela had seen her mom get involved in helping people. Usually, it went well. She didn't see this as an easy fix.

When her mom didn't say anything, she said, "Mom, promise me you won't try to help the Cristos."

"Fine. I'll not try to help the Cristos."

"Thank you. I need to either get more sleep or find something quiet to do while Heath sleeps. Have a good day."

"You too. And give Heath a hug from me. I'm thankful he saved my daughter."

The emotion in her mom's voice reminded Dela of what she could have lost. "Me, too."

The call ended and Dela looked up to find Heath watching her.

"Why aren't you in bed sleeping?" he asked, lowering onto the closest chair. Purple bruising was starting to show around his eyes and on his cheeks. He was bare-chested. There was a tiny bit of discoloration on his pecs.

"I picked up my phone to put it on Do Not Disturb and saw that Zaria had left a message." She went to voicemail and played it on the speakerphone for him.

"You upset her. What did her husband do in the casino?"

Dela told him about the altercation and what she'd said to Darren and Louisa.

"I think your mom's matchmaker genes are flaring in you." He grinned and stretched his hand across the table toward her.

She grasped it and said, "I don't care to match up people. I was just telling them what I saw." She pushed the play button on the threat she received. "I got this too."

Heath's eyes blazed with anger as he listened. "We need to get this to the police."

"I was going to ask you who to send it to. I did send the number to Quinn to see if he can find out where it came from."

"Good idea. He has more resources. But I bet it comes back a burner phone." Heath pulled her around the table and down onto his lap. "I don't want anything to happen to you. If we have to, we'll stay locked up in here until they find Gus's killer."

Dela peered into his eyes. "As nice as that sounds, you and I will not be able to sit still and let someone else solve this."

"True but it was nice thinking about time alone with you."

"You can keep thinking about it and come up with where we can go on our honeymoon."

Heath's face lit up. "Does this mean you're ready to marry me?"

"Once we discover the truth about my father and if you still want me, I will marry you."

"I've told you before, that nothing we find out about your father will change my mind. So we might as well do it now rather than later." Heath held her head in his hands. "It doesn't matter to me how you were conceived. What matters is your truth and heart. Finding out about your father isn't going to change that."

Dela reveled in the truth in his gaze. "I know. But what about how I will feel?"

"Your father hasn't been in your life. He hasn't made you who you are. You and your mom have done that. I love the person you are. Your warts and all." He smiled.

Dela grinned and pushed to stand. "Rosie gave me information on Dory last night. I'll go get it." She grabbed her crutches and swung down the hall. On her way back to the kitchen the aroma of coffee filled the air.

Heath sat at the table with a cup of coffee in his hands and one on the table at her spot.

"Thank you. I didn't want to make it and wake you up." She settled onto her chair, sipped the coffee, and unfolded the pages Rosie gave her.

"How did Rosie find out information on Dory?" Heath moved his chair over next to Dela.

"She's been helping to digitize the tribe's records. She came across the Thunder family and wrote down what she found." Dela pointed to the information about Leo. "Dory and a cousin, Leo, went to Vietnam together. Leo didn't come back."

Heath studied the pages and said, "That could make a person change."

"That's what I thought when I heard this information." She began reading the pages. When she finished one, she handed it over to Heath. When she'd read both sides of the pages, she leaned back in her chair and picked up her coffee.

"We need to check into both their histories in the Army. I can ask the V.A. how to access Dory and Leo's military records. Something I haven't done is look at school yearbooks. It wouldn't hurt to learn more about them before they went into the military." Dela felt energized at the possibility of looking into her father and cousin's lives.

"We can do that, but we also need to figure out who is threatening you and who killed Gus," Heath said, squashing her enthusiasm.

"Yes. I can't find out about my relatives if I'm not alive." Dela pulled a notepad over to her and picked up a pen. "We know that the car that drove away from here when we had a near break-in was at the brewery yesterday when Marty and I were there. They followed us." She wrote each thought on the notepad. "Which I think means Gus's death has to do with the brewery."

"That's a good connection. But what could Gus have seen that had him call you to discuss?" Heath asked, rising and putting bread in the toaster.

"My guess is it had to do with drugs. The one thing he was staying away from. He wanted to keep his nose clean for Evelyn's sake. She told him no more drug dealing." Dela listed those things.

"Tell me what you saw when you were at the brewery," Heath sat down, buttered his toast, and listened as Dela described everything she saw.

She added, "Stan said they planned to be open by the Stampede."

"That would bring in the most revenue the quickest." Heath offered her a slice of toast.

Dela took the triangle, bit into it, and thought. "We

need to ask Stan more questions about Gus's visits to the brewery." She snapped her fingers. "I forgot, he said a guy named Balto, the beefy guy who tried to run us off, works for Keenan. Stan said he's been the foreman on every Cristo brewery that was built."

"Did you get a last name?" Heath asked.

"No. Stan or Evelyn might know." Dela picked up her phone. "I'll call Evelyn and ask her."

"That may not be a good idea. She knows you're trying to find her father's killer. She might think you think it's him and mess things up."

That's why they made a good team. She could be impulsive and Heath thought things through. Thank goodness he hadn't thought anything through last night when he put his truck between her and the car.

"You're right. I'll try Stan first. If he doesn't know we'll find a way to ask Evelyn without making it look like we're interested in Balto."

# Chapter Sixteen

Dela called the casino and let them know she wouldn't be in for two days since she had to watch Heath for any reactions to the concussion. Chief Steele called to check on Heath and told him to take the week off. He'd rather have him working at full capacity than be there at half.

"Now I can stay with you all week," he said, as they were dressing.

"Then you'll be following me around as I try to find out who is after me and who killed Gus." Dela would have normally been upset to think Heath thought she needed protection. But after last night, she would let him follow her all he wanted. As long as he didn't hurt himself.

"Where are we going first?" Heath asked as he put Mugshot out in the yard with Jethro, after giving the donkey a flake of hay.

"Let's see if we can talk to Stan again. He should

be at the brewery." She grinned.

"You like poking the bear, don't you?"

"I want to talk to Stan. And maybe we can get a little more conversation out of Balto. Or at least see what his expression is when he sees me." Dela took her purse off the coat rack and opened the door. "I think we'll stop by Molly's and have Travis keep an eye on the place with our cameras. If that's okay with you?"

"They missed you with a car last night, I wouldn't put it past them to try to get you from home. That's a good idea. We'll be busy and can't keep an eye on things. If he sees something suspicious, he can call the tribal police." Heath locked the door behind them.

Once they were in the car and headed to Mission Street, Dela glanced at Heath in the passenger seat. His face was getting darker, but he had a determined set to his jaw. "Do you feel okay?"

"I'm fine. Just a faint twinge in my head. It's more irritating than painful." He smiled.

"If you aren't up to this today, we can wait and do it tomorrow." She didn't want him to suffer because she wanted to get the tension out of her neck and back and make her stub quit aching. When she was tense or upset, the phantom pains would worsen. Usually, Heath could ease her tension and make them go away. But she didn't want to burden him with her discomfort after what he'd done for her.

"I'm good. Just don't piss anyone off, because I don't think I could throw good punches today. The jarring of my hand meeting someone's jaw would hurt my head."

"I'll try to be on my best behavior."

Heath laughed. "Then you wouldn't be you if that

happened."

She chuckled. He did know her too well.

At the vet clinic, Molly cornered them. "How are you both feeling?"

"We're fine," Dela said.

"Heath doesn't look fine. He looks bruised and tired. You should take him back to your house and both of you sleep." Molly had her hands on her hips, scowling.

"We aren't going to rest well until we have whoever is trying to hurt Dela locked up," Heath said. "We're here to see Travis. We'd like him to keep an eye on our place while we're out running around."

"He's in his office. The middle bedroom," she amended when Dela started to ask where the office was.

They walked down the hall and found him busy working numbers.

Dela knocked on the doorjamb.

Travis spun in his chair. His eyes were lit up and his smile welcoming. Both dimmed when he saw them. "Oh, I thought it was Cammie."

"That must be your girlfriend's name." Dela sat on a chair and pulled out her phone. "We want you to keep an eye on our place while we're out investigating today. Do you know how to get this app? I'll give you the security codes to access our cameras."

"Piece of cake," Travis said, reading her phone and then typing in the search bar of his laptop. "I'm putting it on here in case someone gets a hold of my phone they won't have access to your cameras."

"Smart thinking," Heath said.

Travis grinned at him. "I come up with a good idea now and then." He continued downloading the app. In minutes he had their cameras showing up on his laptop. "I'll leave it up and running while I crunch numbers on Mom and Marty's house."

"Thanks, Travis. Good luck crunching those numbers." Dela and Heath left the clinic after saying goodbye to Molly and catching a glimpse of Cammie.

The drive to Pendleton and the brewery took twenty minutes.

At the brewery, she noted two Sander Construction vehicles and a black passenger van that could hold about eight people. As well as the two black sedans. Walking up to the entrance, she didn't see the SUV today.

"Hey! No one's to come into this building." A man, not as burly as Balto, shouted and stepped into the doorway. He wasn't wearing a hard hat. And he wasn't dressed like he worked construction. He looked like a bouncer at a nightclub.

"We need to speak with Stan Gould. He's one of the Sander Construction crew members," Dela said.

"Why do you need to see him?"

Heath held up his badge. Dela noticed he had the word Tribal covered with his finger.

"We need to speak to him about an incident that happened last night. He was one of the witnesses."

The man studied them. "He in trouble?"

"No, he was a witness. We just need to clarify something he said."

"You're not wearing a uniform. And you look pretty beat up. You sure you aren't here to cause trouble?" The man stood with his arms crossed and his feet spread apart. He didn't seem to be in any hurry to get Stan for them.

"I'm Detective Seaver. I was in an automobile accident last night. Could you please get Stan? I have several other people I need to speak to this morning." Heath put his badge away and pulled out a notepad and pen. "Can I get your name?"

The man uncrossed his arms and glared. "You don't need my name. I'll get him."

When he disappeared, Dela said in a whisper, "I hope they don't think Stan is snitching on them with me coming yesterday and then today to talk to him."

Heath nodded as the bouncer returned with Stan.

"What?" Stan asked, looking at her with confusion.

Dela stopped him with a shake of her head. Then she led him over to the trees at the far side of the outdoor seating. "Sorry to have to bother you again," she started. "We need to know Balto's last name, and did Gus have an unusual interest in this building?"

Stan studied her and then Heath. "What happened to you?"

"I kept a car from hitting someone. What is Balto's last name?"

"I think it's Henry or Harvey…Herman. It's Herman. Balto Herman. Strange name if you ask me."

Dela nodded. "And did Gus come here a lot?"

"A couple of times. I overheard Balto telling someone he'd seen Gus in here with the blueprints. Like he thought it was wrong for the head of the construction company to have the plans. It didn't make sense to me. But, hey, I'm getting paid well and keep my mouth shut if I see something that looks off."

Dela picked up on that. "What do you mean by off?"

Stan took his hard hat off and scratched his head. "I

saw the blueprints when we started this building. The measurements at the back of the building don't make sense. The last two rooms should be larger than they are."

"Thank you for answering our questions. Each witness to an accident is crucial. Every little bit of information helps us to piece together what really happened," Heath said and closed his notepad.

Dela glanced behind Stan and realized why Heath had said that last part so loud.

"Gould, get back in there and get to work." Balto stomped up to them. His eyes widened at the sight of Dela. "What are you doing back here and with a policeman? I thought you were cable or something."

"We had a mishap that happened yesterday. Mr. Gould happened to be passing by at the time," Dela said, hoping the man would buy it.

"Who are you?" Balto asked, studying Heath.

"Detective Seaver." He flipped his notepad open. "And you are?"

"None of your business." Balto pointed a stubby finger at Dela. "If I see you around here again, I'll be calling this guy to arrest you for trespassing."

"Advice taken," she said as a black SUV pulled into the parking lot next to her car. Dela started to gasp but caught it, and asked, "Are those men working here too?" She pointed at the vehicle.

Balto swung his head around, saw the car, and growled, before heading back into the building.

Dela grasped Heath's hand. "Let's go. I want to get a good look at them." She glanced at the empty license frame on the front of the vehicle. "This is the car that keeps following me."

They hurried across the seating area to the parking lot. When they started toward the car, it backed up and accelerated out of the parking lot.

"I don't think they want us to see who they are," Heath said, as they slid into Dela's car.

"How come the city police and the state police haven't pulled them over yet?" Dela wondered where they were staying that no one had seen the car.

"Let's try to follow them." Heath pointed. "They went through the Walmart parking lot."

Dela started the car and headed to the parking lot entrance.

"They are headed out the other side," Heath said.

Dela drove around the building, and they caught sight of the car going down a street. She followed, staying just far enough back they could see the car. After zigzagging through town, the vehicle drove to a house in the area where Vivian Sander lived.

The car pulled into a driveway, the garage door opened, and the car pulled in, disappearing behind the closing door. Heath wrote down the address and Dela drove by, parking on a side street where they could keep an eye on the house and garage.

"Can you find out who lives in that house?" Dela asked.

"I'll call Fletcher and see if he can get a name." Heath pulled out his phone and called the detective. He told Fletcher about the attempt on Dela and that they had followed the car without a license that had been following her. He gave Fletcher the address and said he'd wait for the detective to call him back.

Ten minutes went by and nothing from Detective Fletcher.

"I'll just go knock on the door and see what I can find out," Dela said.

Heath put a hand on her arm. "No. You are not going up to that door when the people inside have been following you."

The door opened and Annie walked out to the sidewalk, looked both directions, and started up the road toward them.

"Is that where the Cristos are staying?" While she knew that Keenan's business was under suspicion by the DEA, she hadn't thought he would be the one who wanted her dead.

A city police vehicle pulled up to the house. Detective Fletcher and an officer walked up to the door.

"You keep an eye on them, I'm going to catch up to Annie and see which person she is today." Dela exited the car before Heath could say anything. She jogged the best she could without her running foot until she could walk fast to catch up to the woman.

"Annie?" Dela called out.

The woman swung around, fear wrinkling her face and widening her eyes.

"Don't be afraid, it's me, Dela. We met the other night at my mom's dinner party." Dela stopped in front of the woman.

She could see Annie was searching her memory. Did that mean she didn't recognize her as the person at the river parkway either?

The fear dissipated from the woman's face and she smiled. Then she nodded her head and the smile lit up her eyes. "Yes, Deborah's daughter. It was a lovely evening. You and that hunky Tribal Police Officer made a beautiful couple."

Dela's cheeks heated. She thought she was the only one who thought Heath was a hunk.  To hear this woman a good ten years older than she and Heath say that about him made her proud he wanted to be with her.

"What are you doing walking around up here?" Dela asked.

"Oh, the house we rented while Keenan works on his brewery is just down a couple of blocks. I prefer walking in a park but Keenan doesn't have time to go with me, so I sneak out now and then and walk a few blocks up here."

"When it gets hotter, you'll need to start out on a walk earlier in the day. It can get up around the hundreds in the summer here." Dela started walking back the way they'd come and the woman followed.

"I hope we aren't here that long." Annie put a hand on Dela's arm. "I don't like it here. I've had more bad days than good while we've been in Pendleton."

"I'm sorry to hear that. Are the bad days brought on by stress?" Dela wanted to help this woman who seemed to lose the memory of her actions when she was psychotic.

"I don't think it's stress. Though I don't like it when Balto visits. Keenan is always upset when he leaves." Annie looked up and spotted the police car. "Why are the police at our house?"

"I don't know. Do you want me to go in with you?" Dela glanced across at the Rav4 and saw Heath was still seated in the car. He was on his phone. He gave her a thumbs up. She took that to mean he believed it safe for her to walk into the house.

"Do you mind? I don't know what to do." Annie

stood on the sidewalk staring at the house.

"Let's go see what's going on. Knowing the truth is better than making up worse stories in your head." Dela started toward the house as the door opened.

Detective Fletcher had one man in handcuffs and the officer with him had another man. They both appeared to be in their twenties with black hoodies, jeans, and athletic shoes. Either one would fit the person she saw running away from Gus's body. They both stared at her, but they couldn't say anything or they'd give away they had been following her.

"The car is in the garage," she said, smiling at the two young men who stared at their shoes.

Keenan stepped out onto the porch. "Annie! Where did you go?" He hurried down the sidewalk to his wife.

She flinched at his shouting her name but put a smile on her face when he stopped in front of her. "I needed fresh air and look who I ran into. Do you remember Dela from Deborah's party?"

Keenan studied Dela. "Yes, I remember her. What are you doing in this area of town?"

Dela smiled. "I followed your friends who have been following me." She faced Annie. "Call my mom. She's worried about you." Dela walked away from them, a smile on her face. Keenan was involved in all the things that had been happening to her. She knew it by the actions of his wife and the way he'd studied her as if he were trying to figure out how she was so lucky.

In her car, she asked Heath, "Who were you talking to?"

"Quinn. He said the threatening call was made from a burner phone, but they pinged the towers and triangulated and the call came from the brewery." Heath nodded toward the police car pulling away from the curb. "Shall we go see what those two have to say?"

"That was my plan." She glanced at the Cristos. She didn't like the hold Keenan had on Annie's arm. "We need to figure out how to get Annie away from Keenan."

# Chapter Seventeen

At the police station, Detective Fletcher wouldn't let them sit in on the questioning. But he allowed them to watch the video after he'd finished. Neither one of the men said much. They kept their mouths shut except to say they wanted to call their lawyer.

"They were driving the car that has been following me around." Dela knew it was her word against the two men. Well, her and Marty's word. He took the photo that showed the car.

Heath messed with his phone and then showed it to Fletcher. "That is the man running from the car that tried to run down Dela last night. Look at how he's dressed. Just like the two you picked up at Cristo's house."

Fletcher nodded. "I agree they look the part, but without evidence it was one of them and without them talking, I can't hold them for anything."

"Not even the fact they both fit the description of

the person I saw running away from the crime scene?"
Dela asked.

"I wish I could lock them up because they fit the description but that isn't evidence." Fletcher raised his hands. "I can only keep them for so long and I'll have to let them go."

"Can't you tell each one of them that I picked him out as the killer?" Dela asked. "Maybe that will get them talking."

"Or say you're going to turn them over to the Feds or DEA," Heath added.

Fletcher cocked his head and studied Heath. "What do you know that you're not telling me?"

"Not my story to tell. Just a rumor." Heath glanced at Dela.

She understood what he was doing. He was playing on Fletcher's desire to rise in the ranks to get him to dig a little deeper into the two he had in custody.

"Let's go. I promised Special Agent Pierce we'd catch him up on what we know," Heath said, standing.

"Wait, what do you know? Why are you working with the FBI?" Fletcher asked.

"Talk to the men you have in custody. You'll get more out of them than you will me." Heath motioned for Dela to walk to the door.

Once they were sitting in her car, she shifted sideways and peered at Heath. "Did Quinn tell you more?"

"No, but he did want to meet us for lunch in fifteen minutes." Heath smiled. "I think I gave Fletcher enough to make him try harder to get information out of those two."

Dela grinned. "I think you might have."

At the restaurant, they found Quinn already seated with his partner Milo. They were both reading files when Dela and Heath walked up to the table.

"Ouch, that looks painful," Milo said, pointing at Heath's face.

"It doesn't bother me until someone points it out," he replied, holding a chair for Dela to sit.

She took the seat across from Milo with Quinn and Heath on either side of her.

"What did Fletcher find out about the two following you?" Quinn asked.

"Nothing. He barely questioned them and they lawyered up," Dela said, disappointment lacing her words.

"Heath sent us photos of the two. My contact in DEA recognized them. They are part of the drug cartel that the DEA believes Keenan is working with. And the Balto Herman character, he's definitely in the drug cartel. Has been for decades according to my contact." Quinn slid his file into a briefcase as the waitress came over to take their orders.

When she left, Milo added, "They've tried to find the connection between the breweries and the drug cartel through Cristo's finances but they haven't been able to find a connection."

Dela listened to what the Feds had to say. It made sense that Balto would oversee the construction of buildings that were being used for drug transactions. But why was he so secretive about the building?

"Did you learn anything about the vehicle or person who tried to run me down last night?" she asked.

"The VIN was registered to a Morgan Trice. We located him. He's staying at the Spotted Pony Casino over the weekend. He had no idea his car had been used in an attempt to run you down." Milo shrugged.

"The car belongs to a casino patron? How did they get the keys to the car? Why did they pick that one?" Her head was spinning with all kinds of questions. She knew who to contact for more information now that she knew where the car came from. "I'm going to make some calls."

She walked outside and called Marty first. "Hey, I just found out the car that nearly ran me over was stolen in the casino parking lot from a person staying with us this weekend. Morgan Trice. Find him and then go through the video footage from the time he arrived to when the crash happened to see how the person got hold of his car keys."

"I'll get Farley on it. We did get a sort of decent image of the guy running away from the car. "I'll send it to you. I was waiting until I thought you might be up."

"You didn't need to wait. We've been up since my mom banged on the door this morning. We even caught the two guys who were following us around the other day."

"You did? And what did you learn?"

"Nothing so far. But we put some pressure on Fletcher so hopefully he'll try a little harder. Also, would you see if Alfred was working last night and if he'll be in today?"

"Sure thing. I'll let you know as soon as I find out. Anything else?"

"Not that I can think of. We're having lunch with the Feds, that's where we're getting most of your leads. The City Police are dragging their feet for some reason."

"I'll get that sent over. How's Heath?"

"He doesn't look very good, but he says it doesn't hurt that bad."

"I'm glad he was there."

Dela sighed. "You and me both. I'll catch up to you when you get some info on the video."

"Copy."

Dela ended the call and returned to the restaurant. The men were all staring at their meals waiting for her to return.

They fell to eating and when they had sated their hunger, they all started talking again.

"Who did you call?" Heath asked.

"Marty. I wanted him to find Morgan Trice and watch video from the time he arrived to after the car attempted to run me down and see if anyone came in contact with him that might have nabbed his keys."

"Good idea," Milo said.

"I'm also going to talk to Alfred. He would know if someone was messing around in the parking lot. He'd be able to point out when any person of interest, like the two at the City Police Station, had come and gone during his shift."

"He'll know if anything was going on in the parking lot," Heath said.

"Who is Alfred?" Milo asked.

"The valet at the casino. He remembers everyone and sees everything." Dela picked up her iced tea. "What did I miss while I was gone?"

All three men exchanged glances and Heath said, "We were discussing how to find out about Cristo's involvement in the cartel."

Quinn put his fork down and studied her. "Heath said you've made friends with his wife."

Dela shook her head. "I am not going to use that poor deranged woman to get information on her husband. If he found out, who knows what he would do to her. For all we know, he's the reason she is the way she is. Mom thought he'd been abusing her when they were at the dinner party the other night."

"But it sounds like she trusts you," Quinn said, picking up his drink and sipping. He held her gaze as he drank.

He wasn't above using whomever he needed to get what he wanted. That was the flaw in him that Dela hated. It was that trait which had kept her from swooning at his feet in Iraq and falling for him when she met up with him again here.

"Yes, she trusts me and that's why I'm not going to do anything that will get her hurt. It will not happen by my actions. I will not use down-and-dirty ethics like you." Dela threw her napkin on her plate. "Are you ready to go?" She glared at Quinn and shifted her gaze to Heath. Her gut seized at the determination shining in his eyes. "Shit! You think I should get closer to the wife too?" Her heart felt as if someone had stabbed it with the knife that had killed Gus. "How could you stoop to his caustic level of using people?"

"Dela, listen. Quinn and Milo will keep an eye on Annie. They'll make sure she isn't harmed, but you are the only one who can get close to her. The night Gus was killed, you said she was talking about how she knew where the bodies were buried. What if, she is so traumatized by the things her husband has done that she goes into these fugue states to leave reality behind?"

Heath put a hand on her arm. "You would be helping her if we can put her husband in jail and get her the help she needs."

She shook off Heath's hand. "Did he tell you to say that?" She glared at Quinn. "It sounds like one of his slick speeches to get someone to help him ruin a life so he can get the person he's after."

"No, he didn't tell me to say this. It's what I was thinking when you were talking to Annie today. She trusts you. You are the one person who could get close enough to her to help her." Heath again put his hand on her arm. "I'm not trying to get Keenan for anything unless he is the one who sent people to kill you. Then, yes, I don't care who might get hurt if they are in my way to get him." He pulled her toward him and whispered in her ear, "You can't save everyone."

She leaned back and peered into his eyes. Something had happened. She expected in Pine Ridge when he went looking for his father. Someone he cared about had been hurt by him. His eyes held the loss and the regret. She'd ask him about it when they were alone.

"I'll help but I want to go on record to say, I think this is a bad idea."

# Chapter Eighteen

After lunch, Dela and Heath went to the casino to see how Marty and Farley were coming on the video footage and to speak with Alfred. She parked in front of the casino since she wasn't working, just checking on the events of the night before.

Heath had dozed off as they drove to the casino. She was angry that he'd talked her into befriending Annie, but she cared for him and knew he needed his rest, so she didn't bring up the question she had about what had caused him to sacrifice someone in Pine Ridge.

"Huh, What?" Heath woke up as she turned off the engine. "Hey, sorry about that. I couldn't keep my eyes open any longer. I'm surprised you didn't doze off too."

"I have a lot of short nights and long days. My body has become accustomed to less sleep." She nodded toward the casino. "Are you awake enough to tackle this?"

"Yeah. Can we talk to Alfred first in the coffee shop?" Heath grinned at her.

"I see, you want to jolt yourself awake with some caffeine."

"The stronger the better."

They exited the vehicle and entered the casino. Alfred sat to the right on his stool. He slid off and walked over to her. He wrapped his skinny arms around her. "I'm glad nothing happened to you last night." Then he faced Heath and held out his hand. As he pumped Heath's hand he said, "Thank you for saving our *wišaaníkt*."

"I'm happy I was there," Heath replied.

Dela studied the two of them. What did *wišaaníkt* mean? "Heath needs some coffee to stay awake. Can you take a break?" Dela asked.

"Yes." Alfred talked to the young man also doing valet service. "Jerome said no problem." Alfred led them to the coffee shop.

They sat at a booth with Dela in the middle. After the waitress had poured coffee all around and walked away, Dela asked, "What does *wišaaníkt* mean?"

Alfred smiled and said, "Treasure. You are Nixyáawii's treasure. You came back and you have been helping people."

Dela glanced at Heath. He was grinning and nodding his head. She shook hers. "I don't feel like a treasure. Right now, I feel stupid that I can't figure out who would have wanted to frame me for Gus's death." Rather than go into that with Alfred present, she asked him, "Did you see anyone messing around with cars in the parking lot last night?"

"I heard it was a stolen car that they tried to run

you over with." He shook his head. "I didn't see anyone milling around like they were casing the cars. It was a busy night. The casino was packed. I saw lots of regulars and many more new faces."

"Did you see anyone come in wearing a black hoodie, jeans, and athletic shoes?" Dela wished she had paid more attention to the person running away from the bridge. But at the time, she hadn't known he was a murder suspect until she landed on the body.

"Half a dozen. Mostly teenagers passing through with their families." Alfred sipped his coffee.

"What about alone and older? In their twenties?" She wasn't giving up on finding someone who might have seen one of their suspects in the City Jail.

Heath pulled out his phone and scrolled through the photos. "Either of these guys look familiar?"

Alfred studied them for several minutes. He pointed to one of them. "He looks familiar. I think he's come in here a few times."

"Alone?" Dela asked.

"Yeah. One night I watched him go into the Sports Bar. That was a night when we weren't very busy. Slow nights I get curious about where everyone is going and who they are meeting up with. From my post at the entrance, I can see a lot of the floor on a slow night." He grinned and took another sip of coffee.

"Do you remember what night that was?" Heath asked.

"It was before Gus was killed. One maybe two nights before." Alfred nodded. "Yes, no more than that."

Dela pulled out her phone to call Marty when it buzzed and showed his name. "Marty, I was just going to call you.”

“Good timing,” he said. “We think we’ve found the key thief. You aren’t going to believe who it is.”

Dela stared at Heath and asked, “Who is it?”

“Come to the surveillance room and see.” He ended the call.

“That was mysterious. Marty said he knows who swiped the car keys but wouldn’t tell me. He said I’d never guess.” She finished off her coffee. “Thank you for the information and the lovely comment about me.” She hugged Alfred and bumped Heath to move him out of the booth ahead of her.

When they were walking across the casino floor, Heath said, “You are a *wišaaníkt.*”

“Please don’t bring it up again. I don’t feel like one and it makes me uncomfortable.”

He strode alongside her. “Any time anyone gives you a compliment it makes you uncomfortable. Just hold it in your heart and know.”

Even after knowing Heath as long as she had, there were times when his words and wisdom surprised her. He was an old soul. That was one of the reasons she’d been drawn to him in high school. She was more mature than girls her age, and Heath wasn’t like all the other teenage boys. He had more respect for people and treated everyone as if they mattered.

She dug in her purse for her security badge and tapped it on the square on the wall. The surveillance door opened and they walked in.

Clapping started and resounded through the room. Dela glanced around and saw everyone was watching them walk across the room. “What’s this all about?”

Lionel stopped clapping and so did everyone else.

"It's for Heath for being brave and saving you. We've all watched the video and thought he should get some recognition."

"I couldn't agree with you more." She glanced at Heath and smiled inwardly. Now he was the one squirming under the high praise he was being given.

The door at the end of the room opened and Marty waved them over. "You are not going to believe this."

"So you keep saying." Dela walked to the door and into the back room Marty used as an office.

Farley sat in front of the three monitors on the wall. "Keep an eye on the dark-haired man in the blue shirt and gray slacks."

Dela sat in the chair Marty provided for her and watched the man enter the Sports Bar. He sat at a tall table in front of one of the televisions. He ordered a drink and then became engrossed in the basketball game on the screen. When the waitress returned with his drink, he emptied his pocket to get to a money clip. He paid and slipped the clip back into his pocket but left everything, including his car keys, sitting on the table.

He finished the drink and motioned for the barmaid to get him another one and it appeared he ordered food from the length of the one-sided conversation. The keys were still sitting on the table when a waiter arrived with food. After the waiter left and the man started eating his food, the keys weren't on the table.

Dela faced Marty. "Who is the person who delivered the food?"

He grinned, "Boone Bellamy. And he's got a couple of drug violations on his record."

"Is he working now?" Dela asked.

"He'll be in at three."

Dela glanced at her watch. Another hour. "Then we have time for you to try and find this guy." She motioned for Heath to show them the photo of the person Alfred said he saw a couple of days before Gus's death. She told Farley and Marty what Alfred had said about the man going into the Sports Bar.

"We could go talk to the bartender and see if he remembers this guy," Heath said.

"We could. Do you know if Dexter is on duty?" Dela asked.

"If he isn't, he should be coming on. It's Saturday and he likes working the busy nights," Marty said.

"Let's go." Dela led the way back through the surveillance room and out onto the gaming floor. She walked left along the conference rooms and past the Stallion Restaurant. They stepped into the Sports Bar to a roar from the crowd. Half the patrons were gathered around a screen at the back of the bar watching a horse race.

Dexter was at the bar. It appeared he was taking inventory of the stock.

Dela and Heath sat on stools near where he was counting bottles.

"Dexter, can we talk to you for a minute?" Dela asked.

Heath held out his phone when the bartender faced them.

"Sure. What do you need?"

"Do you remember seeing this guy in here at the first of the week?" Heath asked, showing the photo of the guy.

"I don't work Monday and Tuesday if that's the

days you mean." He studied the photo. "I might have seen him in here last night. He wasn't wearing that hoodie. He had on a nice shirt and slacks. He met a woman and they sat in a booth over there for an hour then left." Dexter pointed to the booth not far from the bar. "I noticed them because I thought they were an odd pair."

"How so?" Dela asked.

"He looks like he's in his twenties and she was mid-forties, I'd guess. They could have been mother and son."

Dela stared at Heath. "Do we have a photo of Annie?" It was a long shot Annie would have been the woman, given how the sports bar had upset her that morning. But the young man had been picked up at her house.

Heath typed and scrolled on his phone and came up with a photo of the Cristos at a fundraiser several years ago. "Was it this woman?" He showed the photo to Dexter.

"Yes, that was her."

Dela felt her jaw starting to drop and forced it shut. How had the woman made it to the casino without her husband and then carried on a lucid visit with the young man? "Thank you. You've been helpful."

She walked out of the sports bar in a daze. Was the woman that good of an actress? "We need to go to the police station and talk to the person she was with."

"Let's wait until after we've talked to Boone," Heath said. "No sense in bouncing back and forth between here and the police station."

Dela agreed. They walked over to the Pony to see if Boone had arrived for his shift. She asked to talk to the manager.

"Dela, I heard about last night. I'm happy to see you are okay." The manager's gaze drifted over Heath. "Are you the person who saved her?"

Heath nodded.

"Thank you. What can I do for you?" The manager asked.

"We'd like to talk with Boone Bellamy," Dela said.

"You'll have to try him at home. He called in sick."

Dela and Heath exchanged a glance as they walked out of the bar and grill.

"That's not a coincidence he didn't show up for work today," Dela said.

"No, it's not." Heath maneuvered them along the wall away from the growing crowd of people.

"I'll call HR and get his address," Dela pulled out her phone. After a brief conversation, she had the address. "Shall we tackle him now?"

"No. We're both tired. He'll be there tomorrow. Especially if he's getting high today off his pay for getting those keys."

Dela nodded. "Let's go to the coffee shop and rehash what we know. I'll call Marty and see what he found out."

"Sounds good. That first coffee is wearing off." Heath grinned.

They took a seat away from the other patrons in the coffee shop. After the waitress brought their coffee, Dela called Marty. "What did you find out?" she asked.

"The guy in the hoodie was in the casino on Tuesday. He met up with Boone and it looked like he slipped him drugs. Anyway, it was a small square envelope that went from palm to palm."

Dela nodded. "Probably the advance for lifting someone's keys." She thought about that. "Wait, that was before the murder. Do you think Boone killed Gus?" The more she thought about it, she didn't think so. He was smaller than the person she saw running away from the bridge. She shook her head. "He's not the right build."

"No, but you have him connected to the hoodie dude and the car that nearly ran you down," Marty said.

"Yes, and we have the hoodie dude connected to Annie Cristo. They met in the Sports Bar last night."

"Isn't that the lady whose husband pulled her out of here yesterday?" Marty asked.

"Yeah. And who was sane this morning when I talked to her."

Heath touched her arm and wiggled his phone.

"I have to go, Heath found something he wants me to look at." Dela ended the call and scooted closer to Heath. "What did you find?"

"I asked Quinn about the guy Dexter saw with Annie. His name is Wallace Tiller. He's her son from a previous marriage. Turns out he's been in and out of rehab for drug addiction the last five years."

Dela stared at the text on Heath's phone. "She didn't even blink an eye when the cops hauled her son away this morning."

"Maybe she's used to it." Heath pulled out his notepad and pen. "Let's make a list of what we know so far."

"But why would she let her son work for her husband if Wallace had a drug problem?" Dela mulled this over as she sipped her coffee.

"Here's what I have, what am I missing." Heath

turned the notepad toward her.

*Wallace gave Boone drugs on Tuesday.*

*Gus is killed Wednesday with Dela's knife.*

*Dela sees suspect run away.*

"You should put between these two that I saw a confused Annie at the river parkway." She pointed her finger between the last two sentences she'd read.

*Someone tries to enter Dela's house early Thursday morning. Unlicensed SUV.*

"Presumably to make sure I can't identify the killer."

*Thursday, discover Gus had a lover, Annie isn't crazy all the time, and the brewery could be a storehouse for drugs.*

*Friday noticed Annie fall apart at the casino. That night Dela is almost run over. Learned the keys were taken by Boone and given to ??*

"Don't forget that weird scene in the casino with Darren and Louisa."

"Do you think they figure into this?" Heath asked, adding them to the list.

"He is married to Gus's lover. We can't rule anyone out just yet." She continued to read his list. "I need to have Farley follow Boone after he takes the keys and see who he gives them to." Dela pulled out her phone and texted Farley. *Follow Boone after he takes the keys and see who he gives them to.*

*Already on it.* 😊

"Farley is already looking to see who Boone handed off the keys to." She continued reading.

*Stan Gould says there is a discrepancy in the blueprints and the size of the back rooms at the brewery.*

*Unlicensed SUV shows up at the brewery. We follow it to Cristo's house. Dela talks to Annie. Fletcher takes the two in hoodies in. Discover they work for a drug cartel. One is named Wallace Tiller and he is Annie's son.*

"If I were to go on the information we have now, I would say Gus figured out the extra space in the brewery and asked someone about it. I'm guessing it's for the storage of drugs or money. They could have just told him storage for brewing supplies, I wouldn't think Gus would think anything of that. He must have overheard something. But what?" Dela thought about what Stan had said. "Stan said Gus had only been to the site a few times. What if he went back at night and overheard or discovered something?"

Heath started shaking his head. "We're not going snooping around the brewery tonight. We're both tired from no sleep last night and the fatigue of your near death. It can wait until we've had a night's sleep and are thinking clearer."

Dela had to agree, her brain wasn't working as well as it should due to lack of sleep. "I agree, but we will go tomorrow night." Her phone buzzed. It was Farley.

"Hey, Farley, what did you find?"

"Nothing. I haven't seen him hand the keys off to anyone before the crash."

"Then he must have left them somewhere. Did he go into the restroom? Or deliver food to a room?" Dela asked.

"He did both. I'll rewatch the video and see who goes in and out of the restroom before and after him and who is in the room he delivers food to."

"Good thinking. Who he passes the keys off to is

most likely the person who was behind the wheel of the car." Dela ended the call and told Heath what Farley had found.

"You're right he must have passed them off by leaving them somewhere." He picked up his notebook and finished his coffee. "It's close to dinner. Let's grab something here and go home early. I'm starting to have trouble keeping my eyes open."

"Let's just go home and I'll pop a pizza in the oven. Then we can both relax."

"Sounds like a plan."

Dela's phone buzzed as they were walking out of the casino. It was Travis. "Hey, what's up?"

"Someone just opened the gate by the shed and is trying to get Jethro out. Mugshot is trying to bite the person."

"Keep watching, we're headed home."

# Chapter Nineteen

Dela jogged toward the car calling to Heath over her shoulder, "Come on. Someone is trying to hurt the boys." She slid into her car and started it as she closed the door. She put her foot down on the accelerator and didn't let up until she rounded the corner onto her road.

A blue compact car burst out of their driveway, heading in the opposite direction. Dela pressed on the accelerator, to get close enough to read the license plate, but as she passed her house, she saw Mugshot on the ground and Jethro sniffing him. She slammed on the brakes and backed up, revving to a stop in the driveway.

She exited the car and ran to her dog. He lay whimpering on the gravel. Tears burned her eyes as she tried to figure out what was wrong with him. "What did they do to you?" she asked, petting him and checking him for blood.

"Call Travis and ask him what they did to Mugshot," she said to Heath when he walked up and put Jethro's halter and lead rope on him.

She cradled Mugshot's big head in her lap, smoothing the hair between his eyes, and telling him he was a good boy. Listening to Heath's side of the conversation she wasn't sure if Mugshot's condition was fixable.

Heath ended the call and sat down beside them, holding onto Jethro's lead rope. "He said it looked like the person jabbed him with a syringe. We're to load him up and get him to Molly so she can figure out what was used."

"I don't understand. Why hurt my animals?" Dela used Jethro to help get on her feet while Heath opened the back door of the car. Together they picked up and carried the eighty-pound limp dog over to the car and put him in. "I don't like leaving Jethro here alone." She peered into Heath's eyes. "I don't suppose you'd stay here with him while I take Mugshot to the clinic."

"No, I won't. We can lock him in the shed until we get back. Does that make you feel better?"

"As long as they don't set it on fire or use bolt cutters to get him out."

A vehicle pulled in beside her car. It was Jacob.

He rolled down his window and smiled. "I came over to see how the two of you are doing after last night."

Relief flooded through Dela. "We need to get Mugshot to the clinic, someone stuck him with a syringe. But I didn't want to leave Jethro alone."

"I'll stay here until you get back." Jacob stepped out of his vehicle and grasped Jethro's lead, scratching the donkey around his ears.

"Here's the key to the house. Help yourself to any

food you want," Heath said, settling in the passenger side of Dela's car.

She hugged Jacob and whispered, "Thank you."

He squeezed her with one arm and said, "Any time."

She slid into her car and sped off toward the clinic. The thought someone would hurt defenseless animals to get to her, made her blood boil. "There better be a good photo of the person who did this to my dog and donkey."

Heath put a hand on her arm. "Travis said from what his mom could see on the video, she thinks it's just a tranquilizer, but it's best to get a blood sample and find out."

"I don't care if it is just a tranquilizer. I'm tired of this person harassing me. Us." She ground her teeth and felt a headache coming on.

At Mission Market she turned left, headed toward Riverside over the speed limit.

"You better slow down or someone may pull you over for speeding," Heath joked.

"They won't stop me until I get to the clinic," she said. The building came into view. She pulled off the road and stopped in front of the door to the clinic.

Travis and Molly met them as Dela opened the back door of the car. The mother and son carried Mugshot into the clinic and lay him down on a metal examining table. The young woman they'd glimpsed earlier in the day, walked in with a large empty syringe.

"Cammie, we need to draw enough blood to do a full screening," Molly said as she checked Mugshot over.

Cammie drew the blood and left the room. Travis

remained, helping his mom as Heath stood beside Dela with an arm around her shoulders.

She'd been ready to call it a day when they'd left the casino. She wanted food, a shower, and a bed. Now she would be worried about Mugshot and how the animals weren't safe at her home when she wasn't there.

She leaned her head against Heath and let the salty tears trickle down the sides of her face and pool in the corners of her mouth. Life had been good until she started looking into Dory Thunder. Was this the Creator's way of telling her to let go of the notion Dory was her father?

"You two look beat. Leave Mugshot with us, we'll keep an eye on him. You have had too much trouble lately to have to deal with watching him. You both need rest." Molly turned them toward the door. "Go home and know he's in good hands."

"But Jethro isn't safe," Dela blurted out.

"Keep him in the yard overnight. Travis will come get him in the morning. Your pets can hang out with us until you catch whoever has this vendetta against you." Molly nudged them out onto the porch. "Is Jethro alone now?"

"No. Jacob showed up to check on us as we were loading Mugshot. He said he'd stay until we got back," Heath said, lowering Dela into the passenger seat.

"Then you can go home and not have any more worries." Molly smiled and waved.

Heath slid into the driver's seat and started the car. "I didn't think you felt like driving."

"Thank you. I don't. I just want a shower and to go to bed." Dela wiped at her wet face. "Sorry, I'm blubbering. It just feels like I did something wrong to make all these bad things happen."

"You haven't done anything wrong. Someone is trying to drive you crazy or kill you, I'm not sure which." Heath reached over and took her hand. "We'll get to the bottom of this after we've had a good night's sleep."

Dela stepped onto the front porch and smelled something delicious. She opened the door and the aroma caused her stomach to grumble.

"What smells so good?" Heath asked, walking by her and into the kitchen.

She found Jacob stirring a pot of sauce. "You didn't have to make dinner, but I'm glad you did."

"Molly called and said you two were worn out, could I find something for you to eat? I just threw some of your cans of tomatoes and sauce together with herbs and spices. Mom taught me how to make spaghetti sauce when I was in high school." He picked up a plate heaped with spaghetti noodles and spooned on the sauce. Jacob handed the first plate to Dela and then made one for Heath and himself.

When they were all settled at the table eating, he asked, "Do you have any idea who would do all of this and why?"

Dela shook her head. "I don't understand. If it was the person who killed Gus, they would know by now that I didn't see them, or else the police would have arrested them. It doesn't make sense." She chewed on a bite of spaghetti and said, "It all started with my knife being taken from my car. Who knew I had a knife in my car and how did they get the key to take the knife out?"

Heath held the fork full of spaghetti halfway to his mouth. "Those are good questions, and where we should start tomorrow morning. Tonight, we need sleep."

"If it will help you rest easier, I can sleep on the couch," Jacob offered.

Dela wanted to tell him it wasn't necessary, but she knew once she and Heath went to sleep they would be dead to the world and not know if anyone was entering the house until their throats were being slit. "Do you mind? I know I'd sleep better knowing someone who wasn't as tired as the two of us would be on guard."

Heath studied her. "If Dela wants you to stay, I'm good with it."

"Molly said to keep Jethro locked up in the yard for the night and Travis will come over tomorrow morning to get him. They are going to keep Mugshot and Jethro until we catch who is doing all of this." Dela sipped her iced tea and held back the tears she felt building in her eyes.

"Don't worry. I'll make sure Jethro and the two of you are safe."

When they finished eating, Jacob shooed them off to shower and go to bed. It was only seven but Dela felt as if it were midnight. They showered and fell into bed, sleeping as if they hadn't slept for days.

Dela woke to the sound of two people talking. She glanced at her watch and sat up. It was after nine. Heath wasn't in bed. She dressed, prosthesis and all, and walked down the hall. She'd expected to see Jacob, instead it was Travis.

"Good morning, sleepyhead," Heath said, kissing

her and handing her a cup of coffee.

Travis grinned.

"What's so funny?" she asked, glaring at the young man, whom she'd known his whole life.

"Just you letting someone call you sleepyhead. If I'd said that you'd have bit my head off or slugged me."

She glanced at Heath who was hiding a smile behind his raised cup of coffee. "That's because I know Heath says it with love and you say it to get me riled." She asked Heath, "Were you up when Jacob left?"

"Yeah, he had to go to work. Jethro misses Mugshot but other than that he's fine." Heath plucked the toast, that popped up in the toaster, out and buttered it. He placed the slices on a plate and set it in front of her.

Travis motioned to Heath's phone on the table. "Have you had a chance to look at the video from the cameras last night?"

"I looked at it but wanted Dela to have a look before I said anything." Heath picked up his phone and began scrolling and clicking. He held it out in front of Dela. "Can you tell who that is?"

She put down the piece of toast she'd been nibbling on and grasped the phone. She studied the person as they tried to get the donkey out of the gate, and then pulled the syringe out of their pocket and jabbed it into Mugshot. Her hand clenched the phone as she watched Mugshot go down.

Hands massaged her tense shoulders. "Don't look at the animals. Look at the person," he said close to her ear in a soft soothing voice.

She started the video over and forced her gaze to stay on the person. They were wearing a dark hoodie which hid their face. Especially when they were looking down at the animals. "The person is taller than me. He or she tips their head more to look at the animals than I do. The build is similar to the person I saw running from the bridge where Gus was killed." She continued watching until the person ran to get away. "Yes, they run just like the person I saw that night." She peered into Heath's eyes. "This is the person who killed Gus."

# Chapter Twenty

"We know that whoever is trying to hurt you is the person who killed Gus," Heath said as Dela watched the video again.

"I don't understand why they keep coming after me. They should know by now that I can't identify them." Dela handed the phone back to Heath.

"Two times they tried to get into the house," Heath said. "Maybe they are just trying to plant evidence that would make you the suspect in Gus's killing again."

"But why run me over?" Dela asked.

"To incapacitate you and drop the evidence with your injured or dead body. That would close the case on Gus's murder." Heath shrugged. "We won't know why this person is doing what he's doing until we catch him."

"I'll catch Jethro and leave you two to your crime solving. I have to purchase lumber for Mom's house so we can get started on it." Travis opened the French doors and was met by Jethro.

Dela followed. She hugged Jethro and told him he'd come home soon before Travis loaded him into the small horse trailer.

She walked back into the house. Heath had his laptop open on the table. "What are you looking up?"

"Not looking up. I'm making a timeline to connect what we know and try to figure out who is involved and maybe also get some hint as to why you are being harassed."

"I'm trying to figure out who knew about my knife in my car. It had to have been someone close to me." Dela made a list of names and one by one ticked them off, knowing they wouldn't have told someone about it. Her eyes kept going back to Rosie's name. She knew her friend wouldn't have told anyone, but… something in the back of her mind said Rosie knew who it could have been.

Dela picked up her phone and dialed Rosie.

"You've called Rosie, leave a message at the beep and I'll get back to you as soon as I can." The phone beeped.

"Rosie, it's Dela. Give me a call, I have a question for you." She ended the call and sighed. "Shouldn't we go talk to Boone?"

Heath glanced up from the laptop. "Why did you call Rosie and have you heard anything from Farley?"

"I think Rosie is the clue to who knew about my knife."

Heath closed the lid on his computer. "Rosie? You think she mentioned it while talking to someone?"

"No, for some reason I have a memory of being with Rosie and I showed it or said something about it to someone." Dela kept getting small flashes of a memory. She shook her head. "Anyway, I'll call Farley and see what he came up with."

She dialed Marty's assistant.

"Yo, Dela!" he answered. "I followed all the men who went into the restroom before Boone went in and came out either while he was in there or after he left. None of them left the building before that car tried to run you down. So, I looked into who reserved the room where he delivered the food. The name was Jane Smith."

Dela groaned. "Did you get a visual of her?"

"Yeah, but you aren't going to like it."

"Because it's someone I know?" she asked, dreading who it might be.

"No. She checked in wearing a pink hoodie with the hood pulled up and large sunglasses. Like an actress would wear to keep people from recognizing her. She also wore them when she left the room fifteen minutes after Boone delivered the food. Get this. She never came back to the room."

"Send me some footage of her, please. And thanks for putting so much time into this for me."

"Hey, no problem. It's more fun than what Marty gives me to do."

She laughed and ended the call.

"What did he say?" Heath asked.

"He's sending over footage of the woman who reserved the room." Her phone buzzed and she pulled up the video, showing Heath.

"That doesn't help us much. Her hair and face are covered so much you can't see any features."

Dela ran it again. When the woman stood at the

registration counter the counter hit her mid-chest. "She's short. Which means it isn't Annie." That lightened Dela's heart. She didn't want to think the mentally tortured woman had anything to do with trying to harm her.

"I'll look and see if the female cartel members wear pink hoodies." Heath opened up his laptop and started typing.

"When you finish, we need to talk to Boone." Dela rose to get another cup of coffee when there was a knock on the door. She pivoted to walk into the living room.

"Wait. I'll see who it is first." Heath messed with his phone and smiled. "It's Rosie."

Dela crossed the room and opened the door for her friend. "You didn't have to come over."

"I was on my way here when I got your text. I wanted to check and see how you two were doing after the other night. I can't believe someone would intentionally want to harm you." Rosie pulled her into a hug.

Dela wrapped her arms around the barrel-shaped, cushiony body, hunching a bit to rest her chin on the shorter woman's shoulder. Rosie had always been a good friend, even in school when other Umatilla kids weren't as accepting of the girl whose mom was a teacher and non-tribal member. Rosie's mom was a teacher too. She understood the other student's distrust of teacher's kids.

They parted and Dela asked, "Want a cup of coffee or tea?"

"Tea would be great," Rosie said, following her into the kitchen. "Oh! Heath your face is blue."

"I'm hoping to get a part in the next Avatar movie." He winked.

Dela made a cup of hot water for Rosie and placed a dish with various teas in front of her. "We're doing fine, considering. I have a question for you. We've been trying to figure out how someone knew about the knife in my car. In the back of my mind, I remember talking to someone about it when you were with me. Can you remember who it was?"

Rosie nodded and her expression sobered. "It was Daisy. When you helped us move her. She saw the knife and asked you about it because it was unique." Rosie glanced at Heath. "The antler with the carved initials and who gave it to you makes it hard to forget."

"I know Daisy wouldn't tell anyone about it to cause trouble but who would you think she'd tell?" Dela had to find out who knew about the knife.

"I'll ask her." Rosie pulled out her phone, scrolled through the contacts, and tapped on the screen. "Hey, Daisy, I have a question for you. Remember when Dela helped with your move?" She listened. "Yes, and we talked about the antler handle knife in her car." Rosie nodded. "Did you tell anyone about the knife and that she kept it in her car?" She nodded her head and said, "uh-huh," several times. "Thanks. No, it's okay. Dela knows you wouldn't go around telling everyone about it." Rosie rolled her eyes and said, "I'll see you at Mom's later tonight. Bye."

Dela waited wondering who Daisy talked to. "Did she talk to someone?"

"Yes, a woman at work. Millie Frank." Rosie studied Dela. "Does that help?"

"Not really. I've never heard of her." Dela tapped

a finger on the table, thinking. How would someone she'd never heard of have something to do with Gus's death and implicating her?

"Where do they work?" Dela asked. Maybe someone overheard the conversation.

"Stage Technology." Rosie sipped her tea. "There are about twenty people who work there. Do you think someone could have overheard their conversation?"

"That's what I'm thinking." Dela smiled at Heath. "Think you can look up Stage Technology and see if they have a list of their employees on their website?"

"I'll see what I can find."

"Where's Mugshot?" Rosie asked.

Dela told her about the evening before and that Molly was keeping her animals until they figured out who was out to get her.

Rosie's eyes sparked with anger when Dela finished. "That's just low-down mean to go after someone's animals."

"I agree. I wish we could get this figured out. It's tiring to always wonder if a stranger is out to get you." Dela felt the tension bunching her shoulders and sending pain to a leg that wasn't there. She had an idea. "Do you know anything about Boone Bellamy? He works in the bar and grill as a waiter."

Rosie giggled. "He's not a waiter, he's a busboy. And I know he does drugs. How he passes the drug tests is beyond me. I started a conversation with him one day at the deli and he couldn't keep his mind on what we were talking about. I think he might have been high then."

Dela glanced over at Heath. "That's good to know. He might spill more information than we think."

"Is he messed up in this person trying to get you?" Rosie's eyes narrowed.

"We believe he stole the keys to the car that was used to try and run me down." Dela hoped Boone was the weak link they needed to start piecing things together.

"If I see him, I'll give him a good kick!" Rosie said.

Dela laughed and said, "We plan to go see him when Heath gets off the computer. Have you had any luck with the employees at Stage Technology?"

Heath glanced up. "I've scrolled through the whole website and wrote down the names I saw." He spun the notepad around for her to take a look.

She shook her head. "None of those look familiar. We're going to have to ask Detective Fletcher to get us a list of the employees."

"Why do that? Daisy works HR for the company. I'll text her and ask her to send you the list. It's the least she can do if her conversation gave someone information they used against you." Rosie picked up her phone and began texting.

"Can she do that?" Dela asked.

"They don't do anything top secret at that place. They're a think tank that tries to come up with better ways to conserve and make electrical power." Rosie shoved her phone back into her dress pocket. "I'll get out of here so you two can go talk with Boone. But I swear when I see him, I'm going to kick him. Just because I think he needs it." She stood and walked to the front door.

Dela followed her friend. "Thank you for coming over to check on us."

"Everyone at the casino is worried about you. When you show up there, you'll probably feel all their eyes on you. Everyone is watching out. We're a family and no one messes with a family member." Rosie hugged Dela and walked out the door.

"She's a good one," Heath said from the kitchen doorway.

"That she is. From the minute I met her in grade school we've been friends. That she works at the casino is a bonus." She glanced at the notepad in his hand. "Are you ready to go talk to Boone?"

"Even more so after hearing Rosie's description of him."

Dela nodded and grabbed her purse. "I agree."

# Chapter Twenty-one

Heath drove the rental car to Boone's apartment building. Dela wondered if it was a coincidence that he lived in the apartments owned by Delbert Malik.

"Do you think he'll try to run?" she asked as they entered the building.

"I doubt it. He won't know who we are." Heath punched the button on the elevator and they listened to it clank and creak as it lowered to the first floor. For a new build, the elevator didn't sound safe.

"He might recognize me from the casino." Dela was hesitant to step into the elevator.

Heath drew her in and pushed the button with a 2 on it. The building was four levels tall.

The metal box creaked and clanked up to the second floor. Dela was the first one out. What she liked best about the Spotted Pony Casino it had only one floor and she rarely had to go up the elevators to the guest rooms. But those elevators were like floating through air with piped-in flute music to soothe.

She walked down the hall to number 203 and knocked on the door.

"Who's there?" called a drowsy male voice.

"We're giving residents of this building a chance to get a free month's rent," Heath said. He winked at Dela.

She grinned. That should get Boone to the door.

Sure enough, the lock on the other side clicked and the door swung open.

Dela recognized Boone from the video she'd watched of him stealing the car keys.

"What do I have to do for a chance?" he asked, standing in the doorway in plaid boxers and no shirt.

"Answer a few questions," Heath said, stepping in front of the man and forcing him to walk backward into the apartment.

Dela followed, closing the door behind her.

"Hey! Are you really giving away free rent?" Boone asked as he sat on the arm of a stained couch that he probably picked up off a sidewalk with a FREE sign on it.

"No, we want to know who asked you to steal car keys." Heath placed the two kitchen table chairs in front of Boone. He sat in one and Dela in the other.

Boone glanced back and forth until his gaze landed on Dela. "Hey, you're the tough lady who runs the casino security."

She smiled. "That's right. We saw you on a video take car keys off a table in the Sports Bar and take them up to a room on the second floor. Who asked you to take the keys and who did you give them to?"

Boone stared at her. "Why would I take car keys? I have my own car." He grinned with one lip up in a sneer.

Heath scooted closer to him. "Stop trying to act smart. We know you aren't. We also know you bought drugs while on the casino premises. I can take you in for that and we'll find out the rest later." He pulled out his tribal badge.

"Hey, I didn't buy any drugs. Wally gave them to me." Boone wiped his hand under his nose.

"What did Wally want you to do for the drugs?" Dela asked.

"Nothing. He's my friend and when he's flush, he gives me some." Boone stared at her as if she were dumb.

"Did he ask you to steal car keys?" Heath asked.

"No, why would he do that? He has a nice ride. His boss gave it to him."

"Then who asked you to steal car keys?" Dela asked.

Boone tipped his head back and forth from shoulder to shoulder.

"Did you know the car that those keys belonged to was used to try and run someone down?" Heath said. When the words seemed to sink in, he added, "That means you are an accessory to attempted murder unless you tell us who asked you to get those keys."

Boone's eyes widened and his mouth opened slightly.

"Who asked you to get those keys?" Dela asked.

"She said it was a prank. That a man in the bar and grill would order food and when I delivered the food to the table to pick up his keys and bring them up to her when room two-eleven ordered room service." He raised his hands. "I swear I thought it was a prank. Like she was trying to keep her husband from leaving without her or something."

"What did she look like?" Heath asked.

"She had on a pink hoodie, big sunglasses with little diamonds. I thought I saw blonde hair. She wasn't very tall."

"How did she talk?" Dela asked.

"Like a woman." Boone gave her that 'you're dumb' look again.

"Was her voice high pitched, low, raspy, sweet?" she recited.

"Soft."

Dela shrugged when Heath glanced at her. "Thank you for trying to help us," Dela said.

"What about the free rent?" Boone asked.

Heath chuckled and said, "There isn't any free rent. I said that to get you to open the door."

"That's low," Boone said, sitting on the arm of the couch as Dela and Heath let themselves out.

As they dropped to the first floor in the elevator, Dela wondered out loud, "Do you think Morgan Trice was in on it? I mean what are the odds that someone would order dinner and leave their keys sitting on the table when the waiter came by and not look for them when he was ready to leave the bar?"

"I was wondering the same thing. We didn't talk to the man himself. We took Milo's word for what Trice said." Heath opened the passenger door for Dela and went around to the driver's side. He started the car and asked, "Casino?"

"I think so. Hopefully, Morgan Trice hasn't left yet."

At the casino, Dela went straight to the registration desk.

"Dela, good to see you. You haven't been to work since that lunatic tried to run you over," Abby Shanee said when Dela walked up to the desk.

"Yeah, I've been working on finding out who has it out for me." She and Abby were friends in school. Not as close as Molly and Rosie, but still a good friend. "Can you see if Morgan Trice is still here, please?"

"Sure. It'll just take a few seconds." She tapped on the computer and said, "He's still here. He's in room number two-thirteen."

Dela threw a look over her shoulder at Heath. That was right next door to the woman who received the keys. That didn't make any sense at all. If they were in it together, why not just hand the keys to her? This was getting weirder and weirder.

"Thanks." Before they went up to the room, Dela called Farley.

"Yo, Dela. I saw you came in the casino with your bodyguard." He chuckled.

"Funny as usual. Hey, can you show the photo of the man whose keys were stolen to the crew in surveillance and see if any of them see him on the floor right now? If they do, text me where he's at."

"Sure, I can do that." The call ended.

Dela led Heath over to the deli. They bought iced teas and sat down at a table where they could watch people going by. Her phone buzzed. She glanced at the text.

*He's at Carousel 29.*
*Thanks.*

Dela picked up her drink and stood. "I know where

he's at." She sipped her drink as she made her way to the carousel of the largest progressive payout slot machines. In the middle, playing two machines at a time sat Morgan Trice.

Dela took a seat at the machine he was playing next to him. Heath sat in the chair on the other side.

"Hey, that's my machine," he said, in a confrontational tone.

"I don't want to play it. I want to talk to you." Dela held up her security card and then Heath tapped him on the shoulder and showed him his Tribal Police badge.

"What's this about?" He stopped pushing buttons on the machines and looked back and forth from Dela to Heath.

"Your car almost ran me over on Friday night. If Heath hadn't been there to ram his car into it, I wouldn't be sitting here talking to you."

The man threw his hands in the air. "Hey, I had nothing to do with that. My car keys were stolen sometime during the night."

"Were they really?" Dela asked. "We happen to know that the person who had them stolen was in the room next to yours. Coincidence? I don't think so. I don't like looking over my shoulder all the time and since Friday night that's what I've been doing." She rose, getting in his space to intimidate him.

"I swear, I didn't know they were gone until the police called me. I had a lot to drink and was gambling and didn't really pay attention to whether or not I had my keys." The man was blabbering.

"What about the woman next door to you? Did you talk to her?" Heath asked.

"She was on the elevator with me when I arrived.

We walked down the hallway together and she said, "Looks like we're neighbors." His face flushed.

"What else did she say?" Heath asked.

"She mentioned that if I was sitting in the Bar and Grill when she came down, she'd have a drink with me." He squirmed in his seat. "She was petite, pretty. I thought she was coming onto me, so I said sure. I'd be there. But she never showed."

"You said she was pretty. What did she look like?" Dela asked.

"Small, fit. I think blonde hair, I couldn't really tell with that pink hoodie and the big rhinestone glasses."

"Then how do you know she was pretty?" Dela asked.

"She was petite and had a soft voice."

Dela wanted to knee him in the balls. Just because the woman was petite and soft-voiced this lug head thought she was pretty. If a full-figured woman with a voice like hers was wearing a hoodie and large glasses he would have said she was ugly or average-looking.

"How could she have known you would leave your keys on the table when you paid for your drink?" Heath asked.

The man stared at the machine in front of him. He snapped his fingers and said, "She was next to me when we checked in and I left my keys sitting on the counter after I took something out of my pocket. She told me they were sitting there as I walked away."

Dela wondered if the woman was a con artist since she knew how to pick a patsy. But how did she fit into the murder and possibly the drug angle at the brewery?

"Thank you for your time," Heath said.

They both stood and walked toward the gaming

area that was quieter this time of day on a Sunday. When they were standing in a corner of the conference area where it was quiet, Heath asked, "What do you think?"

Dela shook her head. "We are just going around in circles. One dead end after another. And no closer to knowing how or why Gus was killed and why someone wants me dead."

"Let's go for a drive." Heath grasped her hand and led her to the casino entrance.

"Where are we going?"

"To talk to my mom. Since we are against a wall with Gus's murder and who is after you, let's focus on Dory. Or in this case, since no one wants to talk about Dory, let's ask my mom about Leo."

Dela stopped and stared at him. "Do you think she'll talk about him?"

"I don't see why not if he died in the war, he would have been a hero." Heath led her out to the car and they set off for his mom's house out on Cayuse Road.

# Chapter Twenty-two

Mrs. Seaver was happy to see them. Dela had known the woman her whole life, but Heath had spent more time at her house than they did at the Seaver home. She felt awkward around the woman who worked to bring the lost Umatilla language and culture into the schools.

"It's a wonderful surprise to have you two show up today. And you're in luck, I was frying a chicken. There will be plenty of food for us to share a Sunday dinner." Mrs. Seaver motioned for Dela and Heath to take a seat on the couch. She sat in an old willow rocker with a pillow on the seat and one on the back.

"We don't want to be a burden, Mrs. Seaver," Dela said, glancing at Heath.

"We'd love to stay and have dinner with you, Mom," Heath said, placing an arm around Dela's shoulder. His action made his mother smile brighter.

"Good." Her smile faded and she leaned forward in

the chair. "Why is your face a funny color?"

Heath grimaced and said, "I was in a car accident Friday night. Nothing bad, but the airbag deployed and did all of this bruising."

"Did you run into a deer? They have been out and about a lot in the evenings." Mrs. Seaver said.

"No, it was another car. No animals were hurt." Heath drew in a breath and asked, "Mom, what can you tell us about Leo Thunder? We ran across his name the other day and wondered how he's related."

Mrs. Seaver rose from her chair and walked over to a chest that sat by the door with a blanket on it. A sturdy pair of boots and a pair of walking shoes sat in front of the chest. She raised the lid and pulled two books out before lowering the lid and straightening the blanket.

She walked over to the couch and motioned for them to make room for her between them. Mrs. Seaver sat in the space they created and opened the first book. It was a photo album. "This is an album of Silas's brother Paul's family." She opened the book and it started with photos of Paul and his wife, Sara. Then it added photos of three children. She turned the page and there was a group photo.

"This is Paul, Leo, Sheila, Ross, and Sara." Mrs. Seaver pointed out the family members.

Dela's gaze landed on a younger version of Grandfather Thunder. She put her finger on the photo right below his head. "That's Grandfather Thunder. What did his wife look like?" Dela asked, not hiding her excitement. Not only would she see a young photo of Grandfather Thunder's wife, she might be able to pick out Dory.

"That's Martha, there." Mrs. Seaver pointed out a

tall, pretty woman standing above Silas, her hands on his shoulders.

Dela scanned the children around them and stopped on a boy who looked like Leo. "Is this a mistake? That boy looks like Leo."

Mrs. Seaver started to flip the page.

"Mom, why do those two look alike?" Heath asked.

"Silas and Paul married sisters, Sara and Martha. Paul and Sara had Leo a year before Martha gave birth to Theodore. When they were babies there was a slight resemblance but as they grew older, they could have been twins."

"What happened to them?" Dela asked.

"They both went to war. Vietnam. Leo didn't come home, and Theodore came home with evil in him. That's all you need to know." She turned the page and talked about the parents of the family more than the children who would have been her age.

When she closed the book, Dela asked, "Did you like Leo?"

Mrs. Seaver glanced at her son and then down at the closed book. "He could be mean."

"What about Theodore?" Heath asked.

His mom studied Heath. "He was always kind. He stopped Leo when he'd get too rough. But sometimes he was punished for things that Leo did. Someone would point Theodore out when Leo had been the one tormenting them."

"What happened to Theodore when he returned?" Dela asked. "Grandfather Thunder never mentioned him."

Mrs. Seaver put a hand on Dela's arm. "He did

something awful and no one speaks of him. It's best you don't ask questions."

Her answers only frustrated Dela more.

"Here is a yearbook from our senior year." Mrs. Seaver laughed at photos of herself and glossed over ones of Dory and Leo. "Well, I'll go finish getting dinner ready." She rose with the books in her hands.

"I'll put those away for you, Mom." Heath stood, taking the books from her.

"Thank you." She smiled and walked into the kitchen.

"Take photos of the pictures you want," he whispered, handing the books to Dela.

She thumbed through the pages quickly, getting photos of Dory and Leo. "Thank you," she whispered as she handed the books to Heath and he replaced them in the chest.

"We now know that Leo and Dory looked alike. But what does that mean if Leo died in the war?" Dela rose from the couch. "Let's see if your mom needs help."

♠ ♣ ♥ ♦

Driving home, Quinn called Dela. "Have you had a chance to get friendlier with Mrs. Cristo?"

"No, I've been busy stopping people from hurting my pets and getting into my house as well as following leads on how the person who tried to run me over got hold of the knife." She was glad that Heath was driving. Otherwise, she'd have wanted to get out and kick the tires to work out the anger she felt toward the Special Agent.

"What do you mean hurting your pets?" Quinn asked.

She told him about Mugshot and the blue compact car that she didn't get a license for.

"There are lots of compact cars."

"This one belongs to the person I saw running away from Gus's body."

"Unless he stole it. If he's the same person who is trying to cause you harm, he could have just nabbed another vehicle to keep his identity unknown."

Dela huffed out a breath. That was something she hadn't thought of. "What I don't get is why are they after me? I didn't see anything. Heath thinks they are still trying to get me arrested for the murder."

"I think you need to look at your history with Gus. Could be this person wanted him dead and you to pay for the murder since they stole your knife to do the deed."

That made sense. Someone was getting back at her for something that happened in her past with Gus. She'd have to rehash that past with Heath and see what they could come up with. "Thanks, I'll get on that." She ended the call and as she shifted in her seat to talk it over with Heath, her phone buzzed.

A text message from Quinn. *Get close to Annie Cristo, please.*

She snorted.

"What's that about?" Heath asked as they pulled into the clinic to check on Mugshot.

"Quinn actually used the word please when he told me to get close to Annie." Dela shoved her phone in her pocket and opened the door. "He suggested Gus's murder and me being implicated and someone still trying to implicate me, could be because of something from my past with Gus."

Heath knocked on the living quarters at the clinic and faced her. "That's as good a theory as we've come up with. Can you think—"

The door opened, halting their conversation. Cammie smiled at them. "Come in. You'll be happy to know Mugshot is fine. It was a tranquilizer. Molly figures it was someone who didn't know how much a dog his size should have. He was sitting up and wanting attention an hour after you left him here."

She led them into the kitchen.

Molly, Marty, and Travis were all leaning over the kitchen table looking at blueprints.

"We won't bother you. I just want to see my boys," Dela said.

"They're in the exercise area. It's the only fenced-off area we had to put Jethro. He's been making friends with all the dogs we are boarding," Molly said, looking up from the blueprints. "Cammie, will you show them how to get there?"

Cammie led them into the clinic and out a side door. Sure enough, Jethro was playing tug of war with a Great Dane. They each had an end to a four-foot rope in their mouths.

Jethro saw them and dropped the rope, before trotting over. He bumped his head into Dela and she rubbed his ears.

Mugshot having seen Jethro trotting, lifted his head from where he was sniffing and ran/hopped over to them.

"Hi, guys. It's good to see you. And you…" she held Mugshot's head in her hands, "it's good to see you up and around. You had me worried." Dela swiped at a happy tear as she rubbed the donkey and dog's heads.

Cammie had disappeared. It was just Dela, Heath, her animals, and three other dogs in the small grass and dirt area.

"Can we sit with them a bit?" Dela asked.

"We can do anything you want. I don't have work for a week and you don't have to go back to work until Wednesday." Heath found a couple of outdoor chairs and set them near the house out of the wind that had grown chilly as the sun started setting.

Dela and Heath sat down and petted the animals until they both wandered off.

"What do you think about Quinn's idea Gus's murder has to do with something from your past with him?" Heath asked, clasping her hand.

"It could be. Or it could be his way of keeping me out of digging into the brewery." Dela wouldn't put it past the Special Agent to not want her involved in something he had taken an interest in.

"But then why is he asking you to be friends with Annie if he wants you to stay out of the brewery business?" Heath glanced up from their clasped hands.

Dela shrugged. "He probably thinks the harder he pushes for me to get chummy with her the less I'll want to do it." She touched her temple. "You know, that old FBI psychology."

Heath laughed. "What are you going to do?"

"I think I'll see if Annie wants to go on a picnic tomorrow." Dela had wondered if taking Annie for a walk on the River Parkway would make her remember seeing Dela that night and possibly the person who killed Gus.

"You can't go alone." Heath straightened and clasped her hand with both of his.

"I won't. You'll be following us. You can wear a hat and sunglasses and dress differently than you did at Mom's dinner party. I doubt she will recognize you. Though she did call you a hunk…"

Dela laughed at the face Heath made.

"She's not my type," he said.

"What's your type?" she teased.

"You." He leaned over and kissed her.

A door opened to the right of them.

"Hey, you two want to come in and tell us what you've found out?" Marty asked.

Dela chuckled and Heath drew her to her feet.

"Sure. Maybe you can help us figure it all out," Heath said, leading Dela into the house.

Molly had beer set out with crackers and cheese. "I thought you might like a snack."

"We had dinner at Heath's mom's," Dela said, sitting in an over-stuffed chair.

Heath grabbed a beer, handing it to Dela, and sat on the arm of her chair with a glass of water. "We were lucky she was frying a chicken."

Marty studied the two of them and asked, "Is that code for something?"

Dela, Heath, and Molly laughed.

Molly explained. "When you go to visit a relative; mother, auntie, grandmother, if they say you are lucky they made a large amount of something, it's their way of guilting you for not coming over more often."

"Oh! Is that why we haven't been back since your mom mentioned the roast?" Marty asked.

Molly glared at him and he laughed.

"Have you found out who tried to run you over?" Molly asked.

"No. We learned a petite woman in a pink hoodie and large sunglasses found a man who tends to leave his keys lying around. She intimated to him if he was in the bar and grill, she'd join him. Then she asked Boone to get keys from someone he delivered dinner to and when her room number ordered food, he was to bring them up to her." As Dela recited what they'd learned she realized there were too many unknowns.

"That leaves things too wide open," Marty said.

"That's what I think too. How could she be so certain he'd leave his keys for someone to pick up and how could she know that Boone would pick up those keys and not someone else's, not to mention Boone could have not picked up any keys and when she ordered anyone could have taken her the meal and not known anything about the keys." Dela sat up straight. "They are either all in it together or she was lucky."

"You didn't get a good photo of her?" Molly asked.

"She was wearing a pink hoodie and large sunglasses," Heath said.

"Did she walk in with them on?" Marty asked.

"She was wearing them at the registration desk when Trice met her." Dela said.

"We only have his word for that," Heath added.

Marty pulled out his phone, tapped it twice, and said, "Farley, when did you start following the lady in the pink hoodie." He listened. "Well start from when she entered the room and follow her backward to see if she entered the casino with the hoodie and glasses on." Marty ended the call.

"Isn't it late in the day to be asking him to do something so time-consuming?" Dela asked.

"He's a night owl," Marty answered.

"What about Gus's murder? Have you learned anything new there?" Molly asked.

"We discovered that Rosie's sister Daisy told a friend at work about my knife. So anyone who works there could have overheard the conversation," Dela said, reaching for her phone. "Which reminds me, Daisy was supposed to send me a list of the people who work there." She scrolled through her phone and found the email with the list.

Everyone was silent as she read through the list. Two names caught her attention. She studied Heath. "Darren Landis and Louisa Tuttle."

# Chapter Twenty-three

"Why would they frame you? You didn't even know them before this whole thing started," Heath said.

"We need to find out where they were when Gus died, when someone tried to get into my house twice, and when someone tried to run me over." Dela scrolled through her phone and texted Detective Fletcher.

*I want background checks on Darren Landis and Louisa Tuttle and their whereabouts the night Gus was killed and Friday night when someone tried to run me over.*

"It's Sunday night. I'm sure I won't hear from him until tomorrow afternoon at the earliest." Dela placed her empty beer bottle on the table and stood. "I'm ready to go home."

Heath placed his glass beside the bottle and rose. "Thank you for taking care of Mugshot and Jethro. As soon as we get this solved, we'll come get them."

"No problem. Family helps family." Molly hugged

Dela and then Heath. "Take care going home."

On the drive home, Dela didn't say much. She was too busy trying to put what she knew together to make sense.

Heath broke into her thoughts. "How are you going to ask Annie to go on a picnic?"

"I'm just going to show up at her house and ask her." Dela thought that was better than calling ahead and having Keenan say Annie wasn't up to it.

"You're not driving up to that house alone." Heath glanced at her, then back at the road.

"You can follow me in my car, I'll take the rental."

"How about I pick up Marty on the way? She doesn't know him. That way if it looks like we need to get close, he can do that." Heath drove past the casino.

Dela stared at the casino with its flashing lights and wondered when her life would get back to normal.

Monday morning, Dela packed the few items she had in the house for a picnic and then drove to Mission Market to get the rest of the items she needed. When she pulled into the market, Heath drove on by to pick up Marty. They'd called him when they arrived home the night before and asked if he'd be willing to help.

Now with her picnic basket filled with all kinds of finger foods, Dela headed to the house the Cristos were renting. She parked her rental car in front of the house and scanned the streets. Heath and Marty were parked in her car two blocks down on a side street and pointed in her direction.

Dela exited the car and was about to walk up to the house when she spotted Annie walking up the sidewalk from the opposite direction.

"Annie, I was just coming to ask if you would like to go on a picnic with me," Dela said as she walked up to the woman.

She stared at Dela for a couple of blinks and then smiled. "Dela. What a nice surprise. Did you say a picnic?" Her face lit up even more. "Did you invite your mother?"

"I tried but she was busy." Dela felt a small white lie was acceptable since she didn't want her mom to carry the conversation when Dela was digging for information.

"That's a shame. Where are we going?" Annie walked up to her passenger door.

Dela shot a glance at the house and asked, "Do you need to tell Keenan where you're going?"

"He's gone to the brewery and the boys don't care what I do." She opened the door and slid into the car.

Dela wondered if he was at the brewery or at the police station getting Wallace out of jail. When Annie mentioned the boys, she wondered if there was more than one son.

Dela smiled, opened her door, and lowered into the driver's seat. "It's too pretty of a day to not enjoy the outdoors."

"I agree. That's what I miss most because of Keenan's work. We are always moving, never a place with my own things, or my own yard and garden to work in." She sighed and rolled the window down. "As a child, I'd ride my bike or my horse and twirl on a tire swing in the backyard. My family had a farm. I loved all the animals. Keenan won't even let me have a dog or a cat. They would be such good company when he's gone so much."

"How long have you been married?" Dela asked.

"Ten years, and yes, he is a bit younger than me, but we knew we were meant for each other the minute we met."

Dela glanced over at the woman. A soft smile tipped her lips, her eyes were closed as if remembering the moment.

"Was it your first marriage?" Dela asked, wondering how to bring up her son who was in his twenties without giving away how much she already knew about the woman.

"No, it's my second, his first. My first husband was in business as well. We had a son, Wallace. He was a good boy, but lately, he's been staying out late. He didn't even come home the last couple of nights." Surprise laced her words, not worry.

"Who were the boys you mentioned who didn't care where you go?" Dela asked as she parked in the area designated for people using the walkway.

"They hang out with Wallace. Because they are Wallace's friends, Keenan lets them stay at the house."

Dela didn't know if Annie was that clueless as to her husband's dealings or that naïve to think a man of Keenan's age and wealth would let twenty-something hoodlums stay at his house when their friend wasn't there.

"What are we doing here?" Annie asked.

"It's where we'll have our picnic. The trail along the river is beautiful and teeming with birds and some wildlife." Dela exited the car and pulled the picnic basket out of the back seat. As she did this, she spotted her car parking a block away.

By the time she was up on the sidewalk, Annie was

walking up the path to the heron statute. Dela caught up to her and they stood a minute admiring the birds.

"This is one of my favorite places in Pendleton," Dela said. At least until she'd fallen on Gus's body almost a week ago.

"It is special, isn't it." Annie touched the statue and stared at the river.

"Which way do you want to walk?" Dela asked.

Annie glanced toward the bridge where Gus was killed then the other direction. "Let's go that way." She pointed toward the bridge.

Dela had hoped she'd go to the bench where Dela had met her the night of the murder. But she fell into step beside Annie.

Drawing in a deep breath, Annie released it and said, "There is nothing better than being close to nature."

"I agree." As they drew near the bridge, Dela's heart raced. She knew it was stupid to fear the bridge. It hadn't killed Gus, a person had. But that person was still out there and seemed to be gunning for her.

The sound of someone jogging up behind them, had Dela grasping Annie's arm, pulling her to the side, and pushing the woman behind her. When Dela focused on the jogger, he smiled.

"Beautiful day to be out along the river," Marty said, jogging on past.

Dela's heart settled and she watched as Marty jogged out the other side and waved a hand. How had he known she was scared to go under that bridge? She glanced back down the trail and Heath stood at the edge of the trail watching them. He held up a hand.

He had sent Marty ahead of her. He'd known she

would be hesitant.

Annie stepped back onto the trail as if nothing had happened.

"I'm sorry I shoved you to the side," Dela said.

"I heard the footsteps but wondered why you were shoving me nearly off the path when it sounded like only one person." Annie studied her. "Why did you bring me here, really?"

"I'm worried about you." Dela didn't have to fake the emotion in her tone. While the woman had frightened her when they first met, she now understood there was something that triggered the woman's moods. She waved back the way they came. "There's a bench back there we can sit on and talk."

They turned around, without going under the bridge, and walked back past the heron statue and down the path to the bench. Dela sat, placing the picnic basket on the bench between them. She pulled out the different drinks she'd brought with her. "Would you like juice, water, or soda?" She asked, holding each one up.

"It's been years since I had soda. Since this is a special occasion, I'll drink that." Annie took the bottle and screwed the top off. She took one swallow and laughed. "I forgot how bubbly the carbonation is in this drink."

Dela studied her. The woman seemed almost childlike in some ways and yet so sophisticated and worldly in others. "Tell me about your son," Dela said.

"He's twenty-two, I think. I had him when I was thirty. My first husband said we couldn't have children until we had enough money put away to take care of them. Wallace was two when my husband died in a car crash. I never had the chance to have more children."

She thought about that. "Which is probably a good thing. I don't think I've been the best mother. I don't have those instincts."

"I'm sure you've been a good mother. You're so kind and easygoing," Dela said.

Annie peered into her eyes. "Do you think so? Keenan says I can be uncontrollable and delusional." Tears glistened in her eyes. "I don't know why he brings me with him all the time when he is usually not happy with something I've done. I'd be much happier left somewhere all by myself." She scratched at her arm. When she couldn't seem to abate the itch, she shoved her sleeve up and revealed a transdermal patch.

"Why do you have that patch?" Dela asked. "Are you trying to quit smoking?"

Annie glanced up from where she'd been working at the patch. "To be honest, I don't know why I wear it. Keenan said the doctor prescribed it. But I don't know what for."

Dela studied the patch. "Can you take it off and I'll have it tested?"

Annie studied her. "Why would you want to test it?"

"To see what is on it. To see why you need it." Dela fought with her conscience. Did she tell the woman what they suspected of her husband or what she'd witnessed of the woman's craziness? She decided to go with the crazy.

"Annie, the first time we met, you were sitting on this bench, dressed in fuzzy boots, a long coat, and knitted gloves. You were talking crazy. At first, I thought you were a homeless person and the crazy talk was why you were homeless. Then at my mom's party, you walked in and acted like you've been today. I thought, hmmm… were you trying to distract me that night because," Dela took a deep breath and pointed back toward the bridge, "That night I found a man under that bridge with his throat slit."

Annie put a hand to her neck.

Dela continued, "I thought maybe you'd been acting to keep me from finding my acquaintance before he was killed."

Annie's head shook back and forth. "I-I don't remember."

Dela put a hand on her arm. "At my mom's party you were…sane, for lack of a better word. Then about an hour after you got there, you started acting agitated and saying awful things. Keenan made excuses and took you home. Mom had made plans to meet you for lunch at the casino on Saturday. I saw you and Keenan in the bar and grill the next day. You walked in acting fine. An hour or so later you were being crazy again and he left with you and called Mom to tell her you wouldn't be able to meet her for lunch on Saturday."

Annie stared at her, her face a statue in concentration. "I don't remember doing or being that way. Saturday when I was getting ready to meet your mom, Keenan told me she called and canceled."

Dela had wondered if the husband hadn't wanted Annie to meet with the person who accused him of abuse. "The other day when I met you out walking, you appeared sane and today you are doing fine." She nodded to the patch on the woman's arm. "Who puts that on you and how?"

"Keenan puts it on. He uses gloves because he doesn't need the drugs that are on the patch." She said it as if it had been recited to her a million times.

Without asking again, Dela ripped the pad off Annie's arm.

"Ow! I usually soak them off." Annie glared at her.

"Sorry, I figured it was the quickest, easiest way." She dumped the cookies she'd put in a plastic bag out onto a napkin and dropped the patch in. A little sugar shouldn't mess up a test. "I have a question. When you were in a crazy state, you told me you knew where the bodies were buried. Do you have any idea if that was something about Keenan's business?"

Annie stared at her again. She squirmed a bit on the seat and sipped her soda.

Dela dug into the basket and pulled out a salad she'd made, handing it and a fork to Annie. "If you do know things like that, it could be why he doesn't let you see other people."

"When I married him, I knew him to be a businessman. What I didn't realize was a good portion of his income is gotten illegally." She sighed, "I don't know how but I've heard enough conversations that I know it is illegally gained. He has tried to get me to sign over Wallace's trust to him, saying I'm not fit enough to take care of it. But I have my own lawyer who takes care of mine and Wallace's trusts. Even if I'm not fit, he is."

Dela knew why Annie was acting crazy. "Would you like to stay with my mom for a few days while I have this patch analyzed and you see if you don't feel better when not wearing it?"

Annie stopped chewing and swallowed. "Are you saying leave Keenan?"

Dela saw the emotions clashing in the woman's

eyes. "I think if you were free of Keenan you'd feel better. You could purchase a place where you could have cats and dogs and horses. And I believe you will live longer."

"You think he is making me look crazy to get his hands on our trusts." Annie was putting it all together.

"Yes, that's what I think. But that doesn't answer my question of what you were doing down here the night Gus Sander was killed."

"Sander? As in Sander Construction?" Annie asked.

"Yes, does that mean anything to you?"

"Yes, I overheard Keenan and Balto talking. Balto said he thought the head of the construction company had figured out they had changed up the floor plan. And he'd seen the crates with the machines." Annie closed her eyes and opened them again. "I walked into the room and said what did it matter if he saw the brewery machines." She bowed her head. "Keenan grabbed me by the arm and said it was time for my patch. After he applied it, I put on the first shoes and coat I could find and walked out the back door. I don't remember where I walked to or how I got home. But Keenan kept asking me where I'd been and I didn't know."

"Because he'd put that patch on you to make you forget about his conversation and to keep you from going somewhere." Dela put all the picnic items in the basket. "Come on, we're getting you out to Mom's before Keenan sends someone out to find you."

"What about clothes?" Annie asked.

"Mom is resourceful. She'll figure it out. But you'll have to stay at her place, don't come to town or answer your phone until I tell you everything is cleared up." Dela stood and peered into the woman's eyes. "Can you do that?"

"If it means I won't have blackouts and can remember where I've been and what I've done, yes. I want to be a part of the living again." Annie stood and they walked to Dela's car.

Heath leaned against her car. "How was the picnic?" he asked, eyeing Annie.

"I'm taking her to stay with Mom until all of this is cleared up." Dela handed the bag with the patch in it to him. "Take this to Quinn and have it analyzed. Oh, and tell them there had been peanut butter cookies in the bag before I put the patch in it."

"You sure you don't want me to follow you to your mom's?" Heath asked, worry creasing his brow.

"You can come there after you drop that off and follow me home." She kissed his cheek and she and Annie slid into the rental car.

"Don't you need to call your mom?" Annie asked.

"Only to see if she's home." Dela dialed her mom and asked where she was.

"I'm home. Are you coming for a visit?" Deborah's voice was filled with happiness.

"Yes, and I'm bringing a house guest."

"Wonderful! The more the merrier." Deborah ended the call.

Dela chuckled. "I'm sure she's going to make sure the guest room has fresh flowers."

"I do envy your mom and Lance. They seem to be a lovely couple."

"It was a long time coming for Mom. I'm happy for her." Dela thought to herself, especially if I was conceived as the newspaper articles say.

# Chapter Twenty-four

Dela arrived at the ranch and wasn't surprised when Mom hugged Annie and welcomed her into the house without any explanation. Once Annie had excused herself to use the bathroom, Dela leaned close to her mom and told her what she believed and that Annie wasn't to go anywhere and Keenan wasn't to know she was here.

"Not a problem. I'll let Lance know as soon as he comes in the house. That's awful her husband was drugging her to get her trust from her first marriage." Mom had an indignant expression on her face.

"When Heath gets here, I have to go. We're still trying to find the person who has it out for me."

"I understand. We'll take good care of Annie. Let me know what drug he was using. There may be withdrawals I'll need to know about." Mom smiled as Annie returned to the room.

"I don't have any clothes with me. Dela insisted I didn't go home and pack anything." Annie glanced down at the slacks and tunic she was wearing.

"You're taller than me but I'm sure I can rustle up several outfits for you from my closet and I have a friend who I'm sure will donate some clothes and shoes as well."

Barking from Lance's dog, Barracuda, stopped their conversation.

Dela walked to the front window and watched Heath exit her car and lean down to pet Barracuda. "It's Heath. If you need anything let me know." Dela hugged her mom and smiled at Annie. "You're in good hands."

She opened the door as Heath stepped on the porch.

"Are you ready?" he asked.

"Yes. We have one thing solved, and I found out some interesting stuff." She walked by him and out to the rental car. "Call Quinn and ask to meet him somewhere. I'll follow you." She slid into the car and waited for Heath to turn around and head back toward Pendleton. While she'd saved Annie from her husband, she still had to save herself from whoever was out to get her.

♠ ♣ ♥ ♦

Heath pulled into a pizza shop and Dela parked beside him.

"This is where Quinn wanted to meet?" she asked as Heath walked toward her.

"Yep, something about he could walk here from where he was." Heath led the way into the pizza shop. It was dark and had a funky smell that Dela thought was a mix of sewer and burnt pizza crust.

"This place is disgusting. We're not eating anything here," she said as they sat in a corner booth. As she scooted in, she was pretty sure her shoe smeared something on the floor because her foot slipped when she tried to get leverage to scoot.

Heath glanced around. "I think we should leave and tell Quinn to meet us somewhere else."

Dela slid back to the end of the bench and stood. Heath joined her and they returned to the sunny outside and fresh air.

"Hey, I didn't mean for you to go in that sewer pit," Quinn said, straightening from where he was leaning on Dela's car.

"That would have been nice to know before we went in there looking for you," Dela said.

"I only have a few minutes. Our building is only a couple blocks that way." He pointed to the center of town.

"Why did you want to meet here?" Heath asked, now leaning on the rental car.

Quinn settled back against Dela's car and she climbed up to sit on the hood of the rental with her foot on the bumper to keep from sliding off.

"I didn't want anyone to see you coming to our building." Quinn's gaze bore into her. "What did you learn from Annie?"

"I took the patch off when she said she didn't know why she wore it and Keenan put it on her while wearing gloves. Sounds like he is drugging her to make her look crazy. Turns out she and Wallace, her son, have trusts her first husband left for them. Keenan has been trying to get control of the trusts. She said she has a good lawyer who deals with it and he won't let Keenan get near it." Dela gazed up at the sun and then down at Quinn. "As for Keenan's business dealings, all she knows is he does some illegal dealings and she overheard him and Balto talking about Gus having seen the change of building plans and the crates of machines." She studied Quinn. "What kind of machines do you think they're talking about?"

Quinn shrugged. "It could be bottling machines or machines that have to do with the manufacture of drugs."

Dela glanced at Heath. She had a way to find out. "That's all I have for you from the Annie intervention. We need to go see if Fletcher pulled up backgrounds on a couple of people." Dela slid off the hood of the rental car and walked to the driver's door.

"That's all you got out of Annie. You're sure she doesn't know anything more?"

"Positive. But you might try chatting with her son, Wallace. I'm not sure how well he likes his stepfather. Especially if you mention he's been drugging Wallace's mother to get their trusts." Dela slid into the driver's seat and started her vehicle. She didn't drive out of the parking lot until she saw Heath behind her.

She drove out to the police station after making a detour to check out what vehicles were at the brewery. She'd yet to discern what vehicle Keenan drove.

At the police station, she asked for Detective Fletcher.

"I'll call back and see if he's in," the receptionist said.

Dela and Heath waited by the window until she confirmed he was in and would be out to see them. Five minutes later Fletcher pushed through a door to their right.

"Come on back. I imagine you're here for the backgrounds."

"Yes. I would like to stop looking over my shoulder," Dela said, following him down the hall to a small office with two desks.

Fletcher plopped into the chair behind the desk like his legs couldn't hold him up much longer.

Dela sat in the chair Heath set in front of the desk and he stood behind her.

The detective handed her two folders. "This is what we came up with for the two. I'm not sure it's going to be much help."

Dela opened Darren's file while Heath read Louisa's.

She couldn't find anything that would connect him to her through anyone in his family or where he worked. He was what he seemed to be. Though Gus was having trysts with his wife. Jealousy or revenge would be a good reason, and Darren was the right build for the person she saw running away. But how did he get into her car and get the knife?

"Hey, Louisa's uncle is Derick Brown, spelled with one r. Wasn't he the father of someone who died from the meth Gus had cooked on the rez?"

Dela pulled the file from Heath's hands and read the family connection. "That would make her a cousin to Tyler, the son who died. That would explain why she would want Gus dead, but why me?"

"Maybe because you kept Gus from going to jail by allowing his wife to financially ruin him." Heath took the file back. "Did you find anything that connects you to Darren?"

"No. But I think Louisa talked him into killing Gus to get her revenge. All she had to do was tell him if he got rid of the man standing between him and his wife, he'd get her back. Darren is so besotted with Zaria that he would believe it. But that didn't happen and he was pissed and decided I should die too or be implicated in the murder."

Buzzing came from Heath's pocket. He pulled his phone out and read. "It's the house alarm. Someone is trying to enter the house." He slid it to video and they watched a person with his back to the camera, messing with the door before it opened and the invader entered. Dela had been set against having cameras in the house. They waited ten minutes and the person exited the house the way they went in, through the French door.

"How in the hell are they getting my keys? First, they got into my car and stole my knife and now they just walked right in through a door I know was locked." Dela was furious. Blood pounded in her head as she watched the person walk to a black unlicensed SUV. She stared at it and said, "Now they're back to the unlicensed SUV."

"They had to have paid someone to get your keys and then had replicas made. But that would require lots of beforehand thinking." Heath stood. "Let's go have a talk with Darren."

"Wait, this is a police investigation. I'll pull them in and see if I can get one of them to roll on the other." Fletcher picked up his phone and ordered two different officers to pick up Darren and Louisa. "Go see what they left in your house. Photograph it and where they put it, then bag it and take it to the State lab to see if there are any prints or a way to connect it to them."

Dela stopped at the door. "Can we listen in to the questioning?"

Fletcher shook his head. "You can listen to the tape afterward."

She grumbled to Heath as they walked down the hall. "Seeing their reactions is more helpful than trying to figure out things from their tone."

Outside the police station, Heath stopped beside the rental. "This isn't our homicide. You have to abide by Fletcher's rules. Let's see what they left to incriminate you."

♠ ♣ ♥ ♦

At her house, Dela went through the gate into the backyard and checked to see if they locked the French doors on the way out. They hadn't. She faced Heath. "Why do they keep not locking things up? It's as if they are saying, see I can get in and you aren't safe rather than trying to hide the fact they were even here. It's evident they broke in since the door is left unlocked." She didn't like that their leaving things unlocked was like a threat.

"They were in here for nearly ten minutes. Do you think it took them that long to look for a good hiding spot?" Heath entered the kitchen.

"You check here, the living room, and weight room. I'll check the bedrooms and bathrooms." Dela set off down the hall. She went into the guest room, dug through every box in the closet, and looked under every piece of furniture. Then she checked all the places something could be hidden in the guest bathroom, including the water holding tank on the toilet.

"Hey, I found the other fob for your car. It was under the recliner," Heath called down the hallway.

Dela's mind started buzzing with how someone got into her car without the fob.

She moved into their bedroom and bathroom. Anger wrestled in her chest and throbbed in her head that someone she didn't know saw the handicapped bars in the bathroom, and if they looked in her closet, the prosthesis with the running foot. Her privacy had been breached and she didn't like it. That ticked her off almost as much as knowing someone was trying to frame and kill her.

She walked into the bathroom and started pulling towels out of the cabinet and shaking them. Thunk! She looked down and spotted a cell phone. Not hers or Heath's.

Sticking her head out the bathroom door, she called out, "I found it!"

Heath's hurried steps in the hallway announced his arrival. He stepped into the room. His gaze dropped to the phone on the floor. "In the towels?"

"Yes."

He took out his phone and took pictures of the towel cabinet and the phone on the ground. Squatting by the phone, he pulled the latex gloves he'd taken from his work vehicle before they entered the house out of his back pocket. Once he donned the gloves, he picked up the phone and pressed the power button. It didn't go on. "We'll need to charge it to see who it belongs to and what's on it." Heath carried it out to the kitchen.

"It has to be Gus's. Why else would they have hidden it here?" Dela found a cord that worked on the phone and handed it to Heath.

He plugged the phone in and started checking it

out. "They pulled the SIM card."

Dela studied him. "Does that mean we won't be able to find out anything?"

Heath grinned. "No. It means whoever took it or left it isn't very smart. We can still access his emails and texts. All the SIM does is not allow the user to use it like a phone or send texts."

Dela smiled. "Maybe there will be something on there that can help us determine what is going on at the brewery as well as who murdered him."

Heath's phone dinged. He glanced at the screen. "It's Fletcher wanting to know if we found anything." He met her gaze. "We need time for this to charge so we can see what it has. You know they aren't going to let us see it once they get their hands on it."

"Tell him we're still looking." Dela went to the cupboard, took down two glasses, and filled them with iced tea. "While we wait for that to charge, we could try to figure out who helped someone gain access to my keys."

Something clicked in Dela's mind. "Did you remember reading what Louisa Tuttle's father does?"

Heath studied her over the glass of tea he'd raised to get a drink. He set the glass down. "Locksmith."

Dela looked up a locksmith in the Pendleton area and waited for the phone to ring. "I'm going to ask a locksmith if you can duplicate a key fob."

A woman answered.

"Hi, I'm just wondering if a person loses a key fob can a duplicate be made?" Dela asked.

"Yes, there are several ways it can be done," she answered.

"Do I need to bring in the fob I have?"

"That's the easiest way. Or we can use the VIN on the car or just the make and model but that does create a bigger issue and cost."

"Thank you, that's what I needed to know." She hung up and said, "A locksmith can create a key fob with just the make and model of the car."

"That would explain how they were able to unlock the car. But what about the keys to the house?"

Dela shrugged. "Anyone who works for the casino could have been in the security office when my purse was sitting out and no one was watching and made a wax of the keys. Or they could have just picked the locks. We couldn't see his hands the way he was standing at the door."

She rose and walked over to the French doors. Using a flashlight, she studied the keyhole. "There is a bit of scratching as if someone stuck something in to break the tumblers free."

Heath pushed the on button and the phone came on. "We're in luck, it doesn't seem to be face recognition or fingerprint secure. What do you think Gus would use for his PIN number?"

Dela looked up information on Gus and Sander Construction. "Try nineteen-ninety-eight. That's the year he started the construction company."

"We're in! I'll check recent calls." Heath used a stylus to slide and press buttons. "You were the last person he called."

"That was two hours before he was killed." Dela placed a bag of chips on the table between them.

"Wow!" Heath exclaimed. "Do you look at your Hotmail email?"

"No, it's too hard to get to it, why?" She scooted

her chair over next to his.

"Gus sent you a detailed email about what he'd found at the brewery. I'd say it was worth killing for if I were the one making pills in the back of the brewery." Heath swiveled his head and peered into her eyes. "This could be why they wanted in the house, to destroy the email, and why they are trying to kill you."

"But I never saw it?" She walked into the living room and grabbed her laptop out of the hidden drawer under the television stand. Back at the kitchen counter, she logged in and struggled with getting logged into her Hotmail account. When she did get in, there was the email from Gus. She read it and asked, "Do you think I should forward this to Quinn or Fletcher?"

"Quinn. He can forward it to his DEA acquaintance. They'll be the ones who Fletcher would send it to."

She forwarded it and noted the date and time it was sent. "Gus wrote this up and sent it after he called and set up our meeting. Do you think he knew he wasn't going to be alive to tell me?"

"He knew someone was after him to keep him from telling." Heath put the phone in an evidence bag, picked up his phone, and dialed. "Fletcher, we found what is probably Gus's phone. I've put it in an evidence bag. Do you want us to bring it in?" He listened and smiled. "Sure, we can do that." Heath ended the call. "Detective Fletcher would like us to bring the phone to him and fill him in on what we think might make the two he had brought in talk."

Dela smiled. "I guess he should have allowed us in on the questioning. I'm sure my presence in the room would rile them up a bit since they have been trying to implicate me in the murder they committed."

They took her car to the police station knowing the two that may have the duplicated fob were being questioned. Dela and Heath were ushered back to Fletcher as soon as they walked through the front door.

"Let's see what you found," he said, as they sat in his office along with an officer.

Heath showed them the photos of where the phone was found and Fletcher turned it on.

"Damn, it needs a code," Fletcher said, handing it off to the officer. "Randy is our tech genius on the city force."

Dela piped up, "You might look in Gus Sander's file and use dates that were important to him. His wedding day, his wife's birthday, the day his daughter was born. Possibly when he started his business. He wasn't an overly complicated man and I'd say he'd use something he could remember easily."

"Thanks, I'll start there," Randy said, walking out the door.

"What can you give me about these two that might get them to talk?" Fletcher asked.

"What have you gotten out of them so far?" Dela asked.

"They both say they were at home with their spouses the night Gus was killed and the night you were nearly run over." Fletcher ran a hand through his hair.

"Did you check with the spouses?" Heath asked.

"I have an officer doing that now. I'm waiting for him to either confirm or deny what they said." Fletcher studied Dela. "You look like you have something you want to spit out."

"We believe Louisa asked her dad to make a new

key fob that would work on my car. I called a locksmith and it's something that is fairly easy to do."

"How do you know her father made it?"

"In her file, it said her father was a locksmith." Dela leaned back. "Didn't you read their files before you questioned them?"

Fletcher's face reddened. "I've been busy, and we don't usually get such a complicated homicide around here. Mostly it's an overdose or someone is caught shooting or stabbing someone. And those don't happen very often."

"I think you'll get Louisa to crack if you allow me to sit in on the questioning. She's bound to get upset that I'm not more of a suspect than she is." Dela leaned forward. "And it will be fun."

Fletcher shook his head. "I can't have you go in there and irritate the suspect to get answers."

"Where and when were these two picked up?" Heath asked.

"Both were at work," Fletcher said.

Dela and Heath exchanged a look and Dela said, "Then they couldn't have been the ones who broke into the house and planted the phone."

# Chapter Twenty-five

"What are we missing?" Dela asked as she and Heath sat in her car in the Dairy Queen parking lot eating fries and ice cream.

"It had to be Louisa dressed in the pink hoodie who got the keys to the car that ran you down." Heath swirled a fry in his ice cream and ate it.

"And they had to have made the fob that got them into my car to steal my knife. The knife they heard about when Daisy was talking to her friend at work." Dela dipped her fry in the chocolate sauce dribbling down her sundae. "Has anyone found out if Darren or Louisa own a blue compact car? We know who owns the unlicensed SUV that also tried to get in the house and that followed me."

"Let's drive by Darren and Lousia's residences and see if we can see the car. I'm sure Fletcher is still holding them until he can get them to talk." Heath finished off his ice cream and started the car.

"Go by Stage Technology first. Darren and Lousia were picked up from work. Their vehicles should still be in the parking lot. It would save time if the blue car is there." Dela continued to eat her sundae as Heath drove to State Technology.

They did a spin around the parking lot looking for a small blue car.

"There!" Dela pointed to a spot tucked in a corner under a tree. They both exited their vehicle and walked up to the little blue car. Dela looked in the windows. There was a woman's sweater in the back seat and hearts on the seat covers. "I would say this is Louisa's car." She walked to the back of the car and typed the license plate into her phone. Then she texted it to Fletcher and asked him to look up who the car belonged to.

Heath took several photos. "It looks like the one we saw speeding away after Mugshot was tranquilized."

Dela nodded, not wanting to think about what had happened. "We need to see how they would have gotten a hold of a tranquilizer."

Her phone buzzed.

*That vehicle belongs to Louisa Tuttle*. Fletcher texted.

"It is Louisa's," Dela confirmed. She texted back. *Ask Louisa if she has animals, and if she does, what veterinarian she uses.*

*What does that have to do with the homicide case?*

*It has to do with her harming my dog. And it might shake her up to think we know she attempted to get in my house.* She had a thought. *Have you searched Louisa and Darren's houses?*

*No. No reason until we have something more concrete.*

Dela dialed Detective Fletcher.

"Dela, I'm preparing to go back in with Darren. I don't need you harassing me about searching houses."

"This car I'm standing next to is the little blue compact that we saw drive away right before we found my dog drugged and my donkey wandering around outside the fence. The least you could look for is the drug that was used on my dog at Louisa's and possibly any other items that were kept when Gus was killed. It's obvious they kept items to use to frame me."

"All I can do is take it to the DA and see if he feels there is enough evidence. But knowing him, it won't be."

Dela ended the call. "He believes the DA won't think he has enough evidence to get a search warrant."

Heath grasped her hand and walked her back to their car. "Let's go see if Zaria is home and visit with her. After that, we'll visit with Louisa's husband. That will determine if they were telling the truth about being home at the times we believe they were out doing illegal deeds."

♠ ♣ ♥ ♦

Heath parked in front of the Landis home as the sun was setting. The house and porch looked dark.

"I wonder where Zaria is," Dela said as they approached the porch.

The light came on. Dela threw up her hand to lessen the harsh light in her eyes. On the porch, she groped around next to the door until her eyes recovered from the glaring light. Her finger finally found the doorbell and she pressed.

There wasn't any sound coming from the house. Dela walked along the porch to the side of the house and still only saw dark windows. "I don't think she's home," Dela said, knowing they couldn't just let themselves in.

"You looking for Darren?" a male voice asked from the other side of the fence.

Dela walked closer and peered up. She saw a man's eyes and a ball cap. "We're looking for Zaria."

The man snorted. "This time of night you won't find her home. She's out being a barfly. I don't know why Darren stays with her. She has made it pretty clear she prefers lots of men, not just one." The man grabbed his hat brim and scratched his head. "Not sure why Darren isn't home. He's usually here half an hour after he gets off work. But he hasn't come home tonight."

"You keep pretty close tabs on your neighbors," Heath said. "Any chance you know if they were home last Wednesday night?"

"Are you cops?" the man asked.

"We're helping the police with an investigation," Dela said.

"Really? Huh. It must be something Zaria is messed up with. Let's see… last Wednesday, that would be my bowling night. I came home about ten. Both of their cars were in the driveway. But in the morning when I went out to go to work, I noticed that Darren's was parked in a different spot. Like he must have gone somewhere during the night. Which is odd. He usually doesn't go out once he's home for the night."

"Thank you. You've been helpful." Heath led Dela away from the fence. When they were seated in the car, he said, "It sounds like Darren went back out somewhere after ten.”

"My guess would be to steal my knife and kill Gus. He admitted he saw Gus and Zaria come out of the bar together. My guess is he called Louisa, told her what he'd seen and she got him riled up to go do her killing. Maybe even providing the weapon." Dela could see her sneaking up to the car, using the duplicated key fob to open the door and grab the knife, then meet with Darren, hand it off, and get him riled up to kill Gus. Using the very distinctive knife to frame Dela.

Her mind reconstructed the video she'd seen of the car and the person taking her knife. It wasn't Louisa and the car was the black SUV. "We're still missing something. All the pieces aren't fitting together."

"Let's talk to Louisa's husband. Maybe he'll have something to help tie it all together." Heath pulled away from the Landis home and headed to the other side of town where Louisa lived.

When they pulled up to the house, Dela saw six small bicycles and other children's toys strung around the yard. Four cars were parked in the driveway, and three were at the curb. "This is where Louisa lives?" she asked.

"It's what her file said." Heath stepped out of the car and walked around to Dela's door. He opened it and leaned down. "I think more than one family lives in this house."

They walked up to the door. The aroma of chiles, peppers, and spices filled the air. A telenovela was playing on the television and loud discussions in Spanish could be heard.

Heath knocked on the door. Several dogs barked and the door opened.

"Hello?" the older Hispanic man said as he peered at them.

"Hi, we were given this address for Louisa Tuttle," Heath said.

The man shook his head. "No one by that name lives here."

"Does anyone named Louisa live here?" Dela asked.

"Sorry, no."

"Okay, thank you." Heath headed off the porch steps.

Dela lingered on the porch.

"Come on. She obviously gave a fake address," Heath said.

"Where did you get the address?" Dela asked, joining Heath on the sidewalk.

"From the file Fletcher had."

Dela slid into the passenger seat of her car as she stared at the house. The living room shade moved and someone peaked out. "If she doesn't live there then why are they interested in whether or not we leave?"

Heath started the car. "Good questions. I think we'll go down the street and turn around. I'd like to know if someone leaves the house looking for her or to tell someone we were looking for her."

He did a U-turn about three blocks down and then stopped a block away from the house on the opposite side so they could keep an eye on the front door.

"We should have brought snacks," Dela said, leaning her head back, but keeping her gaze on the front of the house.

"I didn't know we'd be doing a stakeout." Heath stretched an arm out towards her. "Act like you're interested in making out."

"Act? Why?" she frowned, watching him smile.

"Because we have a curious homeowner."

Dela didn't look around. She just leaned over the console between them and kissed him. "I can't see if anyone leaves the house."

"I've got my eyes on it." He put his hand on her back, moving it up and down. Then his hand stopped. "Okay, he went back in the house."

Dela fell back into her seat. "I'm glad, it's not easy to look horny with that console poking in my side."

Heath laughed. "I wish you were on all my stakeouts. They wouldn't be so boring." He leaned forward. "We have action."

Dela saw the two men in black hoodies slip into one of the cars parked along the street. They were coming in their direction.

"Duck down so it only looks like one person in the car," Heath said.

She did as she was told, he started the vehicle before they passed and then headed in the opposite direction, making a U-turn as she sat up. "Did you see which way they went?" she asked when she didn't see any taillights.

"I did. Hang on. I just need to get close enough we can keep them in our sights."

He was speeding in a residential area but soon saw their backlights.

Dela typed the car license into her phone and sent it to Quinn since Fletcher wasn't being as helpful as she'd hoped and Quinn would be quicker to get her the information.

Her phone buzzed. Quinn.

"What is this license number for?" he asked.

"I want you to tell us who it is registered to." She didn't add anything else.

"It is registered to Juan Salas. From what I can see he has a long list of priors and is part of the cartel that the DEA has linked to Cristo. What are you doing?"

"We were staking out a house that Louisa Tuttle had down as her place of residence. When we arrived there was a house full of Hispanic people who said they didn't know her. Now we're following Juan Salas and friend to—" She put her hand on Heath's arm. "I think we just found a connection."

"Yes, we did," Heath said, parking the car in a hotel parking lot. They watched Juan and his friend park in the Brewery parking lot and walk around to the back of the building.

"What connection?" Quinn asked.

"We're at the brewery." Dela hung up as Heath slipped out of the car. She followed right behind him using the shadows of the trees to hide them. They went along the side of the brewery that had less windows and stopped at the back corner.

Heath did a quick poke of his head past the corner and then flattened his body to the side of the building and whispered, "They're unloading a truck in the back. There isn't anything to hide behind to get closer, it's just the back of the building."

"Then we wait to take a peek when they all leave," Dela said.

Heath grasped her hand. "Then we need to get away from the building and over there by that bush to watch until we see them leave."

She scanned the area Heath pointed at and saw

what he was talking about. It was an old bush that she was surprised hadn't been torn down by Keenan. It was scraggly and didn't look like much but it would give them cover if they could get to it without being seen.

They backtracked up alongside the building and jogged over to the line of trees that hid the building from the hotel. From there they proceeded slowly toward the bush to not attract anyone's attention.

Once they were settled, sitting on the ground behind the bush, they pushed some branches to the side to watch what was happening.

There appeared to be half a dozen people in black hoodies, unloading the truck and carrying the boxes through a small door at the far back corner. There weren't any windows in the wall, only one door.

"There's Balto," Dela whispered as the large man walked out the door and said something to the workers. They started moving faster.

"I think he told them to hurry up," Heath whispered.

"I wonder why?"

"Maybe he has a hot date."

Dela studied Heath. She could barely see the smile on his face.

"You know that door is going to be locked when they leave and we won't have a way to get into it." She wanted to know exactly what was happening. They knew from the email Gus sent her that the back area of the building had been set up for pill making machines. He'd seen the machines and knew he had to say something to keep his daughter believing he'd changed. But given his history with drug making and dealing, he didn't want to go to the police himself.

Just as the door was swung shut on the trailer, the whole parking lot lit up and people in bulletproof vests and jackets that said DEA on them swarmed the back of the building.

"I guess that answers that," Dela said, standing. "The authorities have their drug makers, but we are no closer to finding out who has been after me and who killed Gus than before."

# Chapter Twenty-six

Dela couldn't sleep. After leaving the brewery, they tried to stop in at the police station and see what Fletcher had accomplished but he'd gone home. With Balto and his group in the custody of DEA, she'd never get to question them about whether or not they had killed Gus.

Using her crutches to pace in the living room, which wasn't easy to do in a 12 by 15 foot room with furniture, she thought about the things they didn't know and how so much of her life was unknown. If Mugshot were here, she could at least pet and hug him as she mulled over what she knew and what she didn't. Mainly she wanted to know who was trying to frame and harm her.

"Hey, what are you doing? Practicing for a marathon. You're going to wear out the carpet where you pivot." Heath walked into the room in his boxers. His loose long hair hung down each side of his chest.

"Do you need a cup of tea to help you sleep?" He headed to the kitchen.

"I need answers. How are we going to get them when Fletcher won't let us talk to Darren and Louisa and the DEA have Balto and crew?" Dela followed him into the kitchen.

Heath had set out a plate of her favorite cookies and a cup of tea. She smiled. "You are too good to me."

He grinned. "I know how to calm you down. Food and chamomile tea." He raised his eyebrows. "And a couple other ways."

Her cheeks heated. "I want answers not a roll in the sheets. Save that thought for when we've discovered who killed Gus and set me up." She sat and picked up a spicy oatmeal cookie.

Heath sat down with a cup of tea and plucked a cookie off the plate. "I think we need to push Fletcher harder to get answers from Darren and Louisa. We know Louisa is living with drug cartel members. We could tell Fletcher if he doesn't let us talk to Louisa we'll go to the DEA and tell them she is involved with the drugs and they'll take her away from his homicide investigation."

"That's a great idea!" Dela smiled at Heath. "I'm sure he doesn't want to lose one of his murder suspects to the DEA." She finished her cookie and drank the tea. "I think I can go to sleep now."

♠ ♣ ♥ ♦

Dela and Heath were at the Pendleton City Police Station at 9 AM. "We'd like to speak with Detective Fletcher, please," Dela said to the officer behind the glass window.

"I'll see if he's available." The officer picked up

the phone, talked, and then shook his head. "He's busy this morning and can't be disturbed."

"Tell him it's Dela and Heath. I should have mentioned our names the first time," Dela added.

"He said he didn't want to be disturbed by anyone. Including you two."

Dread knotted in Dela's stomach. Why didn't he want to see them? Her gaze met Heath's. What was going on? Did he now think she was a suspect in Gus's death?

They turned and walked out of the police station.

"Let's see if Quinn can get us everything we need from Gus's investigation," Dela said, worrying that something had come up that put her back in the crosshairs of the law.

"That would be overstepping Fletcher's authority," Heath said.

Dela studied him. "Are you afraid it will cause problems between the city police and the tribal police if you use a federal agent to help you do a city policeman's job?"

"When you put it like that. Yes. Not to mention getting me reprimanded." Heath slid into the driver's seat of Dela's car and said, "I don't like that Fletcher is closing us out. That means either he is more convinced you did kill Gus or he's letting someone dictate how this homicide case is run. Let's talk with Quinn but don't flat-out ask him to get us the file."

The knot that grew in her stomach when Fletcher refused to see them eased as Heath put his need for justice over the possibility of making his job harder.

They headed straight for the FBI offices in downtown Pendleton. Heath parked in front of the building that housed the offices. They used the elevator inside the doors to the second floor.

Milo greeted them when they stepped off the elevator. "Quinn didn't say you'd be dropping by."

"It was a last-minute thing," Dela said. "Is he here?"

"He won't be in for another hour. He had something to do with Marion. Can I help you?" Milo motioned for them to take a seat. He sat on the edge of a desk.

Dela glanced at Heath. He nodded.

"How much do you know about the Gus Sander homicide and the new brewery?" she asked.

"Quinn's been keeping me up to date on it. DEA raided the brewery last night and confiscated a dozen pill making machines and inventory to make millions of illegal drugs. They took in Balto Herman and eight members of the cartel. So far none of them are talking."

"We were there when they raided the brewery," Heath said. "Was it the email Gus sent Dela that made them move or me telling Quinn that's where we were?"

"The email from Gus. Which also is pretty good evidence against the cartel for killing Gus." Milo crossed his arms.

Dela could tell that Milo was happy with the way things turned out. She wasn't. "Is there any chance you could get us a copy of the medical examiner's report on Gus, and this will be trickier, copies of the questioning of Louisa Tuttle and Darren Landis?"

Milo studied her. "You don't think Fletcher is doing a good job with the investigation?"

She shook her head. "He's not following all the leads and hasn't really used any of the information we've given him." She amended that statement. "He has been good about seeing that I was set up, but that's about it."

The special agent walked around to his desk and sat down at the computer. He started typing and within minutes the printer whirred to life. Nodding toward the printer, he said, "That's the medical examiner's report."

Heath walked over and plucked it off the printer.

"I'm seeing if I can get into the city police records." He glanced up and smiled. "But you didn't hear me say that."

Dela grinned and then sobered as she and Heath started reading the medical examiner's report. She read one line several times and then pointed at it for Heath to read.

"My knife wasn't the murder weapon." She peered into Heath's eyes. It was a relief and also it changed how they'd been looking at things. "That means the person I saw running away from the scene may not have killed Gus. He may have been planting the knife."

Heath pointed to a line in the report. "The M.E. figures he was dead a good hour before your knife was stolen. It was definitely planted on the scene. But why? Anyone, especially the cartel, would know they would discover your knife wasn't the murder weapon and was a plant. That it wouldn't stand up in court."

"Someone wanted to implicate me but not have me go to jail?" Dela was relieved it hadn't been her knife that had been the murder weapon, but she was stunned that someone would set her up knowing it wouldn't stick. "I don't get it."

"Neither do I." Heath continued reading the report. "There really isn't anything else that helps to discover the killer. It was someone who is right-handed. That's most of the population. The upward motion shows the suspect was taller than Gus. But it was a clean, concise cut. Someone who had slit a throat before. That leaves out Darren. Nothing in his background would have prepared him to slit a throat like a pro."

"How does Louisa fit into all of this?" Dela asked.

"I have all of the audio from the two sessions Fletcher had with Darren and Louisa," Milo said, leaning back in his chair and grinning.

Dela walked around to where he sat. "You won't get in trouble for this will you?"

"Only if you tell." He grinned and handed her and Heath each a headset. Then he showed them the keys on the keyboard to play and stop the audio.

He moved to another desk, worked on paperwork, and made some phone calls.

Dela and Heath sat side by side, listening to the sessions. When they finished, Dela said, "He didn't ask them anything. He let them lawyer up and then just sat there saying stupid stuff. I don't get it. How did he make detective if he doesn't know how to question a suspect?"

Heath set the headphones on the desk and asked Milo, "Can you get records on Detective Gene Fletcher?"

"Why do you want records on Detective Fletcher?" Quinn asked as he stepped out of the elevator.

Dela hoped he was in a good mood. If he'd spent the morning with his girlfriend, he should be. "He refused to see us this morning knowing we wanted to listen to the tapes of his questioning Louisa and Darren." She kept her gaze on Quinn. "We just listened to the tapes and he didn't know the first thing about questioning a suspect. We want to know how he became a detective."

"He has a pretty good close rate on his cases," Quinn said. "But I'd be interested, too, since my DEA contact said there were some mutterings by some of the cartel members they picked up that law enforcement was supposed to be on the payroll."

The printer whirred.

Heath walked over and picked up the pages. He sat down beside Dela and they started skimming the file on Gene Fletcher.

"I think we'll need some financial records too," Quinn said, reading over their shoulders.

"He's been awarded well throughout his career in the police," Dela said.

The printer whirred and Quinn strode over and plucked the papers from it. "Looks like he received a large deposit into his account the day after Gus was killed. And another one last night."

Dela walked over to where Quinn stood holding the bank records. "Why would someone as decorated as him take money from, I'm guessing, the cartel?"

Milo cleared his throat and looked up from his computer. "Because his wife is undergoing cancer treatment that's expensive."

Dela felt for the man but not enough to forgive him for taking cartel money and not doing his job. "We need to take this to the State Police."

Heath nodded. "It will have to be dealt with outside of the City Police."

Dela took the papers from Quinn and added them to the ones Heath held. "Thank you for helping us clear that up. We'll go talk to someone at the State Police about investigating Fletcher."

"Do you know who tried to run you down and who has been trying to frame you?" Quinn asked.

"No. From what we've discovered, I'm sure it was Louisa and Darren. But then knowing she is living with the cartel, it could have been her and anyone in the cartel." Dela sighed. "We'll keep digging because I won't feel safe until I know that person has been stopped."

"Let us know if you need any help," Quinn offered.

"Thanks, we will," Heath said, maneuvering Dela to the elevator.

As they lowered to the first floor, she asked, "Why did you hustle me out of there?"

"I didn't want you blowing off Quinn's offer to help because of your past with him. We might need the FBI and I didn't want to make him change his mind."

Dela faced him. "I know he and I have differences, but I want to get to the bottom of this and I'd even go to the cartel to find out who tried to run me down just to ease my mind."

The elevator stopped. They stepped out and walked out into the sunny afternoon.

"Let's grab lunch at Hamley's," Heath said, leading her down the sidewalk.

Now that the Umatilla Tribe owned the restaurant that had been an icon in Pendleton for decades it had become the place for tribal members to eat when they were in town. The old building was only a couple of blocks from the FBI office.

They walked through the tall saloon door and found a table in the corner. The saloon opened at 11 AM and served food until closing. The steak house was only open for dinner.

The waitress arrived and took their orders. The waitress walked away, Heath and Dela picked up the papers they'd brought from the FBI office. Keeping her voice low, she said, "I understand how Fletcher was bought. He needed money for his wife's medical expenses. But what I don't understand is why he allowed us to run all over talking to people when he didn't plan to do anything about the homicide."

Heath sipped his iced tea thoughtfully and set it down. "Maybe he was hoping we'd discover the truth and get the real killer and he could play the part of trying to hide it but not be able to handle what we did. Maybe that's why they tried to run you down? That may not have been Louisa in the pink hoodie at the casino. It could have been any one of the cartel's girlfriends or sisters who got hold of that man's keys."

Dela stirred her straw in her drink and thought about it. "True. But what about Louisa living with the cartel?"

"I think we need to ask her about that. I'll call the jail and see if we can talk to her." Heath slid off the tall chair and walked out the door onto the sidewalk to make his call.

Dela spent the time he was outside, checking out the other people in the saloon. Several groups at the tables looked like business lunches. There were three tables with retirement-age couples and two tables with four guys who looked like they were on their lunch break from a manual labor job. Two women she'd guess in their fifties, sat at the bar visiting with the bartender. The bar was old, heavy, and ornate. The bulky piece of furniture fit the wide-open space of the saloon.

Heath stepped back through the door. She could tell by his creased brow and turned-down lips that something was wrong. He sat on the chair beside her and said, "She and Darren were released last night. Lack of evidence against them."

Blood whooshed in her head as anger boiled in her gut. "He let them out without proper questioning?"

"It looks like we'll have to go see them today and ask all the questions Fletcher didn't and hope they will answer."

When Dela's lunch arrived, she was so furious she could barely swallow the toasted sourdough bread holding her sandwich together.

# Chapter Twenty-seven

As soon as they finished eating, they headed to Louisa's house even though they now knew it was a drug cartel house. Dela went through the classes and tests to get a concealed carry license when she became head of security for the casino. But after practically sleeping with a gun in the Army she didn't like the idea of carrying a dangerous weapon around with her everywhere. However today, she had it in the pocket of her jacket.

Heath parked across the street from the house, since there wasn't any room to park in front. A bad sign. It either meant the owners of the cars were home or they were in jail. Either scenario wasn't good for them since they had followed the car that left here last night and went to the brewery. And were there when the raid happened. She hoped no one in the house knew that.

Heath checked the magazine of his backup gun and

slid it back into his ankle holster.

"I wish we didn't need to go in there armed," Dela said, feeling jitters in her gut. Just like she'd get before they set out on a convoy mission in Iraq.

Heath peered into her eyes. "Be tough and don't let them intimidate you. We're here to talk to Louisa about the murder, not anything to do with the cartel, that we know of." He winked.

"What if she went to work today?" Dela just had that thought. "What if she didn't want to lose her job and went to work to tell them it was a misunderstanding that the police took her away yesterday?"

"Then they'll tell us she's at work and that's where we'll go next." He nodded toward the house. "Let's go."

They crossed the road and walked up the sidewalk to the house.

Heath knocked and dogs started barking.

The door opened. It wasn't the man from the night before. It was a woman whose face had as many crevices and ridges as a dried prune.

She started chattering in Spanish.

"No hablo español," Heath said.

The woman stopped and stared at them.

"Louisa Tuttle?" Dela asked.

A younger woman stepped up beside the older woman. "You are looking for Louisa? Are you the police? She has been missing since yesterday. She didn't come home from work. We are getting worried."

"Does she have any friends she might have spent the night with?" Dela asked.

"Not that I know of. She has always come home from work. Never has she stayed out all night."

"Okay, we'll see if we can find her. Can you tell us how she fits into this household?" Dela asked, wondering if she was married to one of the cartel members.

The young woman glanced at the older woman and stepped out onto the porch. She whispered, "She came here as Balto's mistress but she has been trying to get away from him." The young woman glanced over her shoulder and added, "He is not nice to his women. But his mother doesn't see it."

Dela pointed toward the woman at the door without her seeing. "Is that his mother?"

The young woman nodded. "All who live here are related in some way. I am his niece."

Someone from inside the house shouted.

"You must go. Tell Louisa, I wish her well." The woman scampered into the house and closed the door.

"That's interesting," Heath said as they walked back to the car. "Louisa is Balto's mistress."

"I would say her actions may have been to avoid punishment," Dela added.

"Let's see if she is working and if her car is still in the parking lot." Heath started the car and pulled away from the curb. They didn't say much as they drove to Stage Technology.

They drove by where the car was parked yesterday and discovered it was still there. Hopefully, that meant she was at work.

Dela led the way into the business. At the reception desk, she asked to see Louisa Tuttle.

"I'm sorry, she didn't come in to work today." The woman didn't even look up from the keyboard where she was typing.

"Her car is in the parking lot," Dela said.

"It was there last night after the cops took her away and it was there this morning when I came to work. I would conclude she is still with the police or too ashamed to show her face here." The middle-aged woman finally looked up. The smug smile on her thin lips irked Dela.

"Can you tell me if Darren Landis is here?"

"The other criminal? No. He didn't come to work today either. Maybe they are hiding together."

"Thank you," Heath said, leading Dela back out to the car. "Let's go try Darren's house. Maybe he'll know where Louisa is if she isn't with him."

They drove across town to the Landis residence. Darren's car sat in the driveway. Dela hoped that meant he was here. They walked up to the front door and rang the doorbell. When no one answered they headed around the side of the house and discovered Darren sitting in a lawn chair in the middle of the yard, with a cooler of beer at his side.

They grabbed chairs from the patio and joined him.

"Hey, Darren," Dela said, placing the chair and sitting in front of him.

Heath took up a spot on her left side. "Looks like you decided to take a vacation today."

Darren stared at them. "What do you two want? The police let us go. But not before they'd led us out of work and humiliated us. I can't go back there. What do I say, the police made a mistake?"

"Did they make a mistake?" Dela asked.

The man's eyes narrowed. "What do you mean by that?"

"I'm pretty sure you are the person I saw running

away from the bridge before I fell over Gus Sander's body."

He didn't say anything.

"I think someone, possibly Louisa, asked you to get my knife from my car and place it with the body to incriminate me." Dela let it sit a minute then said, "Or to get me caught up in the murder so I would discover that her lover, Balto Herman, was the killer and she wanted away from him."

Now she had Darren's attention. "At first, I thought I was being framed. But now, after learning about Louisa's lover and his ties to a cartel, I think she thought it was a good way to get Balto finally caught and out of her life.

"Did she pull you in to help her rid herself of a man she despised?" Dela could see he was trying to decide if he should say anything. "I'm not the police. I help them with investigations, but I can't arrest you for anything. And what you tell me is hearsay, so it won't hold up in court."

Darren studied her and then pointed at Heath. "What about him? Isn't he a cop?"

"I'm Tribal Police. I'm not on the reservation and you aren't a tribal member so what you say to me I can't do anything with it other than help Dela discover who is trying to harm her."

"What do you mean harm her? She said that she knew I planted that knife. So does the detective. He said he knew that I left it after the man was murdered. That's why he let me go." Darren's gaze flicked back and forth between Dela and Heath.

"Friday night someone tried to run me down in the casino parking lot." Dela found it easier to say now that she was getting closer to knowing who did it. "If it wasn't you, do you have any ideas who it could have been?"

Darren shook his head. "I didn't do it. But I don't have a good alibi. I was home alone, as usual. Even with Gus dead, Zaria still continues to go out every night as if she is a single woman."

"Do you happen to know where Louisa might have gone after she was released by the police?" Heath asked.

"I heard her ask the policeman who was taking her home to take her to an address on King Avenue. I figured it was where she lived. But I also wondered how she could afford a house in that area."

Dela had a good idea which house Louisa was going to. "Thank you for answering our questions." She stood, as did Heath.

"What about my placing your knife at the crime scene?" Darren asked.

"I think it was placed there to get my help. I'm not upset about that. But how did you get the knife?" She had wondered about that since she'd discovered her less-than-a-year-old car had been broken into.

"Louisa gave me the knife. I'm not sure how she got it." Darren shrugged.

Walking back to the car, Dela said, "Do you think she went to the Cristo house on King Avenue?"

"That's the only one I can think of," Heath replied.

"Me, too. Who did she run to there? Balto's boss? Do you think she and Keenan have been fooling around and she wanted away from Balto and because he was such a good cartel member, Keenan wouldn't get rid of him?" Dela could see Keenan falling for Louisa. She had that sweet innocent act down and could have used it on Keenan. Which would have hastened his need to get his wife put away in an institution. But what about Wallace?

As Heath drove through town and up to the nicer houses in Pendleton, Dela wondered how her mom and Annie were getting along.

At the house, Heath parked in front along the sidewalk. They exited the vehicle and walked up to the front door. Music could be heard faintly. He rang the doorbell and they waited. When no one answered, he rang the bell and pounded on the door.

Dela tried to look in the front windows but the shades were drawn. She started around to the left side of the house, rather than go all the way around the garage on the right. At each window she tried to see in but the blinds were all drawn.

At the back of the house, Heath joined her from the opposite side. "All the blinds are closed."

She nodded and placed her ear against the crack between the door and the jamb. "There is music playing. Someone could have left a radio on, I guess."

A crash sounded from inside.

Heath tried the door, then using the bottom of his foot kicked right beside the door handle and the door flew open. He raced in ahead of Dela.

"In here," he called out as she jogged down the hall.

Wallace was tied to a chair. Blood spilled down the side of his face from a cut on his scalp. He was unconscious.

Dela pulled out her phone and dialed 9-1-1.

Heath was untying Louisa, who also had blood and

bruises on her, but she was conscious. It was evident she had knocked over a table to get their attention.

Dela began untying Wallace. "What happened?"

Louisa fell to her knees in front of Wallace, tears streaming down her face. "I came here to tell Wallace that we could leave. Balto was in jail. But when I arrived, Keenan was in the middle of beating him to find out where Annie was." She hiccupped and continued. "We didn't know where she'd gone. I was glad she finally got away from him but neither Wallace nor I had any idea where she could be. But Keenan didn't believe us. He tied us up and after he received a call, he was really mad."

Louisa wrapped her arms around Wallace's waist. "Keenan accused me of going to the DEA and telling them about the brewery. I told him I didn't. He hit me pretty hard and when I came to, he had us tied and Wallace was unconscious and bleeding. I think he tried to stop Keenan from hurting me more."

The sound of sirens grew.

"I'll go direct them in," Heath said, leaving out through the front of the house.

Dela watched the young woman. She was in love with Wallace. "Did you have Wallace steal my knife so you could give it to Darren to leave with Gus's body to get me involved in the case?"

Louisa sniffed, wiped a hand under her nose, and peered straight into Dela's eyes. "I heard Balto tell someone Gus was meeting a threat at the Riverpark and he was going to make sure the meeting didn't happen." She shrugged. "I'd had my dad make a key fob for your vehicle when we first moved here. I figured there would be a time when I'd need to get your attention to help me take down Balto. My family talks about how even when you were accused of murdering the meth cooker on the reservation you kept digging until you not only cleared your name but took down the drug dealer. I thought by implicating you, you would dig until you came up with the truth and I'd be free of Balto."

The paramedics followed Heath into the room.

"He needs to be attended to first," Dela said, moving to give them a clear path to Wallace. She led Louisa down the hall to the front room. Heath followed them.

"Did Wallace get the knife and hand it over to you, who in turn gave it to Darren?" Dela asked as the paramedics rolled Wallace out the front door.

"Yes. Can I go with him? And please, find Annie. She's been tormented by Keenan and doesn't deserve to have him find her. There is no telling what he might do." Louisa started to leave.

Dela grabbed her by the arm. "Did you try to have me run over?"

The woman's face paled. "I helped steal the keys for the car, but I didn't know it was going to be used to try and run you down. Balto told me to find him car keys from a car at the casino. I thought he needed a vehicle to deliver drugs or something illegal. I had no idea it was for a hit and run."

"Did you do illegal things like that often for him?" Heath asked.

"It was do them or suffer the consequences. Then Wallace and I fell in love. We had to keep it hidden to not get one or both of us killed. We were working to get enough information so we could go to the police and get into witness protection. But Keenan didn't leave things about his illegal business lying around the house." She walked toward the door as a paramedic came back in to check her out.

"Go," Dela said. "But be careful." As soon as Louisa and the paramedic left, Dela pulled out her phone.

"Who are you calling?" Heath asked.

"Quinn to send some DEA people to go through this house and to keep watch over Louisa and Wallace."

# Chapter Twenty-eight

"We know the truth about the knife and who tried to run you down. Balto is in the hands of the DEA. What do you want to do now?" Heath asked as they walked out to her car after waiting for members of the DEA to arrive.

"Take what we know about Fletcher to the State Police and then look for Keenan. If he's really worried about or trying to find Annie, we need to make sure she's safe. But if he knows DEA raided his brewery, I'd think he'd be hightailing it out of the country to save his hide." Dela settled into the passenger seat and stared at the road ahead. "After we talk to the State Police, we should let Annie know that Wallace is injured but she shouldn't go near him until Keenan's been caught."

"Maybe you should wait to tell her. If you think she'll run to her son, Keenan may think that too and be watching for her." Heath pulled away from the curb and headed the car downhill.

"That's true."

♠ ♣ ♥ ♦

At the State Police Office Dela was pleased with how interested Lieutenant Keller was in the file and the information she and Heath had on Detective Fletcher.

"I'll get one of my detectives on it right away. I'm glad the DEA could move on the brewery before it opened. It will be a shame if that beautiful building sits there idle but better than having illegal drugs being made there." Lt. Keller stood and shook their hands. "You two have uncovered a lot of crooked people during this investigation."

"We have one more to uncover," Dela said. "When he's behind bars several people will be able to breathe a sigh of relief. Including me. Thank you for taking on this investigation."

"You have come highly endorsed. I'd be a fool not to listen to what you had to say."

Dela stopped at the door and studied her. "Who has endorsed me?"

"Trooper Hawke and Special Agent Pierce. Two people I've worked with often. If they both sing your praises, I'm willing to hear what you have to say."

Dela smiled. "Thank you."

In the car, Heath asked, "Who is Trooper Hawke?"

"I'm sure I told you about him. His mom is Mimi Shumack. She cares for the children of single parents so they can work. He grew up here and is now a State Trooper for Fish and Wildlife in Wallowa County. When I was the Assistant Head of Security at the casino, he came here looking for one of the mothers of the children Mimi watches. When she couldn't get local authorities to take her seriously about the mom being missing, she called her son. He, myself, and Quinn worked to discover a human trafficking ring working out of the casino with the help of the head of security and a few others." She smiled. That had been one of her most rewarding investigations. Not only did they get that woman back but another one who had been abducted earlier as well.

"That must be when you became head of security," Heath said, turning on the vehicle and asking, "Where to next?"

"Mom's."

"Shouldn't we check and see how Wallace is doing and maybe see if we can learn anything from him?" Heath asked.

Dela was torn. It would be good if Wallace could give them some insight into what Keenan might be doing or thinking. If he was up to visitors and talking. "Okay. Let's go to the hospital and see what he knows. I wouldn't mind talking to Louisa some more since she was sleeping with Balto."

Heath drove them to the hospital where they were told to wait until the nurse could escort them back.

They sat in a small waiting area. Dela's phone buzzed. A glance showed it was Quinn.

"Hello," she answered in a quiet voice.

"Where are you?" he asked.

"A lot has happened since we saw you this morning." She went on to tell him about Louisa, Darren, and Wallace. And that they were waiting to talk to Wallace.

"I got the report back on that patch you gave me. There wasn't any prescribed medicine on it. The patch had a gel base laced with ketamine and LSD. He clearly wants her and those around her to think she's crazy."

Anger bubbled in Dela. How could a man do something so despicable to a woman he was married to? A desperate man. "Have you looked into his financials? He must need money if he's trying to get it from Annie without killing her. I'd guess that the trusts can only go to bloodline relatives which is why he's making her crazy to get his hands on them. And he might have hoped by having Wallace in the cartel, he'd end up dead and Annie would get both the trusts."

"We do have his financials. I had Milo pull them up when you gave me the patch. He is hurting. The breweries in his name are not his. The cartel owns them. He is their front man and he's been losing money and borrowing from them. That's why he needs his wife's money, to pay off the cartel." There was a smile in Quinn's voice as he informed Dela about the money trouble.

"You think he needs to be fed to the cartel he's been fronting," Dela said.

"I do. But that's just my twisted sense of justice."

Dela laughed. "We need to find him. Can you get me a description and plate for his vehicle?"

"Yeah. I'll text it to you. My buddy from DEA is calling." The call ended.

Dela told Heath what she'd learned from Quinn. "We need to find Annie. It sounds like Keenan is desperate to get his hands on money. And his wife breaking into her trust is his fastest way to do that." She stood.

Heath grasped her hand before she could walk away. "What about Wallace? He might have an idea where to find his stepfather."

Dela was torn. She felt an urgency to get to Annie but it would help quicken the search if they had some information.

The doors opened and Louisa walked toward them.

"How's he doing?" Dela asked.

"They sewed up his head and he has a concussion. They are watching for internal bleeding. Keenan hit him hard with something that had an edge on it." She shivered. "I knew he had a temper. I'd seen him blow up on Annie before, but I didn't think he was that violent. He looked almost crazy when he left the house."

"Do you have any idea where he might have gone? Did he have a place he went to think or to get away from his problems?" Heath asked.

Louisa shook her head. "I honestly don't know. I was either being manipulated by Balto or hanging out with Wallace. I tried to stay away from Keenan. He and Balto seemed to have a power thing going on and I didn't like to get in the middle of it."

"How did that work? You were Balto's mistress yet you hung out at Keenan's house with Wallace. Weren't you afraid someone would tell Balto?" Dela asked.

Louisa blushed. "Wallace and his friends didn't care for Balto either. They wouldn't say anything. They thought it was funny that Balto thought I was all his and I'd be with Wallace when I wasn't working and Balto was busy. I think Keenan thought it was funny and that's why he didn't say anything."

"Did Balto ever say anything about Keenan owing the cartel money?"

Louisa's eyes widened. "Does he? Oh. My. God.

That would be why he's been so crazy lately. I heard Balto on the phone and he said, he'd get the money if he had to kidnap the old lady."

Dela exchanged a glance with Heath. If she hadn't hidden Annie with her mom, she may have been kidnapped by the cartel. Right now, Balto wasn't a threat but if the cartel sent more people to do it, they might pull it off.

"Thank you." Dela fished in her purse for a card and wrote her cell phone number on the back. "Call me when Wallace feels up to talking. I need to go somewhere. But I'll be back." She spun around to leave and then pivoted back to face Louisa. "Did DEA send someone to keep an eye on you and Wallace?"

"Yeah, someone is standing outside Wallace's door."

"You need to stay in the room or close by. The cartel could send someone to take revenge if they think, like Keenan did, that you and Wallace turned them into the DEA."

Louisa's mouth opened and then she nodded. "I'll head back there now."

Dela grasped the sleeve of Heath's jacket. "We need to get to Mom and Lance's. Keenan may have figured out by now that Mom was an ally to Annie. And we don't know who could be following him."

# Chapter Twenty-nine

Dread gurgled in Dela's gut as gravel crunched under the tires on the driveway leading up to Mom and Lance's house. A fancy car was parked in front of the walkway to the front porch.

As they parked behind it, she received a text from Quinn. She read the text and the license on the car.  She told Heath, "Keenan is here," as she texted it to Quinn.

*Where are you?* Texted Quinn

*Mom and Lance's ranch.*

Heath opened the glove compartment and put his backup weapon in the ankle holster. "I hate we have to go in your mom's house with guns."

"I'm leaving my gun in the car. I know where Lance keeps his guns. If I sneak around the back, I can pick one up on my way through the house." Dela wasn't sure what they would find. But she knew Mom wouldn't like whatever she and Heath had to do to keep her, Lance, and Annie safe.

"He won't buy me walking into the house without you. You take your gun and go in the front. I'll go in the back." Heath started to pull his Glock from the ankle holster.

"You're right. He will expect me to come through the front door. You go to the back. There should be a pistol in a holster hanging from a hook on the back porch. It's Lance's rattlesnake pistol. He wears it when he's walking through the fields. Grab it. When you get the chance, try to get it to me." Dela opened the car door and walked up to the front door. She waited until Heath had made it around the side of the house before she knocked and tried the door latch. It wasn't locked.

"Hey, Mom. I thought I'd come by and see what you've been up to," she said loud and joyfully to not let on she knew that the car out front belonged to Keenan.

"Dela don't—" Lance's voice was cut off.

She found Mom, Lance, and Annie tied to dining room chairs. Keenan stood beside Lance.

Annie's bloody face told the story of what she'd been putting up with.

"What the hell! Keenan, if you touch her one more time, I'll kill you with my bare hands!" Dela said. Anger pushed her toward him, her hands balled in fists ready to punch.

He raised his hand as if to strike the woman again and Dela lunged. She collided with his belly, catapulting both of them backward. As they landed on the floor she caught sight of Heath charging into the room.

He stepped on Keenan's wrist and shoved the snake pistol in his face. "I'd advise you to drop the weapon in your hand and roll over onto your stomach."

Dela stood and as soon as the man was on his stomach, she grabbed his thumb and wrenched the arm behind his back. He screamed in pain and she smiled. But not so her mom could see it. As she kept him on the floor with the thumb hold, Heath untied her mom and then used that cord to tie Keenan's hands behind his back.

Once his hands were secured, they raised him to his feet and sat him in the chair her mom vacated to untie Annie and then Lance. They used the rest of the cord to tie Keenan to the chair. When that was done, Heath pulled out his phone and called the sheriff and the state police.

"We need to call nine-one-one. Annie needs to be looked at," Mom said, dabbing at the cuts on Annie's face with a rag and water Lance brought in from the kitchen.

"I'm fine. Why is he so angry?" Annie asked, her wide eyes focused on her husband. His gaze was full of hate and fury.

"Because he borrowed money from a drug cartel and needs your trust to pay them back. They plan on kidnapping you to make him pay them what he owes." Dela watched triumphantly as those words brought Keenan's gaze to her. "You didn't know that? They told Balto to kidnap Annie and then you'd pay them what you owed them. But you don't have any money. Your breweries have all failed. Anyway, the front of them where you make beer and sell it has failed. The back of the buildings where the drug cartel makes illegal pills and sells them is doing just fine. Or it was until the DEA raided your Pendleton brewery last night."

Keenan's red angry face faded and fear crept into

his eyes.

Dela turned to Annie. "Those patches he told you were prescribed by your doctor? They were making you hallucinate and forget. They were ketamine and LSD patches. There wasn't a prescribed drug in them."

Annie's face paled.

Mom moved to her side.

"He was drugging you to make you think you were going crazy and to get the people around you to attest to it so he could get his hands on your trust, as well as Wallace's. I'm sure when Wallace is feeling better, he'll tell us how Keenan suggested he join the cartel to help him out. When all he wanted to do was get Wallace either killed by the cartel or locked up by officials so he could get his hands on that trust as well."

Annie peered at her. "What do you mean when he feels better?"

Heath stepped up beside Dela. "We found him and Louisa tied up at the house Keenan was renting. Wallace was unconscious with a nasty gash on the side of his head. Louisa said that Keenan beat them up trying to find out where you were. But neither of them knew."

Annie stood, a bit wobbly, and pointed a finger at Keenan. "You hurt my son and you have been drugging me? I thought you were the love I didn't find the first time I married. How could I have been so foolish to think I could love a man who cared only for money and his status." She grasped Mom's arm and said, "I'd like to go to the hospital and see Wallace."

"We can do that," Mom said, then glanced at her husband who had dried blood crusting around his nose. "Oh, Lance! I forgot he hit you when you tried to warn

Dela."

"Annie, you'll need to stay here until the police arrive and get your statement. Then we'll take you to see Wallace," Heath said.

That's when they heard the shrill whine of the sirens.

♠ ♣ ♥ ♦

Over an hour later, the State Police hauled off Keenan and between the troopers and deputies who arrived, they managed to get everyone's statement as to what happened.

"Now, if you want to clean up, we'll take you to see Wallace," Heath told Annie.

She and Mom went down the hall to one of the guest bedrooms.

Lance faced them and asked, "What you said about the cartel kidnapping her? Will that stop now that Keenan is arrested?"

Heath replied with a grim expression. "Only if the cartel can be told that Keenan has been arrested and could turn states evidence against them if they pursue his wife." His gaze landed on Dela.

She understood what he was saying. If she couldn't get someone from law enforcement to contact the cartel and get that message across, it would be up to them to make sure it happened.

"Do I need to have some of the ranch hands keep watch?" Lance asked as the two women walked down the hall toward them.

"It wouldn't be a bad idea," Heath said.

"What wouldn't be a bad idea?" Mom asked.

"I think I'll stay here while you ladies go to the hospital. That whack to my nose makes it feel like it's three sizes larger than before." Lance touched his nose.

"I'm so sorry to have brought this trouble to you," Annie said. "Now that Keenan is arrested, I could go stay at the house. He has it rented until October."

"No!" Dela, Deborah, and Lance all said at the same time.

Annie stared at them. "Why shouldn't I stay there? What else aren't you telling me."

"It would be safer for you to stay here until we get things settled with the cartel," Heath said.

Annie's forehead wrinkled in a frown and then she said, "Oh! You think they could be waiting for me to return to the house. But Keenan doesn't have any money, and he can't legally get mine."

"They don't know that. Yet," Dela said. "Heath and I are going to try and explain how they won't be able to get the money Keenan owed them from you. But it will take us a couple of days to make that happen."

"I see. And you think they won't find me here?" Annie spread her arms. "Keenan found me."

"He knew my mom had befriended you. We're going to make sure the county and state police patrol these roads more until we get things cleared up." Dela grasped Annie's hand. "Please. Stick around until we can make sure you are safe on your own."

Annie smiled. The twinkle, that Dela first noticed, that lit up her eyes when she smiled was there. "For you, my savior, I will stay put until you get the bad guys."

"Thank you."

# Chapter Thirty

Dela and Heath dropped her mom and Annie off at the hospital and drove to meet Quinn and his DEA friend at a park.

Quinn introduced them to Jerry and they all sat at a picnic table. Dela sat on an end where she wouldn't have to try to thread her prosthesis through the bench and the table.

Dela explained that someone needed to get information to the cartel that Keenan was in jail and he didn't have any money to pay them. And his wife wasn't the golden goose that Keenan had made her out to be.

"You think the cartel is going to take anything someone from the DEA tells them?" Jerry asked.

She sighed. "I was afraid you'd say that." She glanced at Heath and said, "Then we'll talk to them and tell them if they don't leave Annie alone, Keenan will tell DEA everything he knows about the operation."

Jerry laughed. "Do you really think they will listen to you without laughing? They could have Keenan killed in prison, that's how powerful they are."

"That won't get them their money either. But I have to persuade them that Annie can't help them." Dela had to make sure Annie was safe.

"Did you check Keenan's phone? Did it have any phone calls or information that could help in your case against him?" Heath asked.

Jerry rubbed a hand over his chin and said, "We couldn't find anything incriminating on him or in the house."

Dela straightened. "He had to have contacted the cartel some way. Unless it was just through Balto. Annie said the two of them would have heated conversations. Louisa said the same." She shifted to face Heath who sat next to her. "We need to get Louisa and Annie together and see if their knowledge of the two men can help us discover more information or something that will keep Annie safe from the cartel." She slid to the end and stood. "They should both be at the hospital."

Heath rose, stepped over the bench, and said goodbye to Quinn and Jerry.

"You two be careful who you talk to," Jerry called after them.

Dela raised a hand to let him know they heard.

♠ ♣ ♥ ♦

At the hospital, they found both Annie and Louisa sitting on either side of Wallace's bed. The young man was awake, but looked as if he couldn't keep his eyes open.

"How's the head?" Dela asked, walking up to the

bed.

"Feels like someone is in there beating on a loud drum," Wallace said. "Thanks for coming to our rescue."

"You're welcome. Since you're awake, we'll bring you into this conversation," Dela said. "We're working on a way to keep the cartel from coming after Annie for the money Keenan owed them."

Louisa nodded her head and Wallace looked surprised.

"He owed the cartel money?" Wallace asked.

Louisa grasped his hand. "More than I think you and your mom could even get."

"Why didn't you tell me this?" Wallace asked, staring at Louisa.

"I didn't think it would come back on you and your mom. Keenan kept telling Balto he'd have the money soon. I thought he was waiting for it to roll out of an investment or something."

Dela shook her head. "No, he was waiting for his chance to take Annie and Wallace's trusts."

Wallace's eyes widened. "He was using us to get our money?"

"Yes." Dela studied Annie. "How did you meet Keenan?"

"Through an acquaintance."

"Someone who knew you had a trust?" Dela asked.

The pain that flashed through the woman's eyes told Dela the person had.

"Yes. You think Keenan always planned to get his hands on that money?" The sorrow in Annie's voice tugged at Dela but she couldn't let that sway her from digging deep for the answers they needed.

"Yes. You were a means to money. I'm sorry to say." She shifted her attention to Louisa. "I need all three of you to tell me everything you can about Keenan's day-to-day movements. We have to figure out where he kept his dealings with the cartel hidden. Officials haven't been able to find anything on his phone, computer, or in the house. To keep Annie and Wallace safe, we have to find something to use as leverage."

Louisa grinned. "This is why I involved you in Gus's death. I knew you'd help when the police wouldn't care. I learned that about you from my uncle's experience with you."

Dela said, "Sometimes you have to get down and dirty when you can't beat the bad guys legally."

They sat in the hospital room for an hour with Heath writing down what everyone said about Keenan's daily routine and with Wallace drifting in and out of sleep. When they finished Dela said, "Annie, how are you getting back to the ranch?"

"Deborah told me to call her when I was finished visiting. She was going to do volunteer work at the library." Annie pulled out her phone. "I can call her now."

"Okay, but we'd like to follow you back to make sure there isn't anyone from the cartel watching the hospital," Heath said.

Annie's eyes widened. "You think they are watching the hospital to try and catch me?"

Heath shrugged. "Keenan owed them a substantial amount of money and they will do anything to get paid back. Especially now that one of their money-making ventures was shut down by the DEA."

"I'll call Deborah." Annie stepped out in the hallway to make the call.

Dela leaned toward Louisa. "You'll need to be careful. Balto may think you caused them to get picked up."

"I'm staying right here by Wallace until they release him. Then we're giving Annie an email I started today to contact us and we're heading somewhere secluded and hopefully far from anyone connected to the cartel." She grasped Wallace's hand. "He never really wanted to be mixed up in the cartel, but pressure from Keenan to work for him, and Annie thinking it was wonderful, he joined."

"We could see about getting you in witness protection," Heath said.

"I already talked to someone about that. They said we didn't do enough to warrant the taxpayers paying for us to change our identity." She shrugged. "Luckily, I've met people who can do the same thing for a price."

"People you trust?" Dela asked.

Louisa shrugged. "It's hard to trust anyone."

"If you don't feel like someone you know is trustworthy, contact me. I have someone on the legal side of things who can get you set up." Dela didn't look at Heath. She was sure he was wondering who she would get to falsify records and get Louisa and Wallace new identities.

Annie returned. "Deborah said she'll be here in ten minutes." She walked over and kissed Wallace on the forehead. "I'm sorry I brought Keenan into our lives."

Wallace grabbed her hand. "Hey, he made you happy for most of those years. It was the last two that he was getting weird. I should have said something or done something. But I was just trying to keep from getting killed by the cartel."

"We are hopefully free of him now. Or will be as soon as I contact our lawyer and start divorce proceedings." Annie straightened. "Walk with me to wait for your mom."

Dela and Heath walked with Annie out to the front lobby.

"I don't know how to thank you for what you have done for my son and me. I have my life back. I hadn't known I'd lost it. I was so sure that Keenan was doing everything to help me." She shook her head. "I was such a fool to not see all the signs."

"Love has a way of doing that to a person. You're blinded to the truth sometimes." Heath stared out the window as he spoke.

Dela wondered if he was talking about her or someone else.

Mom pulled up outside the doors.

They escorted Annie to the car and told her mom they would follow them to the ranch and then leave because they had things to do.

"You'll come to dinner tomorrow night?" Mom asked.

Dela looked at Heath and he nodded. "We'll be there."

"Good. See you then." She pulled away from the entrance.

Heath and Dela walked to her car, got in, and followed them. Heath watched the rearview mirror and didn't see anyone else following.

After seeing the women drive down the driveway, they headed back to town.

"Let's get something to eat and go over the notes you took at the hospital. We have to find something that will help us negotiate with the cartel," Dela said.

They ended up at their favorite pizza place and sat eating pizza while comparing what the three people told them about Keenan's habits.

"They all say he went to the gym every day. He would have been carrying a bag for his workout clothes. He could have had a laptop or device in his bag that he used to store the information." Dela bit into her second piece of all-meat pizza.

"We don't know which gym," Heath said.

"We could ask Quinn to look up any payments to a gym on his financials." She pulled out her phone and texted Quinn. *Did Keenan make any payments to a local gym?*

*Cross Fitness. Why?* Quinn texted back.

*Working things out.* Dela didn't want to tell him what they were doing. It was bad enough that Heath was going along with her ploy to more or less blackmail the cartel into leaving Annie alone.

Dela closed the lid on the box of pizza and finished her tea. "Let's go talk to the people at Cross Fitness."

They found the gym without any trouble. There was a nice lounge in the front where people could purchase healthy drinks and visit before and after workouts.

Dela walked up to registration and smiled at the fit-looking man about her age who stood behind the counter. "I was wondering if you could tell me when Keenan Cristo usually comes in to work out?"

The man smiled. "He pays a monthly fee. But after his first visit, all he does is walk in the front door and out the back. Then an hour or so later, he comes in the back door and goes out the front."

Dela asked, "What is behind your building?"

"A coffee shop."

"Do you know if he goes in there?" Dela asked, wondering if that could be where Keenan was writing up his illegal business transactions. And could he be leaving the information at the coffee shop?

"I couldn't tell you. All I know is he comes in one door, goes out another, and
then comes back. It's like he wants people to see him coming in here."

"Thank you, you've been helpful." Dela and Heath walked out the front door and around to the back of the building.  Across the street was a coffee shop and a sign on another window that said Computer Doctor.

"Coffee or computer?" she asked Heath.

"Try the coffee shop first. It makes sense he would sit with a cup of coffee and type. But why pretend to go to the gym and then pop in there for coffee?" He started across the street, holding Dela's hand.

They stepped into the small cheery shop and walked up to the counter.

Heath ordered two small cups of coffee and two chocolate chip cookies.

Before they sat down, Dela asked, "Do you have a tall, good-looking man come in here every day and work on a computer?"

Heath pulled up a photo of Keenan.

"Oh, him. He's cream and sugar with a cinnamon twist. Yes, he comes in, orders, then sits at that table over there and works. He said it's more peaceful than at home."

Heath walked over to the table she'd indicated and sat. Dela sat across from him. If Keenan worked in here, they should find an SD card or flash drive that he put everything on. She felt under the table on her side and found a couple of gobs of gum. Yuck! She immediately went to the any-gender restroom and washed her hands.

While in there she checked all the hiding places she could find to see if there was something hidden. Nothing.

When she returned to the table, Heath was smiling. She leaned forward and whispered, "You found it, didn't you?"

He nodded and showed her a magnetized box that an extra key could be put in and attached to the underside of a car. "It was on the backside of that metal flower pot." He pointed to a rectangular flower pot on a shelf attached to the wall.

"Clever. But how did he come up with that, unless he scouted out places when he first arrived? Now to see what's on there so we can scare the cartel into leaving Annie and Wallace be."

♠ ♣ ♥ ♦

Back at the car, Heath pulled out his laptop and slid the SD card into the slot. To their surprise, it wasn't anything written but rather incriminating photos.

"I know which one we need to print out to use as proof we have these." Dela pointed to one where Balto had a man on his knees, his left hand fisted in the man's hair, holding his head back as Balto's right hand held a knife to the man's neck. A dozen men were standing around watching. One of them was the old man who had answered the door when they were looking for

Louisa.

They took the SD card to their house, printed out the photo before deleting that photo, and then slid the card into an envelope and sealed it shut, addressing it to the DEA. If nothing happened to Annie in the next year, they would send it to the DEA. If something happened to Annie, it would go to DEA sooner. Heath put the envelope in their small safe under the floor of their bedroom closet.

"Let's take this to the cartel. I want to be rid of this whole thing as soon as possible and get Jethro and Mugshot home."

They headed back to town with the photo in a large envelope. With Balto and the other eight members with the DEA and the brewery shut down, they figured everyone would be at the house.

They pulled up to find moving vans backed up to the house. It appeared they were moving out.

The older man who'd answered the door the other night, stepped out of the house carrying a box. He stopped and stared at them. "You are brave to show up here after what has happened."

"We wanted to share something with you, that you, in turn, will share with whoever is your boss," Dela said.

Heath opened the envelope and drew the photo out. He held it in front of the man.

"We found an SD card of photos that Keenan took. This is one of them."

The man's eyebrows rose as he stared at the photo. He made to grab it, but Heath pulled it back. "We will hang onto SD card as long as the cartel doesn't go after Annie Cristo or her son Wallace to try and get Keenan's debts settled. If either of them are approached for money or to harm them, we will give the SD card to the DEA."

The man glared at them. "We could just kill you now and get the money that is owed to us."

"You could kill us now but that would mean all of the events Keenan photographed will be in the hands of the DEA within an hour of their discovering our bodies or that we are missing." Heath slid the photo back in the envelope and set it on the box. "It's up to you if you want to bring every law enforcement group in the U.S. down on top of your cartel."

They walked away from the man and the house as casually as they could. Dela's heart raced in her chest, knowing they could shoot them or attack them. But they made it safely to the car and drove away. They'd be looking over their shoulders the next twenty-four hours, but if the cartel was clearing out of the house, it was a good sign they were moving on to some other unsuspecting town to set up shop.

# Chapter Thirty-one

Dela enjoyed herself the next night at her mom's dinner. Wallace and Louisa had also joined them. After the meal, Dela and Heath told them about finding evidence that would keep Annie and Wallace safe from the cartel. They refused to say what or what they did with it but felt that the two of them wouldn't need to worry about the cartel taking revenge or trying to get money.

Annie said she was thinking about staying on in Pendleton. But not in town. She was going to try and find a small parcel of land for a few animals. Mom was delighted to know her new friend would be staying.

"What about you two? Your mom told me you are living together but haven't set a wedding date," Annie said.

"We still have some things to work out before we can commit to marriage," Dela said.

Annie studied Heath and said, "He looks like he's

ready now. What is holding you up?"

Panic gripped her throat as she tried to think of what to say.

"There is some unresolved history that we both need to deal with before we can commit to a lifetime together." Heath grasped her hand and handed her a glass of water.

"Unresolved history? What on earth could that be?" her mom asked.

"Some things I've yet to tell her about when I was in Pine Ridge and things that have happened to Dela that she's still dealing with."

Annie seemed to understand it was something neither wished to talk about. "I understand. I wish I had taken a harder look at Keenan before I'd married him. Now that I look back, there were things that, at the time I ignored, thinking it would change when we were married. But it didn't." She put a hand on both of them and said, "Take your time."

Thank you for reading book six in the Spotted Pony Casino Mystery series. If you enjoyed the book, please leave a review where you purchased *Down and Dirty*. Reviews are the best way to let an author know you enjoyed the story.

As I continue the series there will be surprises about Dela's heritage and more murders that she, Heath, and their friends will solve.

*Paty*

Other books in the Spotted Pony Casino Mystery series:
**Poker Face**
**House Edge**
**Double Down**
**The Squeeze**
**The Pinch**

If you enjoyed this mystery series you might like my other mystery series:

### Shandra Higheagle Mystery Series

| | |
|---|---|
| *Double Duplicity* | *Haunting Corpse* |
| *Tarnished Remains* | *Artful Murder* |
| *Deadly Aim* | *Dangerous Dance* |
| *Murderous Secrets* | *Homicide Hideaway* |
| *Killer Descent* | *Toxic Trigger-point* |
| *Reservation Revenge* | *Abstract Casualty* |
| *Yuletide Slaying* | *Capricious Demise* |
| *Fatal Fall* | *Vanishing Dream* |

**Gabriel Hawke Novels**

*Murder of Ravens*

*Mouse Trail Ends*

*Rattlesnake Brother*

*Chattering Blue Jay*

*Fox Goes Hunting*

*Turkey's Fiery Demise*

*Stolen Butterfly*

*Churlish Badger*

*Owl's Silent Strike*

*Bear Stalker*

*Damning Firefly*

*Cougar's Cache*

## About the Author

Paty Jager grew up in Wallowa County in NE Oregon and has always been amazed by its beauty, history, and ruralness. She has always had an interest in the Indigenous people and their culture and enjoys learning more every time she writes a book.

Paty is an award-winning author of 59 novels of murder mystery and western romance. All her work has Western or Native American elements in them along with hints of humor and engaging characters. She and her husband raise alfalfa hay in rural eastern Oregon. Riding horses and battling rattlesnakes, she not only writes the western lifestyle, she lives it.

By following her at one of these places you will always know when the next book is releasing and if she is having any giveaways:

Website: http://www.patyjager.net
Blog: https://writingintothesunset.net/
Windtree Press: https://windtreepress.com/paty-jager/
FB Page:  Author Paty Jager
Pinterest: https://www.pinterest.com/patyjag/
Twitter: https://twitter.com/patyjag
Goodreads:
http://www.goodreads.com/author/show/1005334.Paty_
Jager
Newsletter- Mystery: https://bit.ly/2IhmWcm
Bookbub - https://www.bookbub.com/authors/paty-
jager

Thank you for purchasing this Windtree Press
publication. For other books of the heart, please visit
our website at www.windtreepress.com.

For questions or more information contact us
at info@windtreepress.com.

Windtree Press
www.windtreepress.com

9 781962 065597